BATTLE SCARS

By the Author

Infinite Loop

The Three

Thirteen Hours

Battle Scars

Visit us at www.boldstrokesbooks.com

BATTLE SCARS

by

Meghan O'Brien

2009

BATTLE SCARS

ISBN 10: 1-60282-129-1
ISBN 13: 978-1-60282-129-3

THIS TRADE PAPERBACK ORIGINAL IS PUBLISHED BY
BOLD STROKES BOOKS, INC.
P.O. BOX 249
VALLEY FALLS, NY 12185

FIRST EDITION: DECEMBER 2009

CREDITS
EDITORS: SHELLEY THRASHER AND STACIA SEAMAN
PRODUCTION DESIGN: STACIA SEAMAN
COVER DESIGN BY SHERI (GRAPHICARTIST2020@HOTMAIL.COM)

Acknowledgments

I want to thank Shelley Thrasher for making the editing process a pleasure. Really. It takes a village to create a book, so I would also like to acknowledge Jennifer Knight, Stacia Seaman, and Sheri, for the great cover. Last but not least, thanks to Radclyffe for helming such a smooth-running ship. Working with BSB is simply awesome.

On a personal note, I want to thank my partner Angie Williams for helping me understand what a person with PTSD feels. I appreciated being able to lift aspects of her own experiences in the military, and I only hope that I was able to capture the reality that so many service members live in a respectful and honest manner.

I also need to thank Ty Justice for always being willing to read my newly finished works and provide feedback. Thanks also to Sandy—I appreciated your offer to beta read, even if we weren't able to find a time to chat. And I think I've always had a shout-out to my sister Kathleen in my novels, so I'm not going to stop now.

Last but not least, I have to mention my own Great Dane Jagger, and his shepherd-mix sidekick Jack. They have provided inspiration, laughter, and much-needed support not only during the writing of this book, but pretty much all the time. I'm lucky to share my life with them.

Dedication

To Angie, and everyone else who serves.
And to the real Jack and Jagger, for being good boys.

Chapter One

Ray McKenna sat on her brand-new leather couch, struggling to breathe with the acrid dust of the Iraqi desert burning her nose. Outside her Bodega Bay home, waves crashed against the rocky shore and set the quiet cadence of beachfront life. Inside her mind, she was thousands of miles away, the explosion that had reduced her unit's Humvee to smoking wreckage jolting her once again. One minute they were rolling through the streets of Al Hillah en route to the local medical clinic, and the next she was crawling in the dirt past a uniformed soldier so disfigured she didn't recognize him. Desperate to help the few men who cried out in pain, she didn't allow herself to mourn the ones who couldn't.

But this was only a flashback. She was safe and nobody could hurt her now. Dr. Evans had told her to focus on her breathing when this happened, but sometimes her body wouldn't obey. This was obviously one of those times.

As the memories took over, despair rolled through her. Rough male hands grasped her wrists and dragged her over the hard ground. They lifted her and threw her into a vehicle, causing a sickening disorientation. She longed to breathe, but how could she with that black hood over her head, suffocating her with its musty heat?

A long, wet tongue worked its way between her fingers, snapping Ray out of the past and focusing her on the heavy, steel gray head on her thigh. She blinked at Jagger, the Great Dane who stared mournfully into her eyes, then exhaled. Wordlessly, she wrapped her arms around his neck, holding on as tight as she could without choking him. He rested against her, as though returning the hug. Soon her breathing returned to normal.

"Good boy," Ray murmured, kissing his short fur. Her heart still pounded like a wild, caged bird's, but the worst was over. "Good boy, Jagger."

After a moment, she pulled away from Jagger and glanced at the clock. Her first online therapy session would start in ten minutes. When she'd moved from Grand Rapids, Michigan, to the Northern California coast, she intended to escape everything—except her therapist. The rapport and trust they had established in the nearly two years since Ray came home from Iraq was irreplaceable. And though Dr. Evans was obviously concerned about her sudden decision to relocate, she seemed to sense what their relationship meant to Ray. So she agreed to continue their sessions over the webcam, even if she didn't think the situation was ideal.

If she was being honest, Ray was just as happy not to have to leave the house for therapy. And she knew that was exactly what Dr. Evans worried about.

Jagger yawned and laid his head on her thigh again. Scratching the top of his broad skull, Ray said, "You do good work, my friend." Did she want to admit to Dr. Evans that she'd just suffered such a severe flashback, the worst she'd had in a while? But Dr. Evans had been right about Jagger. After only three weeks with him as her psychiatric therapy dog, the symptoms of her posttraumatic stress disorder were easing. Even when she had an episode, he could somehow bring her out of it with ease.

He was a miracle, the first she'd enjoyed since the one that saved her life over there.

Ray groaned as she rose from the couch, using Jagger's strong back to steady her as she fought for balance. Though she'd been able to retire the cane almost a year and a half ago, the healed fractures in her left leg still bothered her, especially when she sat for too long. The blustery coastal weather probably didn't help, but she'd always dreamed of living near the ocean. Though her compensation payments from the VA would never make her wealthy, they did allow her to make that one dream a reality, achy joints be damned.

"Come on, boy," Ray said as she walked stiff-legged toward the kitchen. He would follow her whether she asked or not, but she enjoyed talking to him. Before Jagger, she would spend hours or even days alone, in silence. Having him around reminded her of the pleasure of conversation, albeit one-sided in their case. "Let's get something to drink before we log in."

She hadn't been in the new house long enough to stock up the fridge, but she had brought plenty of water with her. She drank it constantly now, having learned true thirst during her time in the desert. The rows of plastic bottles in her fridge were an embarrassment of riches, something she once would have taken for granted but now relished. Grabbing one, she twisted off the cap and took a long, hard pull. She groaned with pleasure at the way the cold water coated her tongue, the sensuous caress of liquid sliding down her throat.

Ray laughed at the heady bliss of the sensation, a sound that came out more humorless than she felt. "Better than sex," she told Jagger, then took another drink. She closed her eyes, forcing her mind away from her melancholy, the awful certainty of her statement. Yes, this water was better than the sex she would never have again, with the unknown man she could never fully trust. Not that anyone would want to put up with her and her many issues anyway. "Way better."

She'd set up her computer in the small room she'd designated her office. That seemed too generous a description for the cheap, pressed-wood desk, the ergonomic chair, and the aging PC she'd put in there. But she would come to do her most serious work here, the arduous task of piecing herself back together again. She'd been at it for eighteen months already and saw no end. Sure, she was better, but she was starting to worry that she'd never approach normal again.

Ray fired up the webcam and logged in to the chat program Dr. Evans had recommended. Seeing that Dr. Evans was already online, she clicked the button to initiate their video conference. After a couple of telephone-like rings, a video window opened and her serious-looking therapist sat staring at her.

"Success," Dr. Evans said, cracking a smile.

"The wonders of technology." Ray adjusted her webcam so she could lean back in her chair, hoping to get more comfortable. "Hi, Dr. Evans."

"Hello, Ray. It's good to see you."

"You, too." And that was the truth. Therapy was painful at times, and Dr. Evans had a tendency to push her in directions she'd rather not go, but it helped to have someone to talk to. "How's the weather there?"

"Two feet of snow this morning, thanks for asking. How about you?"

Ray glanced out the window, grinning as she took in the peaceful sight of sea birds floating on the ocean wind. "Perfect."

"Getting settled in?"

"Pretty well. I've unpacked most of my boxes. Starting to feel more at home."

"Good. Have you had a chance to explore Bodega Bay?"

"A little." Ray had walked around her property, at least. Even ventured down the road during one late-evening walk with Jagger. But she knew that wasn't what Dr. Evans was asking. "I haven't had a lot of opportunity yet."

"You should make it a priority. Remember what we talked about, Ray. This move won't be a positive change if you allow it to push you back into hiding."

"I know."

"Gone to the grocery store?"

Ray thought of her nearly empty fridge. "Busted."

"I think that would be a good first step, don't you?"

She sighed. "You know I hate grocery shopping." Ray always seemed to draw plenty of stares in checkout lines. After all, less than two years ago her face had been plastered on the many magazines sold there.

"That's why I suggested it."

"Remind me again why the VA recommended such an antagonistic therapist?"

"I prefer to think of myself as caring." Dr. Evans moved closer to the camera, staring at her with that sincere gaze that used to make Ray squirm in discomfort. Now she found it strangely reassuring. "I do care about you, Ray. I don't want to see you throw away all the progress we've made."

"Neither do I. Trust me, it's been hard won."

"I know it has. On another subject, how is your therapy dog working out?"

Ray angled the webcam so that Jagger's large, smiling face was in the frame. He sat beside her quietly, as he always did unless she released him. "Jagger. He's amazing."

Dr. Evans chuckled. "Wow. Big dog."

"One hundred seventy pounds. I always wanted a Great Dane, and when I found out they had one in the therapy-dog program, I jumped at the chance." When Ray arrived at the service-dog training facility for her introduction to her new companion and the first of their training sessions together, she had loved him immediately. Every moment since then only served to further solidify her affection for him. "He makes me feel safe."

"I expect he would."

"Not that he has a mean bone in his body." Ray put an arm around him, planting a kiss on a soft, floppy ear. "He'd probably be more inclined to cuddle a bad guy to death than anything."

"How have you been coping with the PTSD? Any flashbacks or panic attacks?"

Ray hesitated, hating to admit that she'd just had a particularly nasty episode less than a half hour earlier.

Dr. Evans gave a knowing nod. "I'll take that as a yes. How was— you said his name is Jagger?"

"After Mick." Classic rock was the closest thing to heaven here on earth, so naming her dog after one of its legends was a no-brainer. "I thought about calling him McJagger, but decided to spare him."

Dr. Evans laughed loud and hard, and Ray swelled with pride. She convinced herself often that she couldn't communicate with other humans anymore, that she was so far removed from social niceties that she was irrelevant, but occasionally she glimpsed her own potential. Making Dr. Evans laugh brightened her day.

"How was Jagger during your episode?" Dr. Evans said when her laughter subsided. "Did he help guide you through it?"

"I had a flashback right before logging in, actually. First one in a while. Jagger put his head on my leg and licked my hand, pulled me right out of it."

"Excellent."

"I'm sleeping better, too. I still have the nightmares sometimes, but having Jagger there with me when I wake up, well, it really helps." Aware that she was nearly gushing, Ray stopped talking and looked at

Jagger for a moment. He gazed directly into her eyes, then opened his massive jaw in a loud yawn. She looked back at the webcam with a grin. "Like I said, he makes me feel really safe."

"I am so happy to hear this."

"I want to thank you for suggesting that I apply to the therapy-dog program. I'll be honest with you. It's only been three weeks, but I'm more hopeful since getting him than I have been since I got home."

"Now we just need to get you to the grocery store."

Ray groaned. "Can't we just focus on my successes for a minute?"

"Absolutely. I'm so happy Jagger is making such a difference. But the world doesn't consist of only you and Jagger, no matter how much you wish it did."

"That's not true." Ray scowled. "I like having you here, too."

"Except when I badger you to go shopping, right?" When Ray didn't answer, Dr. Evans said, "Okay, so let's talk about Jagger. You're taking him on walks, I hope?"

"Of course."

"Off your own property?"

"A little bit."

"How about the vet?" Dr. Evans asked. "Have you taken him to the vet yet?"

"The vet? Why? He's totally healthy. The therapy-dog program gave me his records. He got all his vaccinations a month and a half ago."

"Listen, you've got a dog now. He may be there for your mental benefit, but he's still a living creature, and your responsibility. Companion animals need to go to the vet on occasion. Even if he doesn't need to right now, it'd be a good idea to figure out where the local vet clinic is and take him in for an initial visit."

Ray groaned, and Jagger leaned against her as though sensing her distress. "You're killing me, Doc."

"Listen, don't do it for me. Don't even do it for yourself. Do it for Jagger."

Ray turned her head and found her new best friend staring back at her. He nudged her with his nose, and any resistance she had instantly crumbled. "She's using you against me, buddy."

Jagger's mouth widened into what Ray was convinced was a shit-eating grin, tongue unfurling and nostrils flaring. How could she deny this dog anything?

Narrowing her eyes, Ray looked back at the camera. "Fine, I'll make him an appointment."

Dr. Evans seemed extremely satisfied. "And give that boy a biscuit for me."

"Yes, ma'am."

Chapter Two

R ay sat in her pickup, parked as far from the front door of the North Coast Veterinary Clinic as she could get, trying to stay in the moment. The anticipation of walking inside knotted her stomach, and she was starting to sweat at the thought of actually talking to a veterinarian. What if they expected her to answer a lot of questions? Worries, fear, and doubt paralyzed her and made her breathing rapid and shallow.

She closed her eyes and imagined Dr. Evans telling her to live in the present, to stop focusing on what had happened and what might come next. More than any other symptom of the PTSD, this failure to live in the present was the hardest for her to overcome. It was why she was so often unable to imagine leaving the safety of her own little bubble.

"I can do this," Ray said out loud. Jagger rested his head on her shoulder and whined in a low grumble, clearly sensing her distress.

A refreshing light breeze ruffled her hair and coaxed an involuntary smile from her tense lips. Exhaling, Ray whispered, "I'm okay. Everything is okay." She breathed in through her nostrils slowly, concentrating on the feel of sitting in the leather car seat. Opening her eyes, she studied a eucalyptus tree whose leaves hung over the fence she was parked against. Its intoxicating smell was just what she needed to calm down enough to take the keys out of the ignition.

"You ready to go meet your new doctor, buddy?"

Jagger withdrew his head from between the seats and half stood in the extended cab, clearly eager to get out. Ray put on her favorite pair of sunglasses, needing the tinted barrier between herself and the outside world. Then she grabbed Jagger's leash and opened the truck door.

I can do this.

❖

Dr. Carly Warner grimaced as she examined the skin sample beneath the microscope's lens. She'd known without looking that the boxer puppy in exam room two hadn't yet overcome a particularly bad case of demodectic mange, but hoped that it would've improved more by now. Maybe it was time for a new tactic in the puppy's treatment.

"Damn it," Carly muttered. She hated to suggest Mitaban dip, as it was nasty stuff, but it looked like the ivermectin alone wasn't cutting it. Pulling away from the microscope, she squeezed the back of her neck and closed her eyes briefly. Since when did she get so tired after only six hours of work?

The door to the back room opened and Joyce entered in typical fashion. "You will not *believe* who's sitting in the waiting room right now."

Carly made a note in Boadie the boxer puppy's chart and turned to walk back to exam room two. She hated to tell this young family to bring their new puppy in for relatively expensive weekly dips in a parasiticidal rinse and didn't have much patience for Joyce's reception desk gossip. Usually she tolerated busybodies like Joyce reasonably well, but today she felt more irritable than normal. Maybe she needed to get laid. The thought brought on a twinge of guilt, but it had a ring of truth.

"Who?" Matt asked. An extremely competent vet tech, he never hesitated to snap up whatever tasty tidbit Joyce offered. "Scarlett Johansson?"

Carly rolled her eyes, unable to suppress a smirk. The eternal hope of youth. She put her hand on her exam room's knob, ready to deliver the disappointing news.

"Ray McKenna." Joyce acted as though she were announcing the cure for cancer.

Carly released the knob and stared at Joyce, whose eyes gleamed with solemnity. Despite the histrionics, Carly was suddenly very interested in what she had to say.

"Like, the hostage?" Matt turned his attention away from the cat whose blood sample he was taking, mouth agape. "That Ray McKenna?"

"Who the hell is Ray McKenna?" Susan said. Another very good vet tech, she was twenty years old and clearly stayed away from network news and most other media sources. Probably lived in a cave.

"Are you kidding me?" Joyce seemed to vibrate with the pleasure of being able to deliver such big news. "The American soldier who was captured in Iraq a couple years ago? They cut off her buddy's head? She was in that tape the terrorists made?" Joyce was nearly frothing, as excited as Carly had ever seen her. "Any of that ring a bell?"

"I guess so," Susan said, but she looked uncertain. "So the terrorists let her go?"

"Insurgents," Matt interjected. "There's a difference."

"The marines found where the *insurgents* were keeping her and stormed in. It was this huge rescue mission." Joyce shook her head in disbelief. "You're kidding me that you don't know who Ray McKenna is. Do you ever turn on the TV? Or read a paper? Or a magazine?"

Susan shrugged a little defensively. "Two years ago I had just graduated high school. I was having a lot of sex with my ex-boyfriend then."

"Apparently," Joyce said.

"So what's Ray McKenna doing here?" Matt turned back to the cat, who was meowing loudly on the counter in front of him.

"I'm guessing it has something to do with the Great Dane with her," Joyce said. "It's Dr. Warner's next patient."

Carly maintained an even expression, not wanting to encourage any of her colleagues to react differently to Ray McKenna's presence than that of any other client. "I'm finishing up in exam two," she said. "Susan, why don't you take them to exam one and get started? I'll be there as soon as I can."

"Sure." Susan set aside the medications she was sorting through.

"And all of you, please, try not to make it obvious that you're curious. I'm sure she's gotten a lot of attention since coming home, and I can't imagine that all the morbid curiosity is fun to deal with. Let's treat Ms. McKenna like any other pet owner who comes in here, okay? With respect."

"Yes, Doctor," Susan said as she walked to the door that led to the waiting room. As she passed Carly, she said in a low voice, "I really don't know who she is, anyway."

Carly patted her on the back. "Marathon sex is time consuming," she said in a similarly quiet voice. "I was in college once, I get it." Wanting to avoid the inevitable rush of melancholy that would sweep over her if she allowed herself to dwell on those memories, Carly put on a sympathetic face for Boadie's family and opened the exam room door.

❖

Carly thought she was more than prepared not to react when she saw Ray McKenna in person, but she wasn't expecting the former soldier to be so beautiful. The pictures and videos splashed all over the news and Internet for the past couple of years had alternated between shots of a fresh-faced kid and a frightened soldier. None of those images contained a hint of the alluring woman in front of Carly now. Even with her eyes hidden behind a pair of sunglasses, Ray McKenna was the kind of the woman who would've drawn Carly's attention, no matter who she was.

Ray was studying a large poster detailing the different breeds of domestic cat when Carly opened the door, and she startled visibly at the sound. Her dark hair was cut short, falling just below her ears, and her features were delicate. Pale skinned and slender, and achingly feminine, she wasn't at all what Carly had imagined.

With effort, Carly was able to limit her reaction to Ray's appearance to only a slight hesitation as she walked in, and for that she was grateful. Anxiety was pouring off Ray in waves, and the palpable tension in the room compelled Carly into a familiar air of professional detachment.

Sitting on the floor beside Ray's chair, nearly as tall as her, was an impressive blue Great Dane with natural ears. Carly focused on the dog, which wasn't terribly hard to do, in an effort to make Ray feel more at ease. This appointment was about him, she reminded herself, not Ray.

At her entrance, Jagger stood and placed himself between Ray and the door. Carly noted with interest the red service-dog cape he was wearing, wondering what role he played in his guardian's life. Ray appeared to be in one piece, reasonably healthy, and though she wore sunglasses, she tracked Carly's movement in a way that suggested vision wasn't her problem.

"Oh, you are a handsome guy, aren't you?" Carly bent slightly, reaching out to see if the Dane would come to her. "Good boy, Jagger," she cooed, rattling off the name she had memorized from his newly created chart only moments before. Sparing Ray a brief glance, she said, "Hi, I'm Dr. Warner. Carly Warner."

"Hello," Ray said quietly. Her voice betrayed an obvious case of nerves, but the timbre of it was lovely. Smooth and low, even sexy. She cleared her throat, then said, "I'm Ray."

"It's nice to meet you." Carly grinned down at Jagger, who had left his owner's side to give her a careful sniff and then a slightly wet nuzzle. "I love Danes. And he's absolutely gorgeous."

"He's my first." Ray sat up straight in the chair, looking uncomfortable. Though Carly couldn't see her eyes behind the dark lenses, she sensed that Ray wasn't sure where to focus her gaze. "I always wanted one."

"They're wonderful dogs." Carly ran a hand along Jagger's face, then down to pat his chest. Susan had given her an overview of the purpose of this appointment already, so Carly inserted the earpieces of her stethoscope and smiled at Ray. "We're giving Jagger only a basic exam today?"

Ray nodded. After a slight hesitation, she said, "I just moved to town, so I thought…well, I thought we would come to the vet's office." Scowling, Ray tilted her face, probably looking at the floor. Her cheeks turned an interesting shade of pink, and she swiped at her forehead with the back of one hand. "You know, to meet you. So Jagger could meet you."

Carly listened to Jagger's heartbeat for a few seconds, a steady, strong rhythm, then inspected his ears. They were velvety soft and very clean. As she went through the steps of the simple exam, she tried to decide whether she should attempt to make small talk with Ray, who was clearly not happy to be here. Carly worried that Joyce had given away her intense curiosity at the front desk and caused this obvious discomfort.

"It was a good idea to come," Carly said, keeping her eyes on the Dane as she examined him. "It's nice when people bring their pets in when nothing traumatic is happening. Helps the animal learn to trust the people in the funny blue scrubs." She picked up a thermometer from the counter, giving Jagger an apologetic chuckle. "Well, nothing too traumatic." Jagger cocked his head slightly, looking at the new object in her hand, and Carly said, "I promise you'll get a treat out of it, big boy."

"He never refuses a treat."

Affection rang clear in Ray's voice, and Carly instinctively warmed. Ray was an animal lover. Strangely, not all pet owners were. So that meant she and Ray had something very important in common. Maybe it was enough to help them establish a rapport. "Would you mind petting him while I take his temperature? Sometimes a distraction helps."

For a moment Ray didn't move, looking slightly stricken, but she quickly recovered. She called Jagger to her and he went eagerly. Ray cradled his head in her lap and started massaging behind his ears in a way that Carly knew would make her own dog Jack weak in the knees.

"So is he your first dog, or just your first Dane?" Carly asked as she inserted the thermometer. Jagger took a slight step forward, but otherwise betrayed no reaction.

"My father had a German shepherd when I was a kid," Ray said. "But Jagger is the first dog I've ever had on my own."

"I have a mutt who's probably a German shepherd mix," Carly said. "One of many guesses. Rhodesian ridgeback or boxer are other possibilities. Adopted him from the shelter up in Ukiah. He's a sweetheart."

Ray said nothing, but slowly took off her sunglasses. She fumbled with them a bit as she put them in her front pocket, then, drawing in a breath, she met Carly's eyes. Her mouth moved as she said something, but Carly didn't hear a word.

Ray McKenna was one of the most gorgeous women Carly had ever seen. Her hazel eyes were breathtaking, full of loneliness and sorrow, but also shining with an inner beauty that made Carly feel as though she were gazing directly into Ray's soul. Carly felt lost in their depths, and her professional demeanor slipped for a moment when she realized she was staring.

Averting her gaze, she tried to recall what Ray had just said. *Sorry,*

I'm not trying to be rude. Determined to get ahold of herself, Carly said evenly, "No reason to apologize. They looked nice on you."

"How old is your dog?" Ray asked.

Carly withdrew the thermometer and glanced at the display. "Looks good," she said. "Jack is probably just over five years old. I say 'probably' because I can only guess. He was picked up as a stray, so the shelter didn't have much information on him."

"It's great that you gave him a second chance."

"He deserved it." Carly rose and crossed the exam room to rinse the thermometer in the sink. She kept it under the water a bit longer than she needed, grateful for the breathing room. When the hell had she ever reacted so strongly to a straight woman? This was completely unlike her, and her lack of control irritated her. "Jack's a good boy." Smiling over at Jagger, she cooed, "And so are you, Jagger. How about that treat I promised?"

The moment her hand went into the treat jar, Jagger's ears perked up. Sitting up straight, he watched her face as she crossed the room, easing into an appealing doggy grin.

Because he was already sitting, Carly offered her hand and said, "Can you give me your paw?"

Jagger lifted one heavy paw and dropped it into her hand, drawing a proud smile from Ray. "Good boy." Carly offered him the biscuit, which he took gently, and Ray murmured another "good boy."

"Well, he looks as healthy as a horse," Carly said. Glancing at his chart, she noted, "Almost as big as one, too. One hundred seventy pounds. Wow."

"I told you he never refused a treat."

Carly looked up from the chart and laughed, catching Ray's gaze. In that moment Ray was as unguarded as she'd been since Carly walked into the room. Ray shared a smile with her, then seemed to realize what she was doing and smiled even harder, shyly turning away.

"Well, thank you guys for coming to meet me," Carly said, and rubbed Jagger's floppy ears. "Come see me again, Jagger. I can always promise a treat."

"He will," Ray said quietly. "Thank you, Dr. Warner."

"You're very welcome. You can just stop by the front counter on your way out." Carly gave Ray one last nod, then walked out of the exam room. Once the door closed behind her, she collapsed against the wall and exhaled. "That was ridiculous," she scolded herself. Ray McKenna was straight, she was clearly very introverted, and Carly had read something about a boyfriend in one of those magazines. "What the hell is wrong with me?"

Maybe she really did need to get laid.

CHAPTER THREE

After her last patient of the day, Carly woke Jack from what sounded like one hell of a barking, grumbling nap in the corner of her office and took him to say good-bye to Joyce and Dr. Patterson, who owned the clinic. As usual, they were the last three holdouts at the clinic after a very long day. Normally she would have outlasted even Patterson, sixty years old but still tireless at his practice, but today she was eager to get home, if only to a nice glass of wine and some quality time with her dog.

With Jack secured to the passenger seat in his car harness, Carly cracked the window slightly and pulled out onto Highway 1. As it did every day, the breathtaking Northern California coast made for a pleasant commute home. The three twisting, hilly miles drove more like ten, but the serene beauty of the Pacific Ocean crashing against the rocky shore made it a pleasure. In fact, she often overshot her house on purpose, just so she could keep enjoying the view. Sonoma County was so different from San Francisco, and while she loved the city and all its strange rhythms, she had worked toward an inner peace here that she doubted she could have ever attained in her old apartment in the Castro.

Carly pulled into her driveway at six fifteen, deciding that the glass of wine she had imagined sounded better than prolonging her scenic drive. Besides, the sun would go down in an hour or so, and she wanted to be able to do some agility training with Jack before it was too late. He seemed to relish the brief walks they were able to take when Carly had time between patients during the day, but she knew he was most happy when he could really expend his energy.

Unbuckling Jack from his harness, she patted him on the chest and said, "Let's go!" He hopped out of the car and immediately lunged forward into a rather dramatic stretch. Tail wagging madly, he yawned, then trotted to her side as she headed into the house.

They went straight through to the backyard and Jack ran over to the first obstacle in the modest agility course she had set up, a relatively small A-frame. His entire back end swayed side to side with the force of his wagging tail, and Carly's fatigue began to slip away at the sight of her best friend's obvious joy.

"Okay." Carly pointed at the A-frame. "Go!"

As always, Jack's improvement in running the course impressed her. They didn't get a lot of practice time together, but he learned quickly as long as he was having fun. Carly ran alongside him shouting commands, awed by his pure athleticism. Sixty-five pounds of muscle, he was fawn colored with a black mask on his face and a white muzzle, a handsome, graceful mutt whose incredible speed and strength outdoors belied his absolutely lazy personality in the house.

She took him through the course five times, until he seemed to become more easily distracted by the random bird chirping overhead or a particularly alluring scent on the breeze. When he veered off course to give the corner of the wooden fence that enclosed her yard a vigorous sniff, Carly decided it was time for them both to get something to eat.

"Okay, Jackie," Carly said. "I get it. You're done for today." She walked to the back door and called out, "Dinnertime." Jack nearly broke his neck in his haste to follow.

Once inside, Carly went through her nightly routine with practiced efficiency. She pulled some leftover pasta from the fridge and tossed it in the microwave, then uncorked a bottle of pinot noir. As the pasta heated, Carly filled Jack's food dish with kibble and a bit of soft food, to entice him to eat. Due to skin allergies, he was restricted to a diet of duck-and-potato kibble, which he seemed to find only marginally appealing.

When both of their dinners were prepared, Carly loaded her arms with the food and the bottle of wine, then made her way out to the patio. Jack followed close at her side, threatening to trip her with his eagerness to be with her. He was like a shadow, her constant companion, and despite the times he made her stumble over him, she couldn't imagine not having him there.

Setting Jack's food dish in his elevated feeder, Carly released him to eat almost immediately. Usually she would go through their obedience commands first, but she was too tired. Instead she headed straight for the small café table, dropping into a cushioned chair to pour a glass of pinot noir.

Before she moved to Sonoma County, she hadn't been a big wine drinker. But once she lived here, she felt obliged to learn to enjoy her new home's most famous export. To her surprise, Carly had developed a true appreciation for the stuff—so much so that she sometimes had to remind herself not to overindulge. Especially on an evening like this, when the loneliness she tried so hard not to feel crept in, leaving her hollowed out and introspective.

Carly closed her eyes, trying to appreciate the silence of the evening. Five years ago, she wouldn't have liked this quietness. She'd thrived on the excitement of the city, and she and Nadia rarely spent a solitary evening at home. Now silence was all she had, and learning to find the beauty in it kept her sane.

She had been a different person before Nadia died, someone she hardly recognized after all this time. She remembered what it was like back then, most likely idealized it, but she couldn't come close to recapturing who she had been—how happy she usually was, how certain of exactly how her life would turn out. Back then she still thought she and Nadia would grow old together, raise a couple of kids, and do their best to spread around even a little of their joy.

One of the hardest things Carly had ever learned, and she had only recently begun to come to peace with it, was that life never turns out exactly how you plan it. Even if you're happy. Maybe especially if you're happy.

This was uncharted territory, the task of trying to figure out what her life was supposed to look like without Nadia. So far she had come up with this quiet existence of solitary dinners, evenings spent buried in a good book, and nights curled up next to the only thing that kept her from feeling totally alone. Her dog.

"No offense, Jack," Carly said as she opened her eyes, giving him a wistful smile. "But I miss two-way conversations in bed." Among other things. Shaking her head, Carly took a bite of her pasta and allowed herself to dwell on the most unsettling experience of her long day.

Ray McKenna.

Of course Carly had noticed other women since Nadia. She'd even had sex. Twice. The first time was about a year ago, when Leeann convinced her to go to a lesbian bar in the city. Her best friend and ex had been positively tickled when Carly went home with a delicious butch whose name, she was ashamed to admit, was lost to her memories of that emotionally intense night. Pushing through her guilt at touching anyone except Nadia, Carly was surprised to find that the sex was good. And that it was something she had been wanting and needing for a long time.

But Carly had never been the no-strings-attached type. When she and Nadia met in college, they dated for two months before sleeping together the first time. And until that butch in the bar last year, Carly hadn't been with anyone else. Now she had slept with two women after Nadia, and her desire for release was back again. Though she had never been into casual sex, casual was all she could bear. Even if the brief feeling of connection she so craved was illusory, it would sustain her until she could imagine sharing something more than her body again.

What bothered her about Ray McKenna was that the feelings she had stirred up didn't seem casual at all. Granted, Carly would love to take her to bed. Ray was gorgeous, just her type. But more than just detached lust sparked Carly's interest. She recognized Ray's silence, a long-buried hurt. And though it wasn't the healthiest basis for attraction, Carly was inextricably drawn to it. More than wanting sex, she yearned to get to know Ray.

"She's straight," Carly said aloud. She took another sip of wine, tasting the words on her lips. "She's straight and she's clearly broken. What the hell is wrong with me?"

And I'm not ready to care that much about getting to know a woman yet, Carly told herself, though she certainly felt ready when she allowed herself to fantasize about being happy again. Before the guilt and fear crept in.

Ready or not, Carly knew why Ray McKenna had shaken her up so much. These feelings, no matter how impossible and ill advised, were exciting. That she was even having them was some kind of miracle. Until she saw Ray, Carly wasn't sure she would ever feel that kind of interest in a woman again.

Now that she knew it was possible, she wasn't sure what to do next.

CHAPTER FOUR

So have you and Jagger made it to the beach yet?"

Ray fidgeted in her stiff-backed office chair, unable to look directly at the image of Dr. Evans on her monitor. Even half a country away, she still didn't like giving her therapist answers that were sure to disappoint. "Not all the way, no."

"Part of the way, then?"

Did a hundred yards count? The beach was a half mile from Ray's house, but it might as well have been on the other side of the world. Every time she thought about going, the enormity of the task overwhelmed her. And she was starting to regret ever telling Dr. Evans about her desire to take Jagger to the ocean. "We've gone a little way."

"But not very far," Dr. Evans said. Her tone told Ray that she knew exactly how little progress she had made on this particular item. Though her voice was gentle, it unleashed a flood of guilt that made Ray shift in discomfort.

"I'm sorry, Dr. Evans," Ray murmured. Tears threatened to spill and she blinked them back angrily. "I really do want to go."

"There's no reason to be sorry. This is difficult for you. Let's talk about why this walk challenges you so much, okay? Then we'll figure out how you can gain the confidence to make it all the way next time."

Nodding, Ray dabbed at her eyes. "Okay."

"Do you need a minute to breathe? I want you present here. Let's try very hard not to slip into a negative place while we talk about this, all right?"

Ray nodded again, then closed her eyes and took a deep breath from her abdomen. As she exhaled slowly, the tension began to melt away. Dr. Evans had taught her somatic breathing exercises during their first sessions together, and though she used to feel self-conscious doing them, they had become an effective way to center herself. She concentrated on the sensation of the office chair cradling her body, on the sound of Jagger's deep snoring as he dozed at her feet. After a minute or so, Ray opened her eyes and gazed into the webcam.

"Welcome back," Dr. Evans said, smiling gently. "Take a moment to feel what you feel."

Ray took stock. The tension in her shoulders had eased, and she was more grounded. No longer on the verge of tears, thankfully. She was ready to talk this through. "I tried to walk to the beach yesterday, but we barely got off my property before I had to turn around."

"What happened?"

Ray shrugged, then paused. Though she was more practiced at talking about her fears now, it was never easy to put her thoughts and feelings into words. "I slipped into a state of hypervigilance and just couldn't get out of it. It's hard to make myself leave the house when I'm convinced something terrible will happen."

"Did you use your mantra?"

Early on in therapy, Dr. Evans had taught her to repeat a phrase or a poem when her symptoms appeared. Something with a strong rhythm to help take her focus off the anxiety while reminding her that she was safe in the present. Ray had chosen two lines from the poem "Invictus" by William Ernest Henley, which she first read shortly after being diagnosed with PTSD. *"I am the master of my fate: / I am the captain of my soul."* Usually it worked. This time nothing had seemed to calm her down. "I did, but it was just…too much."

"Did you try to stop and breathe?"

"For a second," Ray said, although that wasn't quite true. She'd let the panic take hold and carry her back in the direction of her house before she'd even had time to try and break its spell. "I didn't do a very good job, though."

"It's tough. You've experienced a great deal of trauma, threats to your personal safety that most people couldn't even imagine. I know it's difficult to make yourself stay in the present in that kind of situation, but that's exactly what will get you through it. And it will just take practice."

"I know." Running her hands through her short hair, Ray grumbled, "But I'm tired of practicing."

"You took Jagger to the vet last month," Dr. Evans said. "That was a big deal. Good for you."

"Yeah." The vet had been a real challenge, that was for sure. Ray straightened slightly, trying to focus on her one real victory. The waiting room had been hell, but Dr. Warner had actually made her feel comfortable. "The vet wasn't too bad."

"And you finally made it to the grocery store."

"I know. It was terrifying." Even behind her sunglasses, Ray had felt as though everyone in the store was looking at her and her dog, wondering why she needed him. Probably trying to remember everything they had read, all the gory details. Calling up their memories of her hostage videos, imagining what kinds of atrocities she'd experienced that they didn't know about.

"But you did it anyway."

"I had to," Ray admitted. "I needed the food."

"You did it," Dr. Evans repeated. "That's something to celebrate."

"I guess so. I was a nervous wreck the whole time. You wouldn't believe how many people stopped to ask me about Jagger. I knew he was gorgeous when I got him, but I didn't anticipate the attention he would draw."

"Well, he's a pretty magnificent dog. I'm not surprised people would be curious about him."

Ray couldn't disagree. "I sewed patches on his service vest that say *Stop. Don't Touch. Service Dog*, but to be honest, I'm not sure how well they work. People ask if they can pet him all the time."

"Think about it this way. When people are looking at Jagger, they're probably not paying much attention to you."

"I guess so." That was a good point and almost made Ray feel better. "But it means I have to interact with people. You know I hate that."

"It's good for you, though. It really is. And would you trade Jagger, if it meant you didn't have to deal with his admirers?"

"Of course not."

Dr. Evans smiled. "So revel in it."

"I don't know about reveling, but I'll try."

"That's where practice comes in. As often as possible. So, back to the beach. When you set out, where does your mind go?"

Ray forced herself to remember how she felt yesterday, careful not to let herself slip back into the panic. She evaluated her feelings as objectively as she could, taking deep breaths as she explored them. "I feel...exposed." Dr. Evans nodded but kept silent, allowing her to expand on her initial observation. "Vulnerable. I feel *danger*. Like anyone could come at me from any direction, so I need to constantly be on guard. It's exhausting."

"Isn't Jagger trained to put himself between you and anyone who approaches?"

"Yes. And he does a good job. He's also trained to watch behind me and alert me to anyone who might be there."

"So maybe you don't need to be so on guard," Dr. Evans said. "When you try this walk next time, I want you to focus on Jagger and his reactions. He's a pretty calm dog, right?"

"Yeah." Ray petted his head, eliciting a grumble that tugged her lips into a smile. Jagger's job was to be calm and watchful, and she needed to remember to rely on his training. "He's downright mellow."

"If Jagger is calm, there must not be any danger. Correct?"

Ray nodded thoughtfully. The service-dog institute had told her the same thing during her orientation training with Jagger. "I need to focus on Jagger and remind myself that if he thinks everything is cool, everything *is* cool."

"That's right." Dr. Evans gazed at her warmly. "You might also want to remember that nobody's likely to harass you with a giant Great Dane at your side."

That's why she had wanted him, wasn't it? Ray took another deep breath, steadying her resolve. A half mile wasn't too bad. And they didn't have to stay at the beach long.

"Okay," she said after a moment of silent preparation. "We'll try again this afternoon."

❖

Carly came out of exam room one riding the high of seeing Apollo, a Siamese kitten with enormous ears, finally go home. He had been found by the side of the road, apparently hit by a car, and he was doing great after a successful emergency surgery she and Dr. Patterson had performed together. The woman who adopted him was clearly thrilled to be able to take him to his forever home after his checkup today, and Carly felt over the moon about it. These were the cases that made being a vet worth all the heartache it could sometimes bring.

After walking to the computer and typing a note into Apollo's file, she clicked the Save button with a contented sigh. Carly checked her watch, pleased to see that she had five minutes until her next patient. That was more than enough time to take Jack outside to go potty.

"Okay, guys," she said to Matt and Susan, who were both drawing blood from a growling, squirming cat. "I'm taking a quick break. I'll be back for my next appointment."

"Sure," Susan said without looking up. "Have fun."

"Smart girl," Carly said, grinning. "Never take your eyes off an angry cat."

"I learned that the hard way, believe me."

Before Carly could reach her office, Joyce made a dramatic entrance into the back room. Carly braced herself for whatever gossip was about to be trumpeted, but instead of the look of conspiratorial glee she normally wore, Joyce's expression was grave. "Dr. Warner, I need your help up front."

Carly instantly changed direction. *Sorry, Jack.* "Emergency?"

"It's Ray McKenna," Joyce said, though her voice lacked the sick pleasure it had the first time she'd broken that news. "Something happened to her dog at the beach, but I'm having trouble getting the details. She's freaking out."

"Freaking out?"

"I told her we don't have an exam room open right now, but she won't let me bring him back here. Causing a bit of a scene, actually."

Carly picked up her pace and jogged to the waiting area. He was a service dog, so it made sense that Ray wouldn't want to be separated from him. She would have to remember to talk to Joyce about being tactful with clients who came in with service animals. Carly doubted that Ray spent much time away from Jagger, if any.

When Carly entered the front lobby, she immediately saw what Joyce was talking about. Ray McKenna was definitely freaking out. Though her eyes were hidden behind dark sunglasses, she wasn't doing a very good job of being as inconspicuous as Carly suspected she would have liked. Breathing hard, Ray held Jagger's leash in a death grip, her hands shaking. Her face, drawn and pale, was the picture of dread.

Two other clients sat staring intently at magazines, trying not to look interested in the drama playing out in front of them.

"Hi, Ray. Hi, Jagger," Carly said calmly, hoping that she could bring Ray down from her clearly agitated state with the appropriate tone. "What's going on?"

Ray jerked her head slightly to look at Carly, and Carly offered her a calm smile. Inside, her heart quickened at the state Ray was in. Jagger didn't appear to be in any obvious distress. What was wrong with her?

Sensing that no explanation was coming, Carly murmured, "Ray?" She touched Ray's shoulder, guessing that the contact might help bring her into focus. "Tell me what happened."

With a start and a gasp, Ray grabbed her hand and squeezed it tight. Carly watched in silence as Ray removed her hand from her shoulder, then let her go. "I'm sorry," Ray said in a tremulous voice. Carly wasn't sure if she was apologizing for her panic or the extreme reaction to being touched. "I think something bit Jagger. Or stung him. I don't know, I don't know what it was."

"Okay," Carly said. Shaking off her surprise at Ray's jumpiness, she hunkered down to Jagger's level, trying to determine Ray's cause for concern. "When did this happen?" Jagger stepped closer to sniff at her hand, and it became clear why Ray was so upset. The left side of his muzzle was badly swollen. He didn't appear to be having any trouble breathing, but his features were distorted.

When she realized Ray hadn't yet answered her question, Carly looked up and found her in the middle of what appeared to be some kind of anxiety attack. Glancing around at the other occupants of the waiting room, she saw three pairs of eyes boring into Ray, no doubt making things worse. Carly rose.

"Come on," she said, and reached out to take Ray's elbow. She stopped before she made contact, not wanting to give Ray any reason to lash out. "Why don't we go to my office and I'll take a look at him? You can stay with him while I do."

Ray nodded, and Carly began to lead her out of the lobby. "Please tell Mrs. Esguerra that I'll be with her shortly," she murmured to Joyce. "I want to examine Jagger for just a minute."

To her credit, Joyce simply nodded. Carly wasn't used to seeing her so subdued. She might have to thank Ray for achieving the seemingly impossible.

Carly led Ray to the back hallway that connected to her office. As soon as they were out of earshot, Carly said, "We'll have more privacy back here, as long as you don't mind meeting my dog Jack."

"I'd love to meet Jack," Ray said quietly.

Carly opened her office door to find Jack wagging his back end so fiercely his entire body moved side to side. "Jack is great with other dogs, by the way. He's just…enthusiastic."

They made their way into the office, Ray leading Jagger past a barrage of butt sniffing and tail wagging. Carly closed the door behind them, letting Jagger sniff Jack and complete their proper introductions before she held out her hand. "May I have his leash?"

Ray relinquished control of him with only slight hesitation. She made a subtle sweep of the room, given away only by the slightest movement of her head. Carly wished she had somehow had the foresight to clean up a bit.

"I made a complete fool of myself out there." Ray's voice was full of shame and, more than that, disappointment.

Carly shushed her gently and gestured at the leather couch opposite her desk. "Please feel free to sit down while I take a look at Jagger. Jack may try to join you, but if you're not interested just tell him, 'Off.'"

Silently, Ray walked to the couch and sank down on one end. She stretched an arm across the top of it, clearly attempting a casual attitude that she absolutely wasn't pulling off. Ray seemed to realize it wasn't working, because she retreated, folding both arms over her chest. Finally she dropped her hands to her sides and looked away, at the University of California Davis diploma hanging on the wall. Carly felt Ray's discomfort like a third person in the room, whose unwelcome presence made them both squirm.

Jack stopped sniffing Jagger and ambled over to the couch, nosing at Ray's thigh. When she didn't immediately take the bait, he rested his chin on her knee and gazed up at her with the soulful eyes that were always Carly's undoing. Jack rumbled contentedly when Ray scratched behind his ears.

"That's his favorite," Carly said. She got on her knees and took Jagger's head in her hands. "Keep doing that and you'll have a friend for life."

"Awesome." Ray's voice was so quiet Carly could barely hear her, but her pleasure at Jack's enthusiasm was obvious.

"And don't worry about what happened up front. A lot of clients who have service animals feel uncomfortable being separated from them. I'll make sure to remind Joyce that a service animal isn't just a pet."

Jack hopped up onto the couch and crawled across Ray's lap, flopping onto his side so she would have better access to his belly. Ray rubbed him with both hands, and Carly could see the beginnings of a brilliant smile tugging at her mouth.

"If he's bothering you…" Carly said, mostly because it seemed like the right thing to do. It was clear that the last thing Ray felt was bothered.

"Not at all," Ray said. "He's helping me, actually."

Carly returned her attention to Jagger. "His face is pretty swollen. It looks like he's having a reaction to whatever got him. Was he in the water at the time?"

"No. We were walking on the beach, near some rocks. He stuck his face in some brush, then yelped and jumped back. Something bit him, but I didn't see what it was."

Carly tilted his chin toward the early evening light that shone in through the office's only window. After a few moments of examining the swollen area, she straightened. "Aha." She retrieved her car keys from her desk drawer, plucking the tweezers from her Swiss Army knife. "I found the stinger. Looks like a bee or a wasp."

"Is it serious?"

"No, I don't think so." Carly knelt in front of Jagger again and carefully extracted the stinger from his muzzle. "He doesn't appear to be in any distress, but I'll give him some Benadryl to counteract the swelling. It could spread to his throat and make it difficult for him to breathe. The Benadryl will help, and you'll need to keep an eye on him until the swelling goes down to make sure he's doing okay."

"All right." Ray was rubbing her thumbs in circles over Jack's cheeks while he lay prone in her lap. She exhaled slowly, staring at Jagger. "Okay."

"Jack's not going to want to come home with me when you're through with him," Carly said lightly, cracking a smile at what an adorable pair the two of them made. To avoid allowing herself to linger too long on thoughts of how Ray McKenna was no less attractive this time around, panic attacks and all, she stood and returned the tweezers to her knife. "He *really* likes you."

"He's a gorgeous dog. Sweet, too."

"He is." Carly looked at Jagger and tried to decide what to do. She didn't want to keep her next patient waiting, but calculating and delivering the correct dosage of Benadryl for such a big dog would take a few minutes. "We need to give Jagger some medicine, but I'm due to see a patient right now. I can either take him back with me and let one of the vet techs take care of him, or I can ask the tech to get the medicine ready and come give it to him in here, with you." She saw Ray swallow, looking at Jagger, then at the door. "Your choice. Whatever makes you most comfortable."

"I guess you can take him back," Ray said after a moment, sounding less than certain about her decision.

"You sure?"

"I just…I haven't been separated from him since I got him."

"I promise to make this Susan's top priority. It won't take long."

"Okay." As Ray nodded, her face became resolute. "It's fine."

Carly wasn't fooled. This would be a difficult task for Ray, and though Carly knew she could never fully understand, she empathized enough to know that Ray needed a little help to get through it. Jack seemed like the perfect candidate.

Walking Jagger to the door, Carly said, "Listen, do you mind keeping Jack company while we take care of Jagger? I intended to take him for a walk, but I didn't have time. He's starved for attention, as you can tell."

"Yeah, that's what he told me." Ray smiled shyly. "I'd love to hang out with Jack, Dr. Warner. Thanks."

"No, thank you. You'll be doing me a favor. And call me Carly, please."

"Okay." Ray caught her sunglasses in her hand and pulled them off quickly. Her eyes shone with so much emotion that Carly's heart nearly stopped. "Thanks, Carly. For everything."

"Not a problem, Ray." Carly tugged on Jagger's leash, leading him to the door. "Jagger will be just fine. And we'll be back shortly."

CHAPTER FIVE

After Carly left the office, Ray sank back against the couch cushions and groaned. "Goddamn it," she whispered to herself. "I'm fucking hopeless."

Just an hour ago, she had been celebrating a major triumph. Finally they'd made it to the beach, and she had stayed calm enough to explore a bit rather than immediately head for home. How proud she had felt as she strolled down the shore, Jagger at her side, almost like a normal person again.

And now here she was in Dr. Warner's office, nursing her mortification at making an absolute fool of herself in front of no less than four people. Including Dr. Warner.

Ray slammed her head back against the cushion, wishing it hurt more. She was in the mood for self-punishment. "I am such a loser."

She couldn't explain her reaction to Jagger's injury. After spending a year elbow-deep in the most horrific wartime wounds, she had suspected this wasn't a huge crisis. After all, Jagger seemed fine, if a little goofy-looking with his swollen face. But the yelp he'd let loose when he was stung sent her into a wild panic. Something terrible had happened, just as she thought it would. Maybe it wasn't a roadside bomb or a physical assault, but her body reacted as though it were.

The tears that burned their way to the front made her feel even more ashamed. *Great.* She closed her eyes, already picturing the trembling, sobbing mess she would be when Dr. Warner returned. That was the last thing she wanted. She liked Dr. Warner—Carly—a lot. And she cared deeply about what Carly thought.

Focus. Ray coached herself, breathing out through her nose.

As though sensing her distress, Jack quickly stood up in her lap and nuzzled her face with his wet nose. He whined, a strange sound that came from the back of his throat, then pawed her arm.

Opening her eyes, Ray couldn't help but laugh at the earnest expression in his chocolate brown eyes. "Okay, okay. I get it." She redoubled her petting efforts, and he slumped against her, thumping his tail against the couch cushion. "Thank you."

Ray stared at Jack, completely charmed. His pretty coat was brown, with a white chest and stomach. His black muzzle faded into freckled white around his nose. Ray assumed he had never undergone any type of service-animal training, yet he seemed to instinctively know what she needed. Amazing.

"Your mommy raised you well," Ray murmured, then gave his ear a quick kiss. "She seems like a pretty nice lady."

Jack drew in a breath then sighed deeply, flopping onto her lap again. He looked up at her as though to say, "Just relax." Remarkably, that's exactly what she began to do.

Closing her eyes, Ray did her somatic breathing exercise, inhaling deeply from her diaphragm, then exhaling. Once she felt centered, she opened her eyes and allowed her gaze to travel over her surroundings.

Nobody could accuse Carly Warner of being a neat freak. Ray smiled at the short, disordered stacks of papers and magazines covering the large wooden desk that sat opposite the couch. The tall bookcase next to the door was crammed to bursting with precariously balanced medical and animal-related volumes. A dog bed sat in the corner next to Carly's office chair, and the floor was littered with chew toys. An empty food dish and a half-full water bowl rounded out Jack's presence in the room.

Ray glanced down at the sleeping dog in her lap, chuckling at his peaceful expression. He cracked an eyelid, then stretched.

"You're a lazy guy, aren't you?" Ray scratched his belly, and he yawned as though answering in the affirmative. "Jagger's pretty lazy, too. I believe the technical term is 'couch potato.' I think you two would get along just fine."

A light knock on the office door startled Ray badly. She jerked, waking Jack but not dislodging him from her lap. Heart pounding, she called out, "Yes?"

The door opened and Jagger poked his enormous head inside. At the sight of his steel gray fur, Ray relaxed. His face was still swollen, but he seemed in good spirits.

"Well, Mom, Jagger was a very good boy." A smiling Carly followed Jagger into the room, tugging her hair out of her ponytail as she walked. "Took his medicine like a champ. You should see a reduction in swelling within an hour."

"Great," Ray murmured. Strawberry-blond locks fell just past Carly's shoulders, and Carly dropped Jagger's leash and swept her hair aside to squeeze the back of her neck. Settling onto the couch next to Ray, Carly sighed and rolled her eyes at Jack.

"You're just embarrassing yourself at this point, buddy." Carly gave Ray a tired grin, then carefully patted Jack's side. Her hand came close to Ray's thigh, closer than Ray had let nearly anyone since Iraq.

Ray was pleased by the ease with which she was able to accept Carly's presence at her side. Her instinctive reaction to Carly's touch in the waiting room had deeply disturbed and humiliated her. What a relief to find that she could hold it together now. *Almost like a normal person*, came the familiar self-deprecatory thought.

Ray looked up to meet Carly's gaze, ready to confess her instant love for Jack, and realized how attractive Carly Warner was. Never one to dwell on another woman's beauty, Ray was inexplicably tongue-tied and more than a little nervous. So much for normalcy.

Body tense, Ray tried to move on without calling attention to the fact that she had just been struck dumb. She had been about to say something. What was it?

Coming to her rescue for a countless time, Jagger loped up to her and dropped his heavy head on her shoulder, nuzzling into her neck. Ray couldn't help but chuckle at the familiar display of affection.

Carly brought a hand to her mouth as though trying to suppress the grin that formed behind her fingers. "Oh, my God, that's adorable."

After she kissed him on the cheek, Ray said, "He's just a big baby." She was proud of her relationship with Jagger. Her strange moment of anxiety passed and she was able to speak again. "Thank you so much for your help today, Carly."

"You're very welcome. Thanks for keeping Jack company. He definitely appreciated it."

Ray stroked the side of Jack's face. "I appreciated him. He's a really good boy."

Jack's tail twitched, then began to thump a steady rhythm against Carly's thigh. Ray recognized the look of pleasure on Carly's face. "He'll do in a pinch."

With a noisy yawn, Jack picked himself up and lumbered across the couch, only to collapse once again in Carly's lap. Carly bent to kiss his head, scratching his chest lightly.

"I think you're still number one," Ray said, observing their closeness with a warm heart. "But I was happy to borrow him for a while. And I'll be honest. He really helped calm me down."

"Yeah?"

Ray nodded, feeling shy about where she was taking the conversation, but at the same time wanting to tell Carly how incredible Jack had been. "Jagger helps me calm down, you know, when I get overwhelmed. And Jack did the same thing. I don't know if he's ever had training for that kind of thing—"

"He hasn't," Carly said quietly, gaze locked on Ray's face.

From the look in Carly's eyes, Ray knew she was putting together just what Jagger's role in her life was. Trying hard not to dwell on what Carly might be thinking, she said, "Well, he's a natural. I was pretty upset after you took Jagger, and he knew exactly what to do."

Carly kissed Jack on the head again, closing her eyes briefly as she did. "Dogs are amazing, aren't they?"

"They really are. I don't know what I'd do without them, honestly."

Jagger took a step backward, then extended his neck so he could sniff Jack. Obviously sensing the scrutiny, Jack licked Jagger's jowls. Ray watched them, happy to see that Jagger knew how to make friends even if she didn't.

"I think they like each other," Carly said. She petted Jagger's head, then Jack's.

"Looks that way." Ray wondered whether she should start asking about payment. Surely she had overstayed her welcome.

"We should get them together for a play date sometime," Carly said suddenly. She kept her eyes on Ray's face, obviously searching for a reaction. "You're new to the area, right? Does Jagger have any other doggy friends yet?"

Ray's cheeks warmed under Carly's scrutiny. "No."

Uncharacteristically candid, she said, "We don't really know anyone here."

"So what do you think?" Carly said, giving her a careful smile. "I could make dinner. The dogs could hang out."

Ray was unsure what to say. The last thing she had expected was a social invitation. Why in the hell would someone like Carly Warner want to have dinner with her? Ray's hackles rose. Was she simply curious about the media story? Or did Carly want something else from her?

"Do you know who I am?" Ray asked. She studied Carly's face, trying to discern her motives. It's not like she had given Carly many legitimate reasons to want to have dinner together, freak that she was.

"I've read the news stories, if that's what you're asking," Carly said in an even voice. "But I wouldn't say that I know who you are, Ray. I was kind of hoping to, though. If you're willing. I'm relatively new to Bodega Bay, too, and I could use a friend. I thought…maybe you could, too."

A friend. Ray was stunned silent. This was the last thing she had expected to find when she packed up and moved across the country. It wasn't a good idea. She was a mess, after all. A fucked-up, embarrassing mess. How could she be anyone's friend? Was it even possible, at this point?

A small piece of her, the part that remained from before Iraq, remembered what it was like. The old Ray would have loved the idea of going to Carly's house for dinner and letting her dog hang out with a canine pal. Even her new, damaged self couldn't deny the idea's appeal. But she was probably fooling herself. She was far too screwed up. She would only scare Carly away.

No negative predictions. Ray could almost hear Dr. Evans's voice in her head, and she tried to imagine what her therapist would make of this unexpected development. Oh, hell, who was she kidding? Dr. Evans would tell her that accepting the dinner invitation was the best possible thing she could do.

Shoving aside the nagging voice of self-doubt, silencing the alarm bells ringing in her skull, Ray reached deep down and drew upon what courage she had left. If things were ever going to change, she would have to be the one to make it happen. "Dinner would be great."

Carly looked pleasantly surprised. "Really?"

"Sure. It sounds like…fun." Ray winced, all too aware that she sounded like she'd rather have her toenails removed one by one. "You'll have to forgive me. I haven't been out much since I got home."

"I'd say I understand, but I'm sure I don't." To her credit, Carly acted as though Ray wasn't hopelessly awkward at this sort of thing. "Do you like Italian food?"

"I love it."

"Are you free Friday night?"

"Let me check my calendar." Ray rolled her eyes at the absurdity of the thought. They shared a chuckle, and Ray reveled in the warm glow their unlikely camaraderie produced. "Yeah, I'm free."

CHAPTER SIX

So this is a date?"

Carly sighed at the predictability of her best friend's question. For the past year, Leeann had made it her mission to get Carly "back in the game." Pity Carly had to disappoint her. "No, it's definitely not a date. Just a friendly dinner. She's straight."

"That's what they all say."

"And some of them mean it." Balancing the phone precariously on her shoulder, Carly tossed an errant dog toy onto Jack's bed. Ray was due for dinner in fifteen minutes, and Carly was still trying to get her house in order. "Seriously, I doubt that romance is a high priority for Ray right now. With a man or a woman."

Leeann sighed. "Well, at least you've found a kindred spirit." In a slightly muffled voice, as though she was covering the phone, she said, "I'll have an Anchor Steam, please. Why, thank you. I'd be delighted."

When it was clear Leeann was listening again, Carly asked, "Get carded?"

"Bless his heart."

At thirty-two, Leeann looked like she was in her early twenties. But she met requests to show her ID with the enthusiasm of a woman twice her age. Carly chuckled as she shelved a stack of books that had been scattered across her coffee table. "Starting a bit early tonight?"

"I'm meeting my accountant for a drink."

"Business or pleasure?" Carly already knew the answer. Leeann didn't pursue business on Friday nights.

"She's lovely. You'd like her."

"I'm sure I would."

"So, Ray McKenna. Interesting. What's she like?"

"Shy. Lonely, I think. I really don't know a lot about her, but I get the feeling we could be friends." Carly walked into her bedroom, casting a critical eye at the pile of freshly laundered clothes she hadn't yet put away. But dinner wouldn't make itself, and she didn't need to worry about how her bedroom looked. She and Ray wouldn't end up in there tonight. "She has the most beautiful blue Great Dane."

"Ah." Leeann sounded as though she'd figured something out. "A dog lover, huh?"

"She is."

"I know how that turns you on."

"It's something we have in common." Carly resisted the urge to give in to Leeann's teasing and admit that she wished this was a date. That was far too personal and touched on feelings that Carly didn't know how to deal with yet. "Look, I don't have a lot of friends up here. I thought it might be nice to have one. And Ray looked like she might need one, too."

"I'm sorry, sweetie." The sudden change in Leeann's tone told Carly she knew she'd gone too far. "I'm not trying to be pushy, I swear."

"Not trying, but doing a damn fine job regardless." Carly decided that the house was as clean as it needed to be. On to dinner. "But I know you push because you care about me."

"I love you. And I hate to think of you up there all alone."

"I'm hardly alone." As if on cue, Jack trotted to Carly's side as she walked into the kitchen. His allergy diet had made him a regular scavenger. "My good buddy Jack keeps me company. And he lets me watch whatever I want on TV."

"You know I love Jack," Leeann said, still serious. "But a dog can never give you some things. I worry about you, Carly."

"Well, don't. I've been dating."

"You've been coming to the city to fuck random women in bars. That's not exactly dating."

"That's what you call it when you're the one doing the fucking."

Leeann snorted. "That's different. *We're* different."

That's why they had broken up back in college. Because Carly was ready to settle down and Leeann didn't want to stop playing. Twelve years later, Leeann still seemed content with casual encounters. And Carly never felt quite right about her couple of one-night stands.

"You're right," Carly said quietly. "We are different. And don't think I don't want to fall in love again, Leeann. It's just…still so fresh in many ways." Maybe that was why she was torturing herself by pursuing a platonic friendship with an unavailable basket case whom she just happened to find devastatingly attractive. Maybe it felt safer than finding someone who could return her feelings. Carly groaned, touching her forehead against the refrigerator.

"What?"

"Okay, you're right. I do find Ray McKenna attractive. But this is definitely *not* a date."

"Oh, Carly," Leeann murmured in an uncharacteristically sad voice. "Don't do this to yourself."

"I'm not." Inhaling deeply, Carly stood and threw her shoulders back. "I'm not," she said again. "I can be friends with a woman I find attractive, right? It doesn't have to lead anywhere."

"Well, you're friends with me. But then you've already sampled these goods."

"Me and half the women in San Francisco."

"Seriously, Carly, be careful."

"I will." Carly already regretted that she'd let slip as much as she had. "It's not like I'm ready for a relationship, anyway." The words came easily, but she knew deep down, she was ready to love someone again. She just needed to remember that it wouldn't be Ray McKenna.

❖

Ray had the kind of stomachache that made her wish she was curled up in bed. Or snuggled under a blanket on the couch, watching *The Golden Girls*. Or pretty much anywhere but on Carly Warner's front porch. Anxiety had been building since she accepted this dinner invitation, and now that she was poised to ring Carly's doorbell, she was sure she'd throw up.

Some part of her knew that when she rang the bell, she would be able to stop worrying about whether she would be able to go through with this. Another challenge would await—making small talk—but at least this first step would be over. Maybe the nausea would recede.

Goddamned ridiculous, Ray scolded herself. She dropped Jagger's leash and rested her hand on his head. Dr. Evans would tell her not to beat herself up for her anxiety, that she needed to nurture the scared inner child. She used to be skeptical about that type of advice, but lately she was trying to pay attention to her reaction to her own fears. These things were hard enough without self-flagellation.

Jagger leaned against her, forcing Ray to widen her stance and brace herself against his incredible weight. It was lucky she was relatively able-bodied. He would be a terrible therapy dog for someone who had worse physical problems than her own slight limp.

"Okay," Ray murmured under her breath. "Everything will be okay." *I am the master of my fate.* Without giving herself time to change her mind, she rang the bell.

Ray's anxiety reached a sickening crescendo as she listened to soft footfalls approach the door. This was it. It was really happening. Social interaction. Dr. Evans had been thrilled, of course. Beneath all the fear, so was Ray.

Carly smiled when she opened the door, and her expression seemed to brighten as she met Ray's eyes. "Hey there."

"Hello." Ray cursed how quietly her voice came out. "You have a beautiful house." In truth, she'd been too nervous to really notice. But it was something to say.

"Thank you. Come inside and see the rest of it." Carly stepped back and gestured for Ray to enter.

With a deep breath, Ray walked inside. Jagger stayed close to her, lending her much-needed strength. Carly patted his chest as he lumbered past, then closed the door behind them. Ray's stomach flip-flopped at being enclosed in an unfamiliar place, but one look at Carly's face helped bring her into the present.

"Were my directions okay?" Carly stuffed her hands into the pockets of her blue jeans. "I know it's not the easiest place to find."

"I have a GPS," Ray said. She didn't leave getting lost to chance. "Led me straight here."

"Great." Laughing, Carly nodded at Jack, who was wagging madly as he sniffed Jagger. To Ray's surprise, Jagger's tail began to wag nearly as hard. "Jack hasn't been able to stop talking about how excited he is about Jagger coming over."

Ray chuckled, already feeling the knot of tension in her stomach ease. "Jagger tried to play it cool, but I could tell that he was pretty geeked about it."

"I'm also glad you're here." Carly took her hands out of her pockets and folded them over her stomach, rocking back on her heels. With some surprise, Ray recognized it as a nervous gesture. "For the record."

"Me, too." Remembering the bottle she held in her hand, Ray offered it to Carly. "It's just sparkling grape juice. I know we're in wine country, but I don't really drink."

Carly took the bottle, eyeing the label warmly. "Perfect. I've learned to enjoy wine since moving here, but I'd be lying if I said that sparkling juice wasn't a hell of a lot tastier. Why don't we go into the kitchen and pour a couple of glasses? Dinner's almost ready."

Ray followed Carly deeper into her home, surreptitiously glancing into open doorways as they passed, scanning a bathroom, then a sitting room. Evaluating. It was habit now, even in her own home. Having Jagger near had lessened her paranoia about being caught unawares, but the compulsion to check for unknown danger still lingered. Carly's home was clean and tastefully decorated, cozy, the kind of place where Ray could imagine being comfortable hanging out. If dinner went well, that is.

When they walked into the kitchen, a pleasant aroma made Ray glad to have rung the doorbell. It had been a long time since her last home-cooked meal. She was more likely to take it from the freezer and throw it into the microwave. Somehow those frozen delicacies never smelled so heavenly.

"Just a disclaimer," Carly said. "I'm not exactly the world's best cook."

"Well, something smells delicious." Ray walked around the bar that separated the kitchen from the dining area, settling onto a tall stool. "And as long as we're making disclaimers, I should warn you that I'm not the world's best conversationalist."

"You're just fine." Looking pleased, Carly cracked open the bottle of sparkling juice. "And thank you. I hope the taste does the smell justice."

"I'm sure it will." Hearing a commotion, Ray glanced behind her and saw Jack facing Jagger, chest practically touching the floor. His butt stuck up in the air, tail wagging even more frantically. Laughing, she said, "What is Jack doing?"

Carly glanced around the bar as she poured a glass. "That's a play bow. He's inviting Jagger to play."

Charmed by Jack's enthusiasm, Ray looked at her own dog, who dwarfed the brown mutt. Jagger's tail was wagging too, but he remained fairly calm, glancing up at Ray's face from time to time. Had Jagger played with other dogs before Ray got him? Probably, Ray reasoned. She was sure the therapy-dog facility would have made sure he was socialized. So why wasn't he taking the invitation?

"Go ahead, Jagger," Ray said. Jagger looked at Jack, then back to her. Was he not playing because he was on duty, still working? Eager to see Jagger interact with his new friend, she said, "Release."

As though that was exactly what he had been waiting for, Jagger immediately sprang into action. Dropping into an identical play bow, he allowed Jack to jump onto him. At once, they were sparring like they had done it a thousand times. To her amazement, Jagger "talked" the whole time, not quite barking, not quite growling. Just vocalizing in a way Ray had never heard. The excited noises made them both laugh, Ray catching Carly's gaze so they could share a smile. Entranced, Ray returned her attention to the dogs and watched until they tumbled into her bar stool enthusiastically.

"Boys! Try not to tear the house apart," Carly said, though her admonishment was full of humor. "What do you say we let them play in the backyard for a bit? They'll have more room, and we'll be able to hear each other."

After a slight hesitation, Ray said, "Sure. I'll let them out." Having Jagger at her side made her feel more confident, but she could hardly deny him the joy that playing with Jack was clearly bringing him. Nothing had made her feel happier in quite some time.

"The sliding door is just through the den," Carly said, pointing behind Ray. "I'll have dinner out of the oven by the time you get back."

"Come on, guys," Ray said as she stood, and to her amazement, the dogs broke from playing so they could follow her. She led them through the dining area into the den, sidestepping their clumsy attempts to stay next to one another. "Good grief," she murmured. They were a force of nature.

Opening the slider, Ray observed Carly's backyard. She had a fair amount of space, which was filled with what looked like obstacle-course equipment. Jack tore across the yard and jumped through a hoop suspended from a wooden frame, then ran back to Jagger before dropping into another play bow. She would have to ask Carly what that was all about.

Ray took her time returning to the kitchen, not only because she was slightly nervous about the prospect of making conversation, but also so she could check out the den without Carly watching her. A big-screen television in one corner was surrounded by various electronics. She saw a DVD player, what was probably a DVR, and, to her surprise, what appeared to be a video game console. She wouldn't have pegged Carly as a video game player.

An overstuffed dog bed sat next to the leather couch that faced the television. In front of the couch was a coffee table loaded with remote controls and a game controller. So Carly really was a gamer. A cabinet full of DVDs—probably some games, too—sat next to a fireplace against the wall.

Ray fantasized briefly about becoming friends with Carly. Maybe she would come over to watch movies. They could make popcorn and stay up late talking and laughing. Ray used to do stuff like that with friends, before Iraq. She'd taken it for granted that she never would again, but perhaps she could once more enjoy something so painfully normal as movie night.

Ray started to return to the kitchen when a framed photograph on an end table caught her eye. Telling herself not to be nosy, she tried to move past it without looking, but when she saw that it was of two people embracing, she stopped. Curiosity drew her to the picture, and she picked it up to study it further.

Carly and a brown-skinned woman with dark, flowing hair stood in front of the Golden Gate Bridge, bundled up in sweaters, wrapped in an intimate embrace. The woman was kissing Carly on the cheek while Carly laughed, open-mouthed. Ray's heart beat faster as she tried to decide what she was looking at.

"Hey," Carly said quietly, startling Ray into nearly dropping the picture. She stood in the doorway, watching. "I thought you'd gotten lost."

"I'm sorry." Fumbling, Ray returned the photo to the table. "I, uh…I was just—"

"It's okay. If you're ready to eat, dinner's on the table."

"Sounds great," Ray said quickly. Embarrassed to have been caught snooping, she resolved to be a normal person for the rest of the evening. This was hardly the way to make a friend.

She followed Carly into the dining area, impressed that the table was set and a casserole dish full of delicious-smelling pasta sat in the center. Next to it was a bowl of what looked like Caesar salad. A wineglass full of sparkling juice sat in front of each place setting. "Wow, this looks wonderful."

"It's roasted vegetable pasta. I hope you like that kind of thing."

"I'm sure I will." Ray waited until Carly pulled out a chair, then sat down opposite her. "You really went all out."

"I usually just microwave my dinner," Carly said as she dished out a portion of the steaming, cheesy pasta onto her plate. "But I figured this was a special occasion."

"I'm a microwave chef, too."

"Jack enjoyed the change. He kept sneaking into the kitchen, determined to hoover up all the goodies I dropped."

"I'll bet," Ray said as she spooned out a generous portion of the pasta. Part of her felt awkward about eating in front of Carly, but the other part of her, which felt almost faint at how good everything looked, was willing to get over it. "If he's half the chowhound Jagger is, I can only imagine how hard it would be to keep him away from a meal like this."

Rounding out her plate with a pile of salad, Ray blew on a forkful of pasta, then took a bite. It was as wonderful as it looked and smelled, and she vocalized her approval with a soft noise that clearly made Carly happy.

"Good?"

Blushing, Ray nodded and took another bite. "This is the best meal I've had in three years."

Carly looked down at her plate. "I'm so glad."

Grateful that she had something to do with her mouth besides talk, Ray ate in silence. To her relief, Carly focused on her own meal and didn't try to force conversation. Occasionally their gazes would meet and Carly would smile, but Ray was surprised to find that she didn't feel uncomfortable. She appreciated that Carly didn't seem to be full of the questions she had gotten used to hearing from everyone else she met. She almost wanted to talk, if only because nobody was trying to make her.

Noticing Carly's empty glass, Ray picked up the bottle. "Would you like some more?"

"Sure." Carly watched her face as she poured. "Thank you."

Emptying the rest into her own glass, Ray said, "I should have brought another. I love this stuff."

"It goes really well with the meal."

Ray set down the bottle. "I was diagnosed with posttraumatic stress disorder about a year and a half ago. A lot of people with PTSD use alcohol to try and cope, so I decided not to touch the stuff. Becoming an alcoholic is, like, the last thing I need on top of everything else. You know?"

"I do." Meeting Ray's gaze, Carly said, "I think that's an incredibly strong position. Good for you."

"Thanks." The disclosure left Ray feeling exposed, and despite being painfully full, she served herself a little more pasta so she would have something to do with her hands. She might have chosen not to abuse alcohol, but overeating was a whole other matter. "I don't know if it's particularly strong, but I know that I'm screwed up enough without that."

"It's hard to be so clearheaded when you're in pain," Carly said, as though she were speaking from experience. "To be able to make smart choices for yourself even in the midst of that kind of suffering is absolutely a sign of strength."

"I'm doing a lot better now, honestly. To tell you the truth, Jagger has been a godsend. I don't know what I'd do without him."

Carly's face lit up. "I know exactly what you mean. Jack has been the same for me. Life would be pretty grim if it weren't for him."

Carly was definitely speaking from a place of experience. By now Ray's curiosity was fully piqued, but she refrained from asking the obvious question. No matter how much she wanted to know what kind of pain Carly had gone through, she knew how upsetting it was for strangers to pry into her own life. She didn't want to put Carly on the spot.

Carly placed her fork on her plate and cleared her throat. "I lost my partner in a car accident five years ago. Nadia, the woman in the picture you were looking at. We'd just found out she was pregnant. In fact, she was on her way to meet me so we could celebrate."

Rocked by the revelation, Ray set down her own fork. "I'm sorry."

"I adopted Jack from the shelter six months later. I was beyond depressed, had just moved to Bodega Bay. He absolutely helped turn my life around. Dogs are incredible friends."

Ray nodded, still trying to process Carly's words. The thought that Carly could be a lesbian had crossed her mind when she'd seen the picture in the den. But she'd tried to dismiss it because she didn't want to believe it was true. As much as she didn't want to let Carly see her struggle with this reaction, Ray was shaken.

"So you're...?" Ray couldn't bring herself to come right out and say it. She waved her hand, hoping Carly understood what she was trying to ask.

"A lesbian? Yes, I am."

Was this why Carly had invited her to dinner? Were they supposed to be on a date? A seed of anxiety took root in Ray's stomach, threatening to bloom into full-blown panic. After five years in the army, she was well conditioned to want to distance herself from even the suggestion of lesbianism. And she certainly wasn't comfortable with being hit on. Suddenly this whole thing felt like a big mistake.

"Oh," Ray said. This explained why Carly wanted anything to do with her. Shifting in her chair, she tried hard to remain cordial as she decided what she should say. "I'm really sorry about your loss. I, uh, didn't realize. That you were...you know."

"Thank you," Carly murmured. Sitting up straight, she folded her hands on the table. "Ray, is this going to be a problem for you?"

Would this be a problem? Ray wasn't sure what this would be, except uncomfortable. "Well, I'm not a lesbian."

"Okay," Carly said. "I assumed as much, honestly. I remember reading something about a boyfriend in one of those articles when you were...over there. He was also in the army, right?"

"Right. Danny." No need to tell Carly how they'd broken up immediately after Ray got home. How she couldn't stand to be that close to anyone, especially a man.

"Right," Carly said. "So I'm gay, and you're straight. I'm cool with that. I just thought we had some stuff in common, that maybe we would have fun hanging out. So I'll ask again, is this going to be a problem for you?"

She could tell Carly yes, Ray thought, but why? It would quickly end a blossoming friendship that Ray had already started to value. Over what? Ray wasn't in the army anymore. Don't ask, don't tell wasn't a concern. She was a civilian. And she could be friends with whomever she wanted. As long as Carly understood that friendship was all she had to give.

"No," Ray said quietly, relieved to find that it was true. "No, it won't be a problem. I apologize."

"Accepted. I'm sorry if I took you by surprise."

Ray shook her head. "The military taught me to be wary of who I fraternize with. You know…guilt by association. But I'm not in the military anymore. I'm sorry I had a bad reaction."

"I get it. And if you're concerned, I promise that my intentions toward you are innocent."

Blushing, Ray looked down at her plate. "I know," she whispered. But she sensed she wasn't fooling Carly. "I do have a problem with trusting people's motives these days. Especially when it comes to why they'd want anything to do with me."

"Don't be so hard on yourself."

"Well, let's be honest," Ray said, forcing a laugh that she knew sounded painfully awkward. "I don't have a lot going for me."

"We need to work on you giving yourself more credit," Carly said. She waited until Ray met her eyes, then said, "Deal?"

Slowly, Ray's embarrassment began to melt away. Carly was moving them past this horrible moment, and everything still seemed fairly okay between them. Amazing.

"Deal." Ray was grateful that one of them knew how to nurture a friendship.

"I bought a strawberry-rhubarb pie for dessert. Are you interested in a slice, or do you need some time to let your food digest?"

Groaning, Ray put a hand on her swollen belly. "Time, please. That was just too good. I'm about to pop."

Carly pushed away from the table. "Then what do you say we go check on the dogs?"

❖

Carly leaned back in her cushioned patio chair, laughing as she watched Jagger hop around Jack. He was doing a damn good job of keeping up with the smaller dog, who she was confident would sleep well tonight. "They've really hit it off," she said, then glanced over at Ray.

Ray hugged her knees to her chest as she gazed out at the yard. She was smiling, but her eyes shone with an emotion that looked close to sorrow. "I wish I could make friends so easily."

"Yeah, there's not a lot of bullshit between dogs. I'll sniff your butt, you sniff mine, now let's go run around like lunatics."

Snorting quietly, Ray said, "Maybe in my next life."

"I think you're doing just fine in this one." Carly studied Ray's face, unsurprised at the shadow that passed over it. Ever since the conversation about her sexuality, Ray had been even more reserved. Carly couldn't help but worry that it was a problem for her. Disappointing, if that were the case. Then again, maybe Ray could sense her lingering attraction. Though Carly would never act on it, she couldn't blame Ray for feeling uncomfortable.

"I'm sorry again that I questioned your motives for inviting me over." Ray kept her voice low, almost as though she didn't want the dogs to overhear. Staring straight ahead, she was clearly avoiding eye contact. "I was completely ridiculous."

"Please, don't apologize," Carly said. Especially not when there was a kernel of justification for her concerns. "I threw you for a loop. You probably didn't have a lot of gay and lesbian friends in the military."

Ray's mouth twitched. "Who knows?"

"Very true."

"I am sorry, though. I feel…pretty stupid."

"Don't."

"I mean, to think that you… Well, I'm not exactly much of a catch." Ray covered her face with her hands, visibly cringing. "I'm such an asshole."

Carly frowned. She didn't like the negative self-talk, but she wasn't sure it would be appropriate to assure Ray there was absolutely nothing ridiculous about the idea that Carly could be attracted to her. Taking a breath, Carly decided that maybe being honest would help ease some of Ray's embarrassment. "Look, you're a beautiful woman. There's nothing stupid about assuming that someone might have a romantic interest. But I assure you, I want you for your sparkling personality. And your fine choice of canine companions."

Ray dropped her hands, revealing red-tinged cheeks. "You're way too nice to have anything to do with me. You know that, right?"

"I have a different opinion," Carly said. "Deal with it."

"Yes, Doctor."

Carly had to suppress a shiver at the way Ray's voice lowered when she used her title. Her intentions were pure, damn it. If she didn't want to chase Ray away, she needed to put a lid on any thoughts of being attracted to her.

"So what's the deal with the obstacle course?" Ray asked.

Carly was relieved that the subject had reverted to dogs. "I'm doing agility with Jack. It's hardly a full course, or even a particularly good one, but I set up some simple obstacles so we could practice at home."

"Agility? They actually have obstacle courses for dogs?"

"Oh, yeah. It's a legitimate sport. The handler directs the dog through a number of obstacles. It's timed and scored."

"Wow." Ray gazed out over the yard again. "I had no idea. I bet Jack would be great at that. He seems very athletic."

"You have no idea." Carly sat forward in her chair. "Want us to show you?"

"Really?" Ray's excitement was unmistakable. "Yeah, please." Whistling, she called Jagger to her. "Sit," she told him, and he plopped down at her side.

Carly stood, scratching Jack on the neck. His fur was soaking wet, evidence that Jagger had used him as a chew toy. "Gross," she murmured, and shook her hand off. "Come on, boy. Let's show Ray what you've got."

She ran him through the course twice, stealing glances at her guest as they went. Ray was clearly transfixed, and her response unleashed an unexpected flood of affection in Carly. That something as simple as a dog running an agility course could make her so excited was frankly charming. She rarely encountered such a lack of pretense in other women.

After Jack completed the course the second time, Carly waved Ray over. "Come on. Why don't you give it a try?"

Ray moved as though to stand, then sat back. "Me? I don't know how."

"I'll show you."

"I've never worked with a dog before."

"You love them. That's the only qualification you need to start learning."

Expecting her to come up with something else, Carly was surprised when Ray stood and joined her. Her enthusiasm was palpable. "Okay. Tell me what to do."

Carly took Ray through each obstacle with Jack, explaining the necessary commands and tips for keeping him focused. Ray listened attentively and asked questions that revealed a deep intelligence and curiosity. Despite Carly's earlier vow to put a lid on her attraction, she grew ever more interested. By the time she stepped back to let Ray take Jack through the obstacles on her own, she was watching the former soldier in awe.

Ray was completely transformed when she worked with Jack. She wore a full, toothy smile, laughing easily when she or he made a mistake or accomplished a goal. The limping gait Carly had been wondering about nearly disappeared as she ran alongside Jack, her entire body seemingly infused with new strength. Ray was glowing, so inexplicably beautiful that Carly's heart hurt.

Oh, she was in deep trouble. And she knew she couldn't turn back now.

"Excellent," Carly said when they finished the course successfully. Clapping, she bent and greeted Jack with a flurry of pats and praise. "Good job, both of you."

"That was fun." Ray jogged over to join them. "He's amazing."

"Thanks." Carly watched Ray scratch Jack's chest, struck by a sudden thought. "I wish I had more time to practice with him. I want to enter him in an agility trial in June, but with my work schedule, I don't think we'll be ready."

"Are you kidding me? He's great! I can't imagine he needs that much more training."

"I haven't even taught him some of the obstacles yet. Like the weave poles. He doesn't know the first thing about weave poles."

Ray frowned. "Is that hard to teach?"

"It can be challenging. And we usually only get a half hour or so of training time in the evenings. We make it to some of the classes on the weekends, but we miss a lot of them."

Something passed across Ray's face, and Carly knew she had guessed where Carly was leading. "Well, could I...I mean, could I help?"

Perfect. Carly grinned, excited at the thought of having Ray spend time with Jack. It would be wonderful for Ray, if these few minutes of practice were any indication. And Carly would feel a lot less guilt over her work schedule if she didn't have to imagine Jack being bored in her office. "Would you want to?"

"Sure." Excitement began to creep into Ray's voice. "I have nothing but time."

"I take Jack to the clinic with me, but he usually ends up napping in my office all day. If you wanted to take him a day or two during the week while I'm at work—"

"Absolutely! Seriously? You'd let me do that?"

Carly laughed. "Are you kidding? Doggy day care? And free training to boot? You'd be doing me a huge favor."

Ray dropped her gaze to her feet. "Well, I don't know about that."

"Trust me, I'd appreciate it more than you know. But if it ends up being too much for you, please tell me. I don't want him to overwhelm you."

"He won't overwhelm me." Ray stroked Jack's head. "I love him. He's great."

"Then it's a deal," Carly said, so proud of Jack for attracting such instant devotion. With any luck, Ray might learn to trust her, too.

Chapter Seven

Carly woke up with a groan, disappointed as hell that Jack had decided to whine to be let out just as she was nearing Ray for a long-anticipated kiss. Her dream slipped away quickly, leaving behind scant traces of the warm intimacy. She longed to stay in that fuzzy in-between place on the edge of waking, to bask a little longer in the sense of closeness she'd lost with Nadia.

Jack whined louder, then scratched at her bedroom door.

"Couldn't you have waited five more minutes?" Carly's lament appeared to have no effect on his bladder, so she threw off her comforter with a sigh. Time to get up, whether she liked it or not. It was probably for the best. She shouldn't be dreaming about her new—and very platonic—friend. "Just saving me from myself, is that it?"

Jack's next noise indicated he couldn't care less about saving her, but if she wanted to save her carpet, she'd better start moving. She hurried to let him out, following close behind as he dashed to the den and pranced around in front of the sliding door. Once he was safely in the backyard, she collapsed onto the couch and closed her eyes, thinking back to the day before.

She'd dropped Jack off at Ray's house in the morning, and when she returned for him after work, Ray had greeted her with dinner for two. Despite her self-proclaimed microwave-chef status, Ray made delicious homemade fajitas, and they'd enjoyed a second meal together that was markedly less tense than the first. Carly was even able to sit back and let Ray carry the conversation with excited chatter about her day's progress with Jack's agility training.

Apparently their first session together had been a success and Jack was getting the hang of the new equipment. To Carly's surprise, Ray had downloaded plans from the Internet and built homemade weave poles from PVC pipe, as well as a tire jump and a teeter board. Ray glowed with an obvious sense of accomplishment, and Jack seemed happy too, and tired, which was always nice.

Carly wished she could share everyone else's contentedness. Though she was thrilled with how well Ray seemed to be doing, and grateful that Jack had something more fulfilling to do with his days than sit in her office, Carly was uneasy about what this friendship meant for her. Her attraction to Ray was growing, no longer within her control, and she suddenly had a gut-churning desire to be in love again, to share her days with someone other than Jack. After she had avoided intimacy for five years, her heart had seemingly decided to betray her and yearn for love. She didn't want to be alone anymore.

"This is stupid," Carly said out loud. "If I really wanted a relationship, I wouldn't be pining over someone so completely unavailable." These feelings were a defense mechanism, nothing more, which could only hurt her more than help. "Goddamn it, Leeann was right."

The phone rang, rousing Carly from her reverie. Suspecting it was Leeann having somehow intuited that Carly had just granted her a point, she reached over the coffee table and fumbled around until she located the cordless handset.

"Hello?"

"Hey," a quiet voice at the other end said, instantly sending a pleasant shiver down Carly's spine. "This is Ray. McKenna."

Chuckling, Carly squeezed her thighs together to ward off the pleasure of hearing Ray's shy voice. "How are you this morning, Ray McKenna?"

"I'm good." Ray cleared her throat. "I hope I didn't wake you?"

"Not at all. Jack took care of that."

"Good. Better his fault than mine."

Carly beamed. This was the first time Ray had called her. She was glad to have some proof that she wasn't simply harassing her new friend, that this thing, whatever it was, wasn't entirely one-sided. "He likes to sleep in on the days we have to get up early to work. But when I have a chance to sleep in, his bladder gets weak."

"Naturally." Ray paused so long Carly considered fishing for the reason behind this unexpected call, but then Ray said, "What are you doing tonight?"

"Nothing exciting." Carly held her breath at the awkward breakthrough she sensed she was witnessing. Did Ray really plan to invite her to do something? "Maybe watching a movie or playing a video game."

"I got some movies from Netflix. I, uh… Did you want to come over and watch one with me?"

Closing her eyes, Carly tried to will her heart not to start beating faster. This wasn't a date, for God's sake. She needed to internalize that this was a platonic friendship, nothing more. If she didn't, she might lose it. "That sounds like fun. Do you want me to bring something?"

"Oh. Um." Ray stuttered like she hadn't been expecting her to accept and was trying to figure out what to say next. "Sure, if you want."

"Anything in particular?" Carly tried not to let Ray hear her smile. This type of thing was obviously difficult for Ray and she probably had no idea how damn cute she sounded. *Yeah, I've got it bad.*

"Oh! Um, popcorn?"

"Perfect. I did tell you that the microwave is my specialty."

"That's what I heard." Ray sounded as though she was relaxing. She was likely stroking Jagger's head as they spoke. Ray always reached out to Jagger when she began to get anxious, and Jagger was always right there waiting when she needed him.

"Five o'clock?" Carly asked.

"That sounds great. Thank you."

The relief in Ray's voice indicated that she was eager to hang up. How hard was it for her to pick up the phone and put herself out there like this? Touched by Ray's devotion to their friendship, Carly vowed to shut down any thoughts of romance once and for all. Ray deserved a friend who respected her limits and truly understood what it took for her to trust.

Humbled, Carly put her hand over her heart, willing it back into check. "No, Ray, thank you."

❖

Ray fell to her knees clapping after Jack tentatively negotiated the homemade weave poles, then braced herself for impact as he raced to greet her. Jagger watched from the pillow she'd placed on the back patio, lazy but interested. Ray endured Jack's arrival, laughing as she hugged him. Jack wagged his tail madly, feeding off her excitement.

"You're brilliant, buddy." After only two weeks of practice, he clearly had the weave poles down. Now they just had to work on speed and confidence. "I'm so proud of you."

More than that, Ray had to admit, she was proud of herself. Three weeks ago, she had no idea dog agility existed. After a lot of research, she had not only built quality equipment, but her dog-training knowledge was really starting to click. Working with Jack felt natural, taking her away from her usual daily worries. It absorbed her totally, and between Jagger's steady devotion and this new hobby with Jack, Ray was experiencing an unanticipated surge of confidence.

Calling Jagger to her side, Ray walked into the house flanked by both dogs. Chest out and shoulders back, she felt tall in a way she vaguely remembered from boot camp. Back when she was certain of everything and totally naïve about just as much.

She felt like she could take on the world. Or at least the grocery store. She was running dangerously low on bottled water, which was as compelling a reason to venture to the store as any, and strangely, Ray barely hesitated before she picked up Jagger's leash and service vest.

"You're coming with me, Jagger." When Jack quickly sat in front of her, Ray chuckled. "Sorry, Jack, you don't have a fancy vest that gets you into grocery stores." Patting Jack on the head, she said, "Feel free to relax on the couch while we're gone."

Predictably, he followed them to the door, but obeyed and stayed in a sit when they walked out. He would probably look for food on the floor for the first ten minutes or so, then veg out on the couch until they returned. Carly said he behaved well in the house alone, as long as nothing edible was within reach.

Ray's spirit soared as she thought about Carly. To think that she'd even considered pulling back from their friendship over something as trivial as Carly's sexuality. Like it mattered at all, between them. Carly had changed Ray's life so much already, and they had been friends for only a few weeks. Though Ray had spent more hours with Jack than

Carly, each meal and conversation together drove home just how much she had missed having a friend.

Carly was funny, she was compassionate, and in a way Ray had never expected, she seemed able to understand and relate to much of Ray's pain. Though their experiences were nothing alike on the surface—Carly losing her partner and their unborn child, and Ray's ordeal in Iraq—they had both suffered tremendously. And not the kind of suffering that one easily leaves behind.

Buckling into the driver's seat, Ray patted down her pocket for her cell phone. Part of her itched to call Carly. Carly was working, of course, and Ray would never gather the courage to bother her for no reason even if she weren't, but she burned to talk to her. Just to chat, to hear her voice. To feel a connection to another human being.

Instead Ray shifted the truck into reverse so she could pull out onto the road. And as she drove she talked to Jagger so she wouldn't think about where they were going.

"Think Carly will stay for dinner tonight? I bet if I make stir-fry she will. She told me she likes stir-fry."

Jagger yawned, no doubt wondering what the hell she was going on about.

"Maybe I can talk her into staying for a movie afterward." That had gone well the first time. Really well, in fact. Sharing the couch with a bowl of popcorn between them, Ray had been surprisingly comfortable. Something about Carly put Ray's entire body at ease.

Most of the time, anyway. Twice now she'd noticed how attractive Carly was, and not in a casual way. First in Carly's office when her realization that Carly was a beautiful woman had struck her dumb. That had disturbed her enough, but the second time, after she knew Carly was a lesbian, really surprised her.

It was during the movie, thank God, and Carly had been engrossed in the action on-screen. Ray had turned her head just as Carly reacted to a funny line and saw Carly laughing in profile. It was like that crazy reaction in the office, only worse. Ray's stomach clenched, her throat went dry, and she felt inexplicably light-headed. She had no idea why.

So Carly was lovely. She was a great person, an amazing friend, and genetically blessed. Sometimes Ray noticed how pretty she was and got nervous. So? Ray was just shy and apparently even more so around attractive women. That had happened even when she was a teenager, hadn't it, like with her senior English teacher. Sometimes Ms. Leah's radiant smiles made Ray a little nervous, too.

"Leave it to me to overthink everything," Ray told Jagger. "I don't know what's wrong with me."

Ray pulled into the parking lot of the local Safeway, only now dreading the prospect of going inside. She drew on the strength of Jagger, calm beside her, and simply breathed, thinking about how confident she felt when she worked with Jack. She was a capable person, damn it.

Surprisingly, she recalled the world-beating attitude that had sent her to the store in the first place. "I can do this," she whispered, and for the first time, she truly believed it. Nothing bad would happen to her. Not today.

Ray got out of her truck, then opened the passenger door for Jagger. He lumbered out and stretched. Ray grabbed his leash and walked toward the front door without faltering.

Ray threw her shoulders back and strode inside the store with purpose. Jagger drew immediate stares. No surprise there. A young couple at the deli counter turned and talked quietly as they stared at Jagger, but Ray ignored them and headed for the beverage aisle. It was ten o'clock on a Wednesday morning, so luckily the store was fairly empty. She was happy to find the bottled-water area deserted, not a soul in sight. She picked up a flat and prepared to make a break for the checkout stand.

Glancing down at Jagger, she halted her escape. Carly had told her about Jack's allergies but admitted that she occasionally allowed him to have a compressed rawhide bone, and that he loved them. Surely Jack's performance with the weave poles had earned him a special treat. Hell, both dogs deserved bones for all the joy they brought her.

Ray walked toward the back of the store, then past the aisles, scanning signs to find the right one. A dark-haired man stood at the far end of the pet-supplies aisle. He glanced up as she approached the dog chews, his gaze immediately drawn to Jagger. Ray ignored him. She would find what she needed and get out of here. She didn't want to blow it by overreacting to innocent curiosity.

Feminine laughter drew her attention to the dairy case at the back of the store, where two women stood holding hands. Ray quickly looked back to the dog bones, determined not to stare. Even a hint of homosexual behavior used to make her nervous, but now that she was out of the military, the idea fascinated her.

At least as it related to Carly. Had Carly and her partner acted like that? The easy intimacy, laughing together in the grocery store? The possibility sent a warm flash of envy to her belly. Danny had been her best friend as well as her boyfriend, but she couldn't remember feeling as comfortable with him as those two women looked together. Or even as comfortable as she felt with Carly. Something about Carly put her at total ease, in a way she never was with Danny.

"Excuse me."

The deep male voice snapped Ray out of her reverie, and she jerked back from the man who had somehow managed to approach. It was the guy from the other end of the aisle, and he put a hand up, smiling apologetically.

"I am so sorry. I didn't mean to startle you. I just…that's an amazing dog."

Ray relaxed slightly, almost amused by the predictability of this scenario and her over-the-top reaction. "Thank you."

The man looked down at Jagger admiringly. "What breed is he?"

"A Great Dane."

"Really? I didn't know they came in this color."

"It's called blue," Ray explained, used to this question. "Black and white, harlequin, is probably the most popular. Blue is a little more rare."

"Wow, he's gorgeous." The man glanced at her. "I know his vest says not to pet him, but could I?"

The guy was attractive, possibly someone Ray would have noticed before she lost interest in that sort of thing. More importantly, he seemed like a nice guy. Recalling Dr. Evans's advice to learn to revel in the admiration Jagger drew, Ray took a breath and said, "Sure."

Jagger seemed to enjoy the attention, crowding in to the man's affectionate caress. Ray felt a swell of pride in her dog, not only his physical beauty, but also his friendly, laid-back demeanor. He really was a good boy.

"He's great," the man said. "I'm not sure how my wife will react when I tell her our next dog should be a Great Dane, but this guy has totally sold me."

"They're awesome dogs. Jagger's a total sweetheart."

"He seems like it. Jagger, huh? Nice." The man pulled back and nodded. "Thanks again. Have a great day."

"You, too."

As the man left, he spared one last backward glance at Jagger. Ray turned back to the bones, snagging two from the shelf. Then she walked Jagger to the front of the store, surprised to find herself fighting back full-on joy.

CHAPTER EIGHT

Are you sure this is okay?" Stopping at a red light, Carly turned to look at Ray, who sat in the passenger seat with her eyes closed. She seemed to be in a trance, complete with deep, rhythmic breathing, and Carly worried that she was pushing Ray too far, too fast. "We could just go back to your place and watch a movie or something. I wouldn't mind at all."

Ray managed a tight-lipped smile. "I'm fine." Opening her eyes, she gave Carly a resolute nod. "I told you. I trust you completely."

Carly felt a powerful rush of warmth, just as she had the first time Ray said it. She knew how difficult it was for Ray to trust anyone and was humbled to have somehow earned such an exquisite gift. But she didn't want to risk losing it by forcing Ray to endure a surprise outing.

"Let me tell you where we're going, at least."

"You said you wanted to surprise me," Ray said quietly. "I don't want you to ruin the surprise."

"Yeah, well, I'm starting to realize that you probably aren't that into surprises these days. It was a silly idea."

"Surprises are fun." Looking out the passenger window as they got off the exit in Santa Rosa, Ray murmured, "I used to love surprises."

Ray obviously wanted to go through with this, so Carly shut up. She didn't want to go too far the other way and have Ray think she was babying her. Carly was determined not to cross the fine line between being considerate and condescending.

"I promise you won't have to really talk to anyone." Carly hated seeing Ray anxious, especially knowing that she was the cause. Yet Ray would love what she had planned for today. "I'll introduce you to a friend of mine, but only for a moment, and I'll do all the talking."

"Carly?"

"Yeah?" Carly glanced over at Ray, searching her face for a sign that her reassurances were working.

"I'm fine."

Carly exhaled. Damn, she needed to calm down. Her own anxiety wasn't helping. "I know you are."

"I really am," Ray said, almost as though she were convincing herself. "I'm doing better lately."

"And I'm proud of you." Without thinking, Carly reached across the console and squeezed Ray's hand. Though Ray didn't pull away or even react, Carly immediately realized what she had done and retreated, embarrassed. "By the way."

"Thank you."

Carly heard something in Ray's voice, but couldn't read its meaning. She hoped the physical contact hadn't made Ray uncomfortable, either because of her aversion to being touched or her fear of being hit on. Carly didn't realize how naturally tactile she was until she met Ray. Now every unthinking gesture put Carly on edge.

"I'm proud of me, too," Ray said, letting go with a real smile. If being touched bothered her, she was doing a good job of hiding it.

Carly took a right turn onto the street where their destination lay. "Okay, we're here."

Ray looked at the building to the left, zeroing in on the sign as Carly slowed in front of the driveway. "Assistance Dog Institute?"

"A friend of mine works here and said they have a four-week-old litter right now that's participating in their puppy-petting program." Carly pulled into a spot near the building. "Is that something you'd be interested in?"

"Is the puppy-petting program just what it sounds like?" A slow grin spread across Ray's face, transforming her from merely beautiful to breathtaking. "That's seriously something people volunteer to do?"

"It seriously is. I arranged for us to spend some time with them, just the two of us. I was telling my friend about Jagger and she mentioned that she could hook us up."

"Awesome." Ray darted a nervous glance at the front door. "I'd love to go play with puppies."

"Right on. I thought you might feel that way."

Carly got out and waited for Ray to unload Jagger from the backseat. Ray stood next to the car with Jagger's leash in hand, mentally preparing to go inside. Her face took on a look of intense concentration, and though she was clearly nervous, she also appeared to have a confidence that hadn't been there when they first met. It apparently began when Ray started working with Jack, when their own friendship took root. The woman who had hidden behind sunglasses for most of Jagger's first vet appointment had ditched her shades and was prepared to let Carly take her into an unfamiliar situation, based on trust alone. Amazing.

"I'm ready," Ray said. "Lead the way."

Carly took them inside, greeting a woman at the desk and asking for her friend Tanya. Ray hung back with Jagger, studying the walls in silence.

Carly had given Tanya a little information on Ray and her PTSD, knowing she would be sensitive to the situation. The Assistance Dog Institute trained all kinds of service dogs, including those who worked with people suffering from PTSD, so Tanya was familiar with the condition. And she was a total sweetheart, a former classmate from UC Davis who chose to work in the service-dog industry rather than complete veterinary school after deciding that she liked to help people just as much as animals. Carly hoped that Ray would feel comfortable with this brief introduction, certain that they would hit it off. Tanya was the nicest person she knew.

Sure enough, Tanya entered the lobby wearing a huge grin and swept Carly into a warm hug. "Hey, girl."

Carly returned the hug, appreciating the human contact. Tanya was straight and Carly would never go there, but that didn't stop her from noticing how nice it felt to be touched. "Hey, yourself. How are you?"

"Busy." Tanya pulled away from the embrace but kept hold of Carly's arms a moment longer. "But things are good." Her gaze flicked over Carly's shoulder. "Wow. Carly was right, he is *gorgeous*."

Carly smiled. Poor Ray couldn't have chosen a more attention-getting companion.

"Thank you," Ray said.

Carly turned to make introductions. "Tanya, this is my friend Ray. Ray, this is Tanya. We were in college together."

"It's nice to meet you, Ray." Tanya took a step toward Jagger. "Do you mind if I greet him?"

"Not at all," Ray said.

Carly watched the pride swell in her eyes as Tanya stroked the top of Jagger's head.

"He's wonderful," Tanya said. "What an unusual dog for service work. You said you got him through an organization?"

"Yes," Ray said. Carly opened her mouth to take over the conversation if necessary, but Ray continued without hesitation. "His breeder's son was killed in Iraq, so she decided to donate a puppy to the service-dog institute specifically to work with a veteran. I always wanted a Great Dane, so—"

"Match made in heaven." Tanya turned back to Carly. "Well, let's go find some puppies to pet."

They followed Tanya farther into the building, to a room with a shiny tile floor, a half-door, and a wire exercise pen filled with six furry yellow puppies. "Four-week-old Lab pups," Tanya said. "We train hearing dogs for the deaf, guide dogs for the blind, and service dogs for people with disabilities or other conditions, like PTSD. When they're eight weeks old, they'll go home with volunteers who will raise them until they're about eighteen months. Then they'll come back to us for advanced training." Tanya opened the door, letting them all inside. "Right now, their job is to be socialized as much as possible, and that's where you guys come in."

Ray put Jagger into a down-stay next to the door, then stepped forward to join them. "They're the cutest things I've ever seen."

Tanya laughed, squirting some hand sanitizer onto her palm, then passing it to Carly. "Have you ever played with puppies?"

"No." Ray used the sanitizer, then handed it back to Tanya shyly. "My dad had a dog when I was a kid, but I don't remember him as a puppy."

"You're gonna love this." Tanya scooped up a puppy from inside the pen, then offered it to Ray. "Don't let them run around the room, but please hold them and play with them as much as you'd like. I'll be back in a while."

Ray took the puppy gently, cradling it as though it might break in her hands. "Oh, my gosh. He's so small."

Carly lifted the tail and checked. "She." She waved good-bye to Tanya as she exited the room. "And yes, she's tiny." She picked up a second puppy, then sat down on the floor next to the pen. "But round."

Ray laughed as she eased down onto the floor cross-legged so they were knee to knee. She flipped the puppy onto her back and stroked her roly-poly belly. "She sure is."

"I can't believe this is the first time you've handled puppies." Carly brought the squirming boy she was holding to her face and breathed in deeply, savoring his puppy breath. That smell never got old.

"Thank you for bringing me," Ray said. The puppy in her arms had fallen asleep, and she gazed upon it with pure love. "This is really cool."

"It's my pleasure." Carly swapped her puppy for another, laughing as the one she released immediately jumped onto a littermate and initiated play. "I raised a puppy for a place like this once, when I was a kid."

"Really?"

"When I was fourteen. For my birthday that year I told my parents all I wanted was to raise a service puppy. I think I was just looking for an excuse to have a baby in the house, but after I went through the orientation and started training her, I got excited about the idea that she would grow up to help someone who needed her."

"What was her name?" Ray carefully laid the sleeping puppy on her lap, then picked up another.

"Lucy. She was a great dog. A golden retriever."

"Was it hard to give her back when it was time?"

"Yes." Carly remembered the tears of that day, as well as the pride she felt at what a good dog Lucy had become. "But it was worth it."

"You sound like you had good parents."

"I have great parents. They live in Portland." Carly hesitated, uncertain whether Ray would feel like she was prying if she asked about her family. She usually tried to stay away from asking so many things she was dying to know about Ray. But they had trust now, didn't they? "How about you? Where's your family?"

Ray swapped pups again, keeping the first snoozing girl in her lap. "Oh, my mother lives near Grand Rapids, Michigan. My younger sister teaches near Flint, and my older sister moved to Boston with her husband. My father passed away when I was a teenager."

"I'm sorry," Carly said.

"Me, too. He was my best friend."

"Do you keep in touch with your sisters or your mom?"

"Not really." Ray shifted a little, momentarily waking the puppy in her lap. "Not lately."

Recognizing discomfort, Carly decided to drop the subject. She hadn't meant to open a can of worms.

To her surprise, Ray kept talking. "My father was in a wheelchair after he came home from Vietnam. He struggled at times, but his service was very important to him. He's one of the big reasons I joined the army. I thought he would be proud."

"I'm sure he would be very proud."

Ray shook her head, smiling without humor. "Yeah." She kissed the puppy in her hands. "I'm sure."

"So what was the other big reason? For joining?"

Ray's expression turned rueful. "Money for college. Not that I'm putting that GI Bill to good use now."

"You're still recovering," Carly said in a low voice. "That takes time. And you've got your whole life ahead of you."

Ray met her eyes and held her gaze for so long that Carly almost looked away. It was too intense. When Ray made eye contact, Carly felt as though she were being laid bare, that all her emotions and desires were on the surface for Ray to see no matter how hard she tried to hide them.

"I'm still trying to get used to that idea," Ray said, finally looking away. "Having my whole life ahead of me."

Carly cuddled the puppy in her arms, but said nothing. If Ray wanted to talk, she didn't want to dissuade her.

"I thought I was going to die over there." Ray returned the second puppy to the pen and resumed petting the one that slept in her lap. "I never even let myself imagine a time after captivity."

Carly's heart thumped rapidly and her throat tightened. Ray had never spoken specifically about her experience in Iraq. Carly stayed very still, afraid that if she moved she might frighten Ray's words away. Even though she was scared to hear the details, Carly needed to know what had happened to Ray over there.

When Ray fell silent, Carly decided to encourage her. "If you want to talk, I'm here."

Ray shrugged. "I've only ever discussed it with my commanding officers and my therapist."

"I'm sure it's not easy to talk about." Carly nodded at the pen full of squirming, yipping Labs. "Puppies are excellent listeners, though."

"I've heard that." Ray sat playing with the sleeping pup's ears. Without looking up, she said, "I was a sixty-eight-W health care specialist. A medic."

"I know," Carly said. Wikipedia had told her that much. "One of the first women to be assigned as an infantry combat medic, right?"

"Right."

"You must have been pretty proud."

Ray's eyes darkened. "Women are in combat over there all the time, no matter what the army says. They need to catch up with the reality on the ground and change their ridiculous policy. It has no bearing on what's really happening."

"Still, to be one of the first officially assigned to a combat unit. That's pretty special."

"I was proud at the time, yes. Still am, I guess. Some people have suggested that what happened to me is the perfect example of why women shouldn't be allowed to serve in combat situations. So I'm not sure it was all that great a thing after all. For women in general."

Carly remembered the debate that raged in the media for a short time after the insurgents released the first videotape of Ray. In between playing the footage over and over ad nauseum, the talking heads pondered whether seeing a woman in such dire circumstances would cause some to reconsider the wisdom of putting female American soldiers in harm's way. The speculation had annoyed Carly at the time, but now she felt downright angry.

"That's ridiculous," she said. "What happened to you had nothing to do with your gender. Would it have been any less traumatic if you were a man?"

"I agree. But some people don't see it that way."

"Some people are wrong."

Ray gave her a humorless smile. "Even so, it sucks to feel like I helped set back that particular issue ten years."

"You didn't do any such thing. Did you like medicine?"

"I'm not sure I'd call what I did medicine, exactly. I reminded the guys to stay hydrated, I patched up holes. I liked it enough, though. At one point I thought I'd go to medical school when I got out."

"Still interested?"

"Not at all."

Carly wished she knew what was appropriate to ask and what she should leave alone. "I bet you saw some pretty horrible things. But I'm sure you did a lot of good, too."

"Well, not when it really counted," Ray said in a husky voice. She shuddered almost imperceptibly, but Carly caught it. Immediately she wished she could take back the words that had clearly triggered a memory.

Instinctively, Carly touched Ray's knee. "Ray, I'm sorry. You don't have to talk about this if it's too hard."

Ray looked down at Carly's hand, something indefinable in her eyes. "It feels good to have someone I want to talk to."

Embarrassed to have been caught touching her again, Carly murmured, "I'm sorry." As she pulled away, Ray's hand landed awkwardly on Carly's, squeezed, then retreated. Carly returned her hand to her own lap, skin burning from the brief contact.

"It's okay," Ray said quietly. "There's not a lot to tell, honestly. An IED disabled our Humvee, and a group of insurgents ambushed us. I broke my leg. A lot of guys were hurt in the explosion, and I didn't even make it to the first one before they grabbed me and put me in a car."

"You can't blame yourself for that. They were waiting for you, ready to take hostages. Your leg was broken. What could you have done?"

"I was trained to respond to all kinds of situations," Ray said tightly. "I should have done something."

Carly detected a faint undercurrent of self-loathing in Ray's voice. Despite the fact that she hadn't been the only soldier taken that day, she clearly blamed herself. And she was the only one to make it back alive. Carly knew better than to press this point. Guilt was tricky, resistant to even the best logic. And once you were intimate with guilt, it was hard to let it go.

"You were very brave," Carly said. "I can't imagine how scary it must have been."

"Pretty scary." Closing her eyes, Ray took a couple of deep breaths. When her shoulders dropped slightly, Carly realized how tense she had been. Ray opened her eyes, clearly done talking about this for the moment. "I'm okay now." Giving Carly a shy smile, she said, "Excellent, actually."

Carly's heart pitter-pattered, silly with excitement over Ray's implied meaning. "I'll say. I can't tell you how proud of you I am. You've been great with Jack, and your confidence is soaring."

Ray's smile turned into a grin. "I've been feeling pretty happy. Strong."

"Jagger and Jack have done you a lot of good."

"Don't give them all the credit." Ray poked Carly's foot with the toe of her shoe. "You've done me a world of good, too."

Face burning, Carly poked back. "Ditto."

Looking pleased, Ray glanced down at the puppy in her lap just as it woke up and began to chew on her finger. "Ouch!" Ray laughed and pulled away. "She's got a mouth full of needles."

"Ah, puppy teeth. I know them well."

"I'll bet." Ray placed the puppy back in its pen with its littermates. She rolled a ball toward the corner of the wire enclosure, sending three puppies stumbling after it. "Courageous woman."

"Worth it, though," Carly remarked, watching the puppies give chase.

"Totally worth it."

Ray brought her injured finger to her mouth, blowing on it gently. Carly's attention drifted to Ray's lips, then she forced herself to look away. No sense driving herself crazy. Her gaze landed on Ray's wrist, where for the first time she noticed a slightly raised white scar set against the pale skin. Carly blinked in surprise. If she didn't know better—

"I didn't try to kill myself or anything," Ray said in a quiet voice. Startled, Carly dragged her eyes away from the scar and found Ray staring at her red-faced. "The plastic restraints they used cut into me." She showed Carly the other wrist, which had a matching scar that actually looked more severe. "I struggled a lot in the beginning, not that it did me any good."

Embarrassed to have been caught staring, Carly felt her cheeks grow hot. "I'm sorry. I wasn't trying to be nosy."

Ray shrugged, clearly trying to act more nonchalant than she was able to pull off. "You would have noticed sooner or later. I don't blame you for being curious."

The two of them probably looked like quite the pair, blushing at one another. Carly imagined that those weren't Ray's only scars, and she tried not to think too hard about where the others might be. Or how she desperately wanted to kiss each one, to take Ray's pain away.

"Like I said, I think you're very brave," Carly said finally. "The real question is, are you brave enough to withstand more puppy teeth?"

Ray visibly relaxed, then raised an eyebrow as she dipped into the pen to pick up the feistiest puppy of the bunch. "Watch me."

CHAPTER NINE

Ray tried to play it cool, but Dr. Evans was good at reading her mood. "You look radiant today," Dr. Evans said, her own joy evident despite the grainy obfuscation of the video chat window. "I take it things are going well."

"Very well." Ray allowed herself to grin. No point in being shy about it. She was feeling better than she had in years. "I'm feeling good."

"Awesome. Any particular reason, or just having a good day?"

"Good day, good week." Ray leaned back in her office chair, dropping her hand to pet Jagger's head. "Great friend."

"Carly?"

Ray laughed. "That's the one. The only one."

"One friend is a wonderful thing. Better than none."

"Definitely. Although I'm forgetting someone." Ray unclipped the webcam from her monitor, aiming it at the second dog pillow that sat next to her chair. Jack lifted his head, looked at the webcam, then settled back down with a deep sigh. "This is Jack."

"Ah, the famous Jack. It's nice to put a face with the name."

Ray laughed as she returned the camera to its original position. "I know it's silly, but I consider him a friend, too."

"Not silly. Dogs can be incredible friends. But I am glad to hear that your human friendship is working out, too."

"It's more than working out. It's amazing. Carly's amazing."

"Tell me," Dr. Evans said.

"She took me to this puppy-petting thing at the service-dog institute the other day." Ray let herself enjoy the memory of that afternoon. Even though she had been scared to let Carly drive her someplace unknown, the experience had turned out to be amazing. Not only the puppies, but the shift in their friendship. "She arranged for us to spend some time with a litter, and it was so much fun."

"That does sound like fun," Dr. Evans said. "She sounds like a very good friend."

"She's incredible. I've never felt like this about anyone. Even before Iraq. I mean, Danny was my best friend, no doubt, but we bonded on a completely different level."

"How so?"

"My relationship with Danny was more of a surface thing. Don't get me wrong, I loved him. We had a lot of fun together. But I'm not sure I ever trusted him as much as I trust Carly. I can't explain it. Something about her makes me want to be with her all the time."

Dr. Evans opened her mouth to speak, then hesitated. Something about that pause put Ray on edge slightly, and she sat back in her chair. She was gushing about Carly, wasn't she? Was that weird?

"What?" Ray asked.

"I was just remembering that you mentioned Carly is a lesbian," Dr. Evans said. "It's interesting that when you talk about her, the first thing that comes up is Danny. That's an intriguing comparison."

"What are you trying to say?"

"I'm not trying to say anything. I'm just making an observation."

"Well, it sounds pretty wrongheaded to me. Danny was my best friend since high school. Carly is my best friend right now. That's the extent of the similarity."

"Of course," Dr. Evans said. "They're both very important people in your life. We're talking about two of the most intimate relationships you've ever had."

"I'm not a lesbian."

Dr. Evans blinked and took a moment to respond. "I'm not trying to offend you, Ray. Or suggest anything that makes you uncomfortable."

"I'm not uncomfortable. It's unfair to assume that just because Carly is gay, me liking her means that I'm gay too."

Dr. Evans raised her hand. "I apologize, Ray. I didn't mean to touch a nerve."

"Well, that was awfully presumptuous." Ray twisted her hands in her lap, so upset she wanted to shut down their session right now. Couldn't she be friends with a lesbian without raising the suspicion that her feelings were something more than platonic? "Plenty of people have gay friends without being gay themselves."

"You're absolutely right. Honestly, Ray, I didn't realize that my comment would upset you like it has. Please accept my apology."

Ray took a deep breath, trying like hell to calm down. Dr. Evans had definitely touched a nerve, and even Ray was surprised by the force of her reaction to the mere suggestion that she was attracted to Carly. Deep down, she knew that her passionate denial hinted at something she couldn't bear to explore very closely. At least not yet.

"I'm sorry too, Dr. Evans." Ray finally looked at her therapist's image on the screen. "I'm a little oversensitive. In the military, that's a serious accusation. Old habits die hard."

"Understood. At any rate, I'm thrilled that you've got this new friendship in your life. She's helping you get out there and experience new things."

"It's pretty cool." Ray took another breath, forcing herself to let down her guard again. "I talked to her a little bit...about Iraq."

"And how was that?"

"Good. A little scary, but she doesn't push me. She just...lets me talk. Or not."

"Sounds perfect."

"She is." Ray felt a niggling of unease, a creeping doubt about the way she talked about Carly. Why did Dr. Evans have to raise the idea that she was attracted to Carly? Now she felt self-conscious, like everything she said was a giant red flag. "It's good to have a friend again."

"It'll be very healing for you to be able to share some of what you've been going through with someone you trust. You're gaining confidence and should find it easier to cope with life when you've got someone on your side."

"You're right," Ray said. "Moving here was the best thing I could have done."

"I was worried about what this move would mean for you. But you're flourishing, and I'm very proud of you."

Ray's eyes filled at the compliment, which meant a lot coming from someone who had seen her at her lowest low. Often she worried that she would disappoint Dr. Evans, so it felt good to have made her proud. And it was even better to be proud of herself.

CHAPTER TEN

P lease just don't tell me you told me so." Carly held the phone to her ear and waited for Leeann to let her have it.

But Leeann must have heard the sorrow in Carly's tone, because she was all sympathy. "Oh, honey."

Carly rolled onto her side and brought her knees to her chest, still huddled under her sleep-warmed comforter. She hadn't been able to get out of bed this morning with the sad longing sunrise had brought. "I knew I was attracted to her, but I didn't think I'd fall in love."

"You're in love with her?"

"I don't know." Every time Carly saw Ray's number on her caller ID, warmth bloomed in the pit of her stomach. Ray was beautiful, pure joy to be around, and as Ray let her guard down, Carly's feelings only grew stronger. Their relationship was possibly more one-sided than Carly cared to admit, but sometimes she thought she saw something in the way Ray looked at her that hinted at possibilities she didn't dare entertain. "Maybe not yet. But I think it's inevitable."

"I know you feel very strongly about her, Carly, but you need to back off a little." Leeann's voice was tight with concern, and Carly knew she was trying to be tactful. "For your own good."

"I can't." The very thought made Carly feel like she couldn't quite catch her breath. "I know it's probably the smart thing to do, but I can't abandon Ray."

"You wouldn't be abandoning her. Just taking a step back. Gaining some distance."

"I don't want distance. She makes me happy, Leeann."

"At what cost?" Leeann's passion was rising, her familiar

protective instincts advancing. "You need someone who can return your love, honey. I don't want your first experience after Nadia to be heartache."

"Neither do I. But I can't control how I feel." Carly pushed her face into her pillow, muffling a groan. "I've gotten myself into this mess and I'm scared to death, but I can't stand not having her in my life. Even as just a friend."

Leeann was quiet, then finally said, "I'm coming up for lunch. I'll be there in three hours."

Carly rolled onto her back. "You don't have to do that."

"Yes, I do."

"Really, Leeann, I'm fine."

"You're not fine. And I miss you. Let me bring you something from the city. How about soup and a bread bowl from Boudin?"

Carly's stomach growled at the thought of sourdough. "Okay, you talked me into it."

"I love you, honey. Everything'll be okay."

"Thank you. I love you, too." Carly hung up the phone and sighed. She really had it bad if she was willing to call Leeann and admit she was in trouble.

Loving Ray McKenna was stupid. Unfortunately her heart wasn't listening to her head. No matter how hard she tried to shove down the feelings Ray stirred, they wouldn't disappear.

She clicked the phone on and dialed Ray's cell number. They didn't have explicit plans for the afternoon, but they had been spending their weekends together almost by default. Maybe it was good for Leeann to come for a visit. Having Ray as her sole social outlet really wasn't healthy, given her conflicted feelings. When Ray didn't answer, Carly left a short voice mail letting her know that Leeann was coming over and she wouldn't be available. Hanging up, she felt a pang of disappointment.

"Pathetic," Carly groaned, then forced herself out of bed.

Three hours later, a hot shower and two cups of coffee had Carly feeling slightly more upbeat. She was running Jack through the agility course in the backyard when Leeann strolled through the side gate carrying a plastic bag, causing Jack to bolt away from the A-frame and over to greet her.

"Careful, puppy dog," Leeann said, lifting the bag of food high into the air as Jack sniffed eagerly. "I didn't bring enough to share."

Carly stepped in and pointed for Jack to back off, which he did with a doggy grin. "Hey, Leeann." Taking the bag from Leeann, she wrapped her in a one-armed hug. "It's really good to see you."

"You, too." Leeann stepped back and looked Carly up and down. "I was expecting red eyes, puffiness, something. Even suffering from unrequited love, you look great."

"Charming as always." Carly tweaked Leeann's elbow, but the compliment warmed her more than she expected, and she couldn't suppress a smile.

"I try."

Carly pulled out a chair for Leeann, then sat next to her. She watched as Leeann arranged their food on the table, touched by the gesture. "Thank you."

"You'd do the same for me."

Carly nodded, but Leeann would never let this happen to her. With her curly blond hair and lithe runner's body, Leeann had no trouble attracting women. She also had no trouble keeping them at a distance. At times Carly thought she envied Leeann's ability to keep things uncomplicated; then again, she wasn't sure whether Leeann had ever been in love. That was a steep price to pay for simplicity.

"I'm an idiot." Carly toyed with her plastic spoon, not meeting Leeann's eyes. "You can say it."

Leeann sighed. "I wish you could've fallen in love with someone else, but this is in no way idiotic."

Smiling again, Carly said, "You're a good friend. The best, actually."

Leeann put down her spoon and took Carly's hand. "I've wanted nothing more than for you to find someone. Or at least get interested. Even though this isn't what I had in mind, it's got to feel good to discover that you can fall in love again."

The last time Carly had felt anything even close to this sweet agony was with Nadia. For five years now she'd believed that her capacity for such deep feeling had been buried along with her partner. So in a way, this was a good thing. At least her heart hadn't been shattered beyond repair. Yet.

"It's nice to know it's possible, I guess." Carly took a bite of bread, and Leeann also ate quietly, letting her think. Carly sighed, then said, "What if I don't want to fall in love with someone who can love me back? Even though a part of me wants that connection so badly, another part is scared to death to ever feel that much again."

"Subconsciously you're falling in love with someone unattainable so you won't have to actually move on?" Leeann nodded. "It makes sense."

Carly paused mid-bite. "Clearly you've given this theory some thought."

"A little."

"I worry that's what I'm doing, but on the other hand…how could I *not* fall in love with Ray? She's gorgeous, she's brave, she makes me laugh. I feel good when I'm with her."

Concern shone in Leeann's eyes. "I'm sure she's a wonderful person. A wonderful *straight* person with a whole lot of baggage. She could be the most incredible woman in the world and I'd still tell you she's a bad prospect."

"I know." Carly set down her spoon. Having her heart broken once was more than enough, so why was she setting herself up for more? Losing Nadia had left her devastated, and she had only recently started putting her pieces back together. "I still miss her so much, Lee."

"I know you do, honey." Leeann put down her own spoon and stood. Taking Carly's hand, she said, "Let's go swing."

Carly let Leeann lead her to the porch swing. They sat close together at one end, and Carly was grateful for the warmth of Leeann's body. It felt good to be with someone who made her so comfortable, and who knew her so well. Though nothing had been resolved as far as her feelings for Ray were concerned, Carly felt better already.

"Nadia would have wanted you to be happy," Leeann said after a few moments of silent rocking. "You know that, right?"

"I know."

Leeann chewed on her lip, clearly weighing whatever she was about to say in her head. "Do you want to be happy, Carly?"

Carly opened her mouth to insist that of course she did, then hesitated. What did that mean, anyway? She could be happy without putting herself out there again. And did she even deserve to find someone else when Nadia and their baby were in the ground?

"Everyone wants to be happy," Carly said finally. "Right?"

"Not necessarily." Leeann grabbed Carly's hand and held it between her own, warming her fingers. "You and Nadia were amazing together, honey. You really were. But you're exceptional. So many other women out there could be good for you."

Maybe, but Carly could think only of Ray, who made her feel something special when they were together, even though their relationship was wholly platonic. Safe. Warm. Almost loved.

Carly closed her eyes and sat back, swept away by a deep, aching need to lose herself in another person. More than just the casual sex she had found in San Francisco clubs. She wanted to be with someone she loved, who loved her back. To experience something more than just the giving and taking of pleasure. Something real.

Leeann squeezed her hand, then wrapped an arm around her, pulling her close. She didn't say anything, and Carly was glad; this wasn't a moment that demanded words. It was enough that Leeann was here next to her, someone who had known her forever and who loved her unconditionally.

Carly opened her eyes and wrapped Leeann in a tight hug. "I don't know what I'd do without you, Lee. I really don't."

"I'll always be here for you." Leeann tucked a lock of hair behind Carly's ear. "Don't you worry about that."

Carly pulled back, intending to give Leeann a silly smile to break the seriousness of the moment, but found herself pressing against Leeann's body, tightening her embrace. As though by instinct Leeann's hands came up and rested on Carly's back, holding her close. Carly shivered at the pleasure of feminine curves against her own, triggering a flash of memory: the two of them making love all night in college, until they were so exhausted they both slept through a psychology exam the next morning.

"Carly?" Leeann asked quietly.

Carly gazed into Leeann's eyes, seeing curiosity, then surprised herself by pressing her lips against Leeann's.

Leeann kissed her back softly, stroking her hair with a trembling hand. Carly deepened the kiss and moved her hand to Leeann's throat, savoring the softness of the skin beneath her fingertips. Placing her own hand on Carly's upper chest, Leeann broke away and rested her forehead against Carly's.

"We can't do this," Leeann whispered.

Blinking through the hurt Leeann's refusal unleashed, Carly tried to retreat. Leeann covered the back of Carly's neck with her other hand, keeping her close. Carly shut her eyes, embarrassed by her moment of weakness. "Rejected by Leeann Hanssen. I'm a member of a pretty small club now, aren't I?"

Leeann stiffened. "That's not fair," she said, but she didn't let Carly go.

Carly sighed and took her hand away from Leeann's throat. "You're right. I'm sorry. I don't know what I was thinking." That was a lie. She knew exactly what she'd been thinking. That she could take Leeann inside and they could make love, and maybe for a little while Carly would be able to forget Ray McKenna. Maybe she would even find some of what she had been craving, with the safest person she knew.

"Trust me," Leeann said in a low voice. "Making love with you is definitely my idea of a pretty awesome Saturday. But you're my friend, you're hurting, and you don't really want to do this." Biting her lower lip, she said, "*I* don't want to do this. You're the one woman I have a real relationship with, and I never want to fuck that up. Especially over a little sex."

Carly nodded. "I'm sorry."

"No reason to be. You're going through a lot right now. And I am pretty irresistible."

Laughing, Carly sagged against Leeann, emotionally exhausted. "Don't forget modest."

"How could I? It's another of my stellar qualities." Leeann played with the fine hairs at the back of Carly's neck. Growing serious, she said, "Are we okay?"

"We're okay. Your heart is pounding."

"That wasn't easy for me. Stopping. I'm sure it was a character-building moment."

Carly chuckled. "I'll bet." Sobering, she buried her face in Leeann's neck. "I just need to be held."

"I can do that."

Leeann started them rocking again, and Carly relaxed, enjoying the intimacy.

Jack tore across the yard toward the gate and broke the tranquility.

Carly looked to see what had spurred him into action, then gasped at the sight of Ray standing just inside the backyard with an odd look on her face. Jagger stood calmly at her side, allowing Jack to sniff him excitedly. Carly sat up straight, pulling away from Leeann a little too quickly. She knew she looked guilty, though she wasn't sure why. Ray was just a friend, and Carly didn't owe her any explanations.

"Ray." Carly cringed at the way her voice trembled slightly. "Hey. I tried to call you earlier."

Ray glanced at Leeann, then shifted her gaze just right of Carly's shoulder. "I'm sorry, I didn't mean to interrupt."

Carly stood abruptly, giving Leeann a quick backward glance. "You weren't interrupting. We were just catching up. Ray, this is my good friend Leeann. Leeann, this is Ray."

Leeann stood and crossed the yard, hand extended. "It's nice to meet you, Ray. Carly's told me so much about you."

Ray looked at Carly briefly, then took Leeann's hand for a quick shake. "It's nice to meet you. I should go."

"Why don't you stay for dinner?" Carly knew Ray wouldn't want to hang out with Leeann, but she needed to ask. Maybe if Leeann got to know Ray, she could tell Carly what to do. Plus, she was proud of Ray. She wanted to show her off.

"Thanks, but I should probably get back. I have some things I need to do today, so—"

Carly knew Ray was lying, otherwise she wouldn't have dropped by in the first place, but she let it pass. "Okay, well…maybe we can see each other tomorrow?"

"Sure." Ray barely looked at her. "You guys have a great dinner."

"Thanks," Leeann said. "It was lovely to meet you."

"You too." Ray turned and opened the back gate, tugging Jagger along with her, while Jack watched them go with mournful eyes. Carly knew exactly how he felt.

Once Ray's car pulled away, Leeann turned to Carly with raised eyebrows. "You're right, she's hot."

"Yes."

"And very shy."

Sighing, Carly said, "Yes."

Leeann took her by the hand and led her to the swing, sitting them down again. "Let me set you up with this girl from work. She's in IT.

Totally cute, in a geeky way. She's hilarious and a freakin' genius. My computer crashed last week and she fixed it like magic."

"I don't know. I'm not sure I'm ready for a blind date." In truth, she couldn't imagine finding anyone as attractive as Ray. But that was a problem, wasn't it?

"No expectations, okay? I just think you two would get along, and maybe it'll help open your eyes to new possibilities. If nothing else, it'll get you out of here for an evening."

Carly covered her face with both hands. She tried to picture making it through dinner with a stranger while Ray ate alone. Right now she would rather be with Ray. How could IT girl possibly compete?

"Please, Carly. Do it for me."

Carly dropped her hands. "Sure. Why not?"

"Really?" Leeann sounded very pleased.

"Yes. If she's interested in having dinner or something, give her my number."

Leeann clapped her hands. "Wonderful. Perfect."

Ready to take her mind off romance, Carly said, "Do you want to go inside and play a video game?"

Leeann wrinkled her nose. Video games had never really been her thing, and she didn't understand why Carly was such a fan. "Would that make you feel better?"

"Yes."

"Okay, then. Video games it is."

Laughing, Carly stood and whistled for Jack. "Don't sound so excited."

"I bet Jessica in IT likes video games."

Carly put on a patient face. "I guess I'll find out."

CHAPTER ELEVEN

R ay?"
      Danny's voice on the other end of the phone caught Ray off guard. How long had it been since they spoke? At least eight months. She should have called him after moving to Bodega Bay, but hadn't worked up the nerve.

"You there, Ray?"

"I'm here." It was unnerving to hear from him, especially after Dr. Evans's comments comparing what she had felt for him to her friendship with Carly. Yet it warmed her that he cared enough to call. She wouldn't have blamed him if he hadn't.

"It's nice to hear your voice."

Ray closed her eyes. "It's nice to hear yours, too." It hadn't been easy for her to end their relationship. Not when he had been her constant companion since freshman year of high school. He had shipped out to Baghdad three months before she had, and they returned home at the same time. By that point they were like strangers.

"How are things in California?"

"Good," Ray said. "I really like it out here." Jagger leaned against her heavily, so she added, "I got a Great Dane."

"Really? Sweet."

"Yeah, he's great. His name is Jagger."

"Nice."

Ray chewed on her lip, unsure what to say. She wanted to tell him so many things. That she was sorry she'd been unable to look at him when he visited her at Walter Reed. That she didn't know why she hadn't been able to stand his hugs or his sympathy. That she really had loved him, but in the end it didn't matter. All she knew after Iraq was that she couldn't be with him. There was no place for Danny in her life anymore.

Instead of saying any of those things, she asked, "How are things there?"

"Oh. Good." Danny cleared his throat, sounding just as uncomfortable as she felt. "Things are great, actually. I, uh, met a girl."

"Oh." Ray forced a brightness into her voice that she didn't really feel. "Wow. That's wonderful."

"Thanks. It kind of is, yeah." Danny paused, then said, "Actually, part of the reason I called was to tell you that I've asked her to marry me."

A pang of sorrow deep in her stomach took Ray by surprise. "Oh." That hadn't taken long.

"For some reason she accepted." Danny waited a moment, and when she didn't speak, he said, "I wanted you to hear it from me."

"I appreciate that." Ray sat down on the couch, no longer trusting herself to stand. The news hit her harder than she expected. It didn't matter that she could never see herself being with him again. They were still Ray and Danny, and she had known since she was fifteen that they would be together forever. That dream had died in Iraq, but she hadn't expected fresh evidence of its demise.

"Are you okay, Ray-Ray?"

The nickname took her back to high school. Saturday afternoons lying on his bedroom floor, listening to Eagles albums. That time they cut class and just drove around in his car, talking about their futures. Counting the days until graduation so they could enlist. Why had she pulled away?

"I'm fine," Ray said. "Congratulations. I'm happy for you."

"I don't expect you to be happy for me."

"But I am." After a moment of reflection, Ray realized it was true. When she broke up with Danny the most difficult part had been seeing the pain she caused him. At that point she felt very little about her own loss. She was totally numb, even about her inability to remain intimate with the only person who'd ever told her he loved her.

"This isn't how I thought things would turn out," Danny said. "In some ways I'm still getting used to that."

"We may not be together anymore, but I still want you to have everything you always wanted." Without her.

"Melissa's a kindergarten teacher." As though uncertain she wanted details, Danny said, "She's very different than you. But she's cool, anyway."

Ray flushed at the compliment. "Well, good." She played with Jagger's floppy ear, still wrestling with all the things she had left unsaid between them. "I really am sorry. About the way I ended things."

"You don't owe me an apology."

"I do." Exhaling, Ray said, "I had no excuse for being so cold about it." She could barely remember what she said, but it had been flat and unemotional. Even after Danny left the hospital room red-faced and teary-eyed, she felt nothing. Like her feelings had been shut off, a switch flipped without her consent.

"You were going through a lot."

"It doesn't matter what I was going through. I was pretty heartless with someone who meant a lot to me."

"War fucks people up. I understand that." Danny's voice broke. "I understand that a lot."

In a flash, Ray heard Danny's own struggle. It took her breath away, though she wasn't entirely surprised that he had been similarly affected. A lot of soldiers came back with combat-related trauma, both physical and mental. It was hard to go through such an experience and not be damaged by it.

"How have things been going for you?" Ray asked.

"Rough for a while. I drank too much for a few months. The army doctor prescribed me a shitload of meds, too, so I was a fucking zombie." Danny laughed shakily. "I mean, *Night of the Living Dead*, right? I was having some fucked-up thoughts at that point, when I could think at all. But I'm in AA now, and Melissa is very supportive. I'm doing better."

Guilt lanced through Ray's gut. "I'm sorry I wasn't there for you."

"Ray-Ray, I saw some fucked-up shit over there, but it was nothing compared to what you went through. God only knows what you're dealing with."

At least she never went down the road to self-medication. "Thank you for understanding. But I still apologize, okay?"

"Okay. Apology accepted."

A warm glow of connection came to life in Ray's chest and she laid her head back, happy to have this moment with Danny. Already she felt like she could start letting go of some of her guilt over what happened between them, which would be a true breakthrough.

"So you can be straight with me," Danny said in a lighter tone, signaling the end of their heavy discussion. "How are you doing, really?"

"I'm okay. It's still hard, but I've been getting out more. Jagger is my service dog, so he goes with me everywhere. He helps a lot."

"Awesome."

"Yeah. He is."

Danny cleared his throat. "How about you? Are you seeing anyone?"

Ray managed a humorless laugh. "No. I don't foresee that happening in the near future." Her conversation with Dr. Evans flashed through her mind, then the memory of finding Carly and her blond friend Leeann embracing on the porch swing. It bothered her how much that upset her.

"Please tell me you're at least making friends out there. It kills me to think of you all alone."

"I'm not all alone," Ray said. "I've got Jagger. And I have made a friend, actually. Her name is Carly. She's a veterinarian."

"I'm really glad to hear that."

He sounded surprised, and Ray wondered if her mother had told him she didn't really leave the house. Maybe she should call Mom and give her an update, too. "I'll be okay, Danny."

"I know you will." She could hear Danny smiling. "You've always been the tough one."

Ray laughed. They had been competitive with one another, particularly when it came to who was tougher. "I can't believe you're giving that title away."

"You've earned it." Danny sniffed. "Anyway, I should get going. Melissa and I are having dinner with her parents tonight."

"Ah," Ray said, her smile fading. "Sounds like fun."

"A blast." Danny paused. "Let's talk again sometime, okay?"

"Absolutely." It was a promise.

Ray hung up and sighed, stroking Jagger's head. For a conversation she had been dreading, that had gone rather well. In fact, a weight had been lifted.

But she also felt she had lost something. Not just Danny, but the girl she had been when she was with him. The girl not afraid of anything, the world hers to conquer. She'd even loved sex then, loved being touched. She couldn't imagine being with Danny like that anymore, but she missed that sense of closeness sex could bring.

The memory of Carly with her friend Leeann returned. Was Carly sleeping with that woman? They certainly looked cozy together. Carly had mentioned Leeann the ex-girlfriend before. As much as she hated to admit it, Ray struggled with jealousy at the very thought of Carly having that kind of intimacy with someone else.

"Stop it," Ray murmured. "Carly deserves to be happy. So does Danny."

Maybe one day, if Ray was very lucky, she would find happiness, too.

CHAPTER TWELVE

Ray tossed a tennis ball down the beach as she walked, sending Jack tearing after it. Jagger stayed by her side, never as interested in balls as in the people who threw them. Carly walked at her other side, so close that her body warmed Ray's in the early morning fog.

They'd barely spoken that morning. Carly never insisted on filling silence with words, which was a good thing. Lately Ray found it hard to know what to say when they were together. Though Carly fulfilled her in a way Ray never imagined another person could, she also caused a great deal of confusion. Ray was conquering an old fear without a glimmer of hesitation—this was the beach where Jagger was stung by the bee—but at the same time she was growing more afraid of the feelings Carly stirred inside her.

"You okay?"

Ray startled despite the gentleness of Carly's voice. "Yeah. Just thinking."

Carly smiled. "Anything you want to talk about?"

Tell Carly that she couldn't stop thinking about seeing her with Leeann? Ray shook her head. "No."

"Okay. I'll leave you to it, then." Jack trotted up to Carly and dropped his ball into her hand, and she threw it for him.

Ray watched Carly laugh as Jack sprinted after his toy, and her stomach clenched. She dropped her gaze to the sand, unbalanced by her visceral reaction to the joy on Carly's face. Why did Carly sometimes make her heart race like this? Ray wanted to chalk it up to nerves over even this social contact, but she knew that wasn't it. There was nothing scary about Carly Warner.

Except the way she was making Ray question everything she thought she knew about who she found attractive and how she saw their friendship.

She wanted to ask Carly if she and Leeann were together. When Carly spoke about Leeann, it sounded like they were just friends. But was it normal for friends to cuddle the way the two of them had? Ray let herself imagine a friendly embrace with Carly and shivered. Not because such contact sounded strange, but because it didn't.

Ray sneaked another glance at Carly's hair, blowing into her face. Carly pushed the locks aside and soldiered on, also looking deep in thought. Ray was so grateful that Carly would just allow her to think and not push to know what was on her mind. Carly appeared happy to be let in, but she always waited until Ray came to her. Ray loved this rare quality about her.

Carly probably never had to wait for Leeann. Ray envied their easy intimacy, which had been obvious the moment she opened the gate to the backyard. She recalled how Carly had looked when she realized Ray was watching. Carly had jumped up like a teenager caught making out by her parents. Had Carly kissed Leeann that day?

The thought slowed Ray down a step, and she stumbled slightly on her weaker leg. Before Carly could react, she made herself keep walking, not trusting herself to explain what was wrong. Sweat beaded on her forehead, though the morning breeze remained cool. She thought about kissing Carly, really kissing her, expecting a wave of revulsion. Instead her belly turned over slightly, sending a rush of pleasant warmth straight between her legs. A tug of arousal, almost like a memory. Something she hadn't felt in at least two years.

Ray stopped, kicking up a spray of pebbles. She knew what would happen even before it started. Her throat tightened. Sweat trickled down her sides, and her heart pounded explosively. She closed her eyes and tried to breathe as one thought raced through her mind. *Please don't let Carly see me like this.*

At once she was back in that filthy apartment in Al Hillah, tied to a chair in a windowless room. Archer's blood still tacky on the tile beneath her feet. Staring down the same video camera that had recorded his beheading. Powerless. Afraid.

"Ray?"

And other times when she felt powerless, times she shouldn't have had to watch her back. When the enemy wasn't someone from another culture. When he wore the same clothes she did.

"Oh, my God, Ray. Are you okay?"

Shaking her head, Ray tried to come into the present. Her legs gave out but Jagger leaned into her, holding her upright. She clutched at his strong back, knowing she was going down, desperate to break her fall.

"Just sit down, honey. Can you tell me what's wrong?"

Carly sounded like she was calling from the other end of a long tunnel, the words indistinct. Dimly aware of the concern in Carly's voice, Ray couldn't make her mouth work. She wanted to tell Carly she was all right, but Carly would know that was a lie.

Ray went down on her knees and brought her hands to her head. Jagger licked her hands furiously, covering her fingers in cold slobber. It brought her back into the present, but didn't stop the panic that tore through her veins. She seemed to be hyperventilating, and even Jagger couldn't make her stop. Worst of all, Carly had a front-row seat for her freak-out.

"You're okay, Ray."

Carly touched Ray's shoulder and Ray pulled away instinctively. She couldn't stand to have Carly so close, not when she was like this. Shame flared in her chest, making it that much harder to breathe. Ray curled into herself, then tried to stand, no longer in control of her body and at a loss about what to do.

"You're all right." Carly wore a look of controlled calm, though Ray knew she was putting on quite a show. "Just sit down for a minute."

Ray's legs trembled and she had to obey. Her head swam, and she still couldn't slow her breathing. Carly took her hand and sat beside her. This time Ray didn't pull away.

"Breathe, Ray. We're alone on this beach. Nobody's here but you, me, and the dogs." Carly's other hand moved to Ray's back and, surprisingly, the contact reassured her. "Take a deep breath and come back to us."

Ray closed her eyes. *I am the captain of my soul.* She could smell Carly's shampoo, the barest hint of raspberry-vanilla over the heady salt breeze. Jagger sat pressed against her side, propping her up.

"I'm sorry." Ray felt lost, adrift, as though she might never find the shore again. "So sorry."

Then Carly's arms were around her, pulling her into a tight embrace. "Hush," Carly murmured. "Just relax." Ray squirmed but Carly held on. "Relax. Let me hold you. Please. Everything is okay, Ray. Nobody's going to hurt you."

Carly's heart beat hard against Ray's chest, a strong and steady rhythm that calmed Ray immediately. Her body relaxed, as though Carly had flipped a switch that cut off her anxiety at the source. Without thinking, Ray brought her arms up and returned the hug. Carly's body felt solid and warm against hers, and softer than she would have imagined.

"Good." Carly's voice shook. "That's good. Deep breaths." She rubbed a trembling hand across Ray's back.

Ray pressed her palm between Carly's shoulder blades, grounding herself in the embrace. She concentrated on slowing down her breathing, like Dr. Evans had taught her. This was real. This was the present. Carly was still there even after Ray fell apart in front of her. In a world where Ray trusted very little anymore, Carly was safety. She was Ray's constant, an anchor to keep the storm of her own emotions from sweeping her away.

"I'm here," Carly whispered. Her words took on a passionate urgency that threatened to take Ray's breath away again. "I'm here for you, Ray. Always."

Ray pressed her face into Carly's neck, then pulled back. Still within the loose circle of Carly's arms, she managed to make eye contact and was humbled by what she saw. Carly's gaze held no judgment, only loyalty. Maybe even love. Her heart rate steadied even as her heart seemed to expand.

Ray opened her mouth to make another apology, then forced herself to smile instead. Carly would tell her it wasn't necessary. And Ray believed her. Looking into Carly's eyes, she realized that Carly cared for her enough to withstand even the worst. Instead of saying she was sorry, Ray spoke from her heart. "You're my best friend."

"I—" Carly shivered, and Ray noticed the too-thin Henley she wore. "I care about you so much."

"You're cold," Ray said thickly. She tried not to stare at the way Carly's hard nipples strained against the fabric of her shirt. Getting to her feet took effort, but Ray suddenly needed distance. She offered Carly her hand. "Let me give you my sweatshirt."

"That would be nice." Carly stood, then folded her arms over her breasts. She broke eye contact to gaze out over the choppy gray water. "It is pretty chilly."

Ray pulled her hooded gray army sweatshirt over her head. She handed it to Carly, giving her what she hoped came off as a teasing grin. It felt like a grimace. "I told you that shirt wouldn't be warm enough."

"You were right." Carly tugged Ray's sweatshirt over her head, then jammed her hands into the front pocket. "Thank you. Should we head back?"

This shyness was new and unexpected, and Ray hoped she hadn't caused it. She hadn't meant to embarrass Carly, only to move past her own moment of weakness. Even though Ray had offered something as simple as a sweatshirt, she felt good taking care of Carly. Especially when Carly was always caring for her.

"Sure," Ray said. Maybe all Carly needed was some time alone to sort out her thoughts. "Let's go home."

CHAPTER THIRTEEN

Carly glanced at the display on her buzzing cell phone. Ray McKenna. A powerful wave of relief loosened the knot that had constricted her stomach for almost a week now. Since Ray's panic attack on the beach, they had been playing phone tag. Jack hadn't even been to Ray's house for the past few days. Was Ray intentionally returning her calls when she knew Carly would be at work?

This morning Carly had decided to carry her cell phone in the pocket of her scrub pants, and luckily Ray's call came between appointments. "I'll be in my office," Carly told Matt as she hurried down the back hallway. She opened the phone quickly, not wanting yet another voice mail that gave her no clue about how Ray was feeling.

"Hello." Carly cringed at the way her voice came out so breathlessly.

"Hey." Ray sounded quiet. Maybe embarrassed. "Caught you finally."

"Yeah, I just finished an appointment. Rhodesian ridgeback, broken leg. Beautiful dog, and so sweet." Carly was babbling, but she tended to do that when things were awkward. What happened on the beach had been emotionally intense, and her feelings for Ray had been close to the surface. How much had Ray seen, and did she understand exactly what it meant?

"I'm sorry. I know you're working. I planned to leave a voice mail."

"It's no problem." Carly closed her office door and sat on the couch next to Jack, who was just waking up. "This is better than another voice mail."

"Yeah, it is." Sounding hesitant, Ray said, "I miss you."

Carly's heart leapt. She had nearly convinced herself that Ray realized exactly how Carly felt about her, and that's why she was so distant. That Ray was avoiding her because she couldn't deal with Carly's feelings, no matter how hard Carly tried to keep a lid on them. Thank God she hadn't sabotaged their friendship with that hug or the arousal their physical closeness had triggered. "I miss you, too."

"Do you want to have dinner tonight? I know it's last minute, but—" Ray cleared her throat. "I could make burgers or something."

Ray would call today, of all days. Deflated, Carly said, "I'd love to, but I actually have plans tonight."

"Oh." Ray didn't hide her surprise very well. "With Leeann?"

Carly couldn't quite put her finger on something in Ray's tone. Could it be jealousy? "Not Leeann. A friend of hers, though. Leeann arranged it."

"Oh."

"Like a blind date, I guess," Carly said in a rush. Why was it so difficult to explain herself? More importantly, why did she feel the need to? "Leeann pestered me to let her set us up, and I finally gave in." She laughed, aware that the sound lacked humor. "Leeann usually gets what she wants."

"That must be nice for Leeann." Ray's voice sounded softer, as though she weren't holding the phone close enough to her mouth. "Well, I thought I'd check, anyway. You have a good time."

Carly would love to cancel her date and see Ray instead. And that was exactly the problem. She needed to start looking at her romantic life as something separate from Ray, and just as important. "We could do something tomorrow night," Carly said. "If you're free."

"I'll call you." It was clear Ray wanted to hang up. "See you later."

Carly knew she was being blown off. She inhaled, stunned by how much the words felt like a slap in the face. "Okay." When Ray didn't say anything else, Carly checked her cell phone display to find that the call had ended. Tears stung her eyes as she flipped her phone closed. Then she kicked off her shoes and curled up on the couch.

Jack crawled toward her from his spot at the other end, stretching so he rested against her body. He had an uncanny ability to offer comfort when she was upset. Wrapping an arm around his strong back, she buried her face in his neck and sighed.

What was going on? Carly apparently hadn't given herself away on the beach, hug and hard nipples notwithstanding. But something had changed between them, and Carly was afraid it had everything to do with the blind date. Things were going okay until she had mentioned her plans. Then Ray just shut down.

"What does she want from me?" Carly mumbled into Jack's fur. She couldn't win. Either she was hopelessly in love with someone who would never love her back, or else she was freaking Ray out by having a love life.

"I don't know what to do." Carly searched Jack's eyes, finding no answers but drawing comfort from the love that shone from within. "Is she really upset that I have a date?" Ray had been uncomfortable with her sexuality, but Carly thought they were over that. "I guess she's never seen it in real life, though," she said quietly. Maybe the thought of her going on a date with a woman was too much for Ray to handle.

Carly pulled away from Jack and stared out at the bright afternoon sunshine. She was exhausted. Blinking back tears, she squeezed the back of her neck hard, trying to pull herself together. Things had been so much easier when Nadia was alive. These were the moments when she missed her the most. When she needed someone to hold her and tell her everything would be all right.

Jack perked up, then jumped off the couch so he could run to the door. The knock came a moment later. "Dr. Warner? Do you have a moment?" Jack's tail wagged fiercely at the sound of Dr. Patterson's voice.

Carly swiped at her eyes, then slipped her shoes on. "Yes, come in."

Dr. Patterson opened the door, offering Jack a greeting just as enthusiastic as the one he received. He grinned at Carly as he scratched Jack's neck with two hands. "I know you're en route to an appointment, but I was hoping you could offer me a consult."

Carly was flattered. Patterson had thirty-three years of experience on her, but from the moment he'd hired her he always made it obvious that he valued her opinion. He was clearly grooming her to take over the practice when he retired. From the growing pile of travel guides she'd spotted in his office, she guessed that would be soon.

"I'd love to, Dr. Patterson." Carly thanked him silently for his timing. Since Nadia had been killed, work was the one thing that could take her mind off everything she couldn't control. Right now escape was exactly what she needed.

❖

Ray shook as she hung up the phone. Carly was going on a date. Tonight. With a woman. She didn't know what upset her more: the idea of Carly going out with a stranger or the fact that it bothered her.

She touched Jagger's back to help ground herself before her emotions spiraled out of control. Grief welled in her chest, so painful that she gasped. It was more than grief. Ray didn't even know how to name it, but she needed to lie down before she fell down.

Using Jagger for support, she began the long walk to her bedroom. So Carly was going on a date. What the fuck was her problem with that? She couldn't expect Carly to live like a nun just so she would have a dinner guest whenever she wanted one. Especially when she had been the one avoiding Carly's phone calls recently.

Breaking down in front of Carly had been embarrassing. And she was terrified to explore the thoughts that had triggered her. So Ray decided that she needed distance to clear her head. Even if it meant not seeing Carly for a few days. Some plan. This had been her worst week in a long time.

And now this. A few days apart and Carly found a girlfriend.

She was immediately shamed. That was fucking selfish. Carly had a life, after all. Like she was going to spend all her time with Ray, who could hardly offer her what her date would.

Ray banged open her bedroom door and walked to her bed, dropping onto the mattress face-first. Jagger jumped up next to her and lay at her side. Angry with herself, Ray rolled to face him.

"I'm sure she wants to get laid occasionally, like a *normal* person." Ray's heart constricted at her harsh words. When she had been normal, she'd enjoyed fucking. How could she begrudge Carly the same pleasures? Was she jealous Carly could do something she wasn't sure she was capable of anymore?

Ray dug deep. It wasn't because Carly would be fucking a woman, was it? But this wasn't about Carly's sexuality. Not even close. In a moment of clarity that sucker-punched her in the gut, Ray understood something that had been niggling at her for weeks now. It wasn't that Carly was seeing a woman. Ray wanted to *be* that woman.

She closed her eyes and let the realization sink in. Her heart thudded, and her breathing caught. Jagger whined loudly, then shoved his heavy head beneath her arm, lifting it from the bed. Ray snapped out of the panic attack she had barely even recognized, then hugged Jagger.

"Thank you," she whispered. Ray started her breathing exercises without letting go of Jagger, drawing from his calm strength. *I need to deal with the present. Stay in the present, no negative predictions.* Ray exhaled slowly, then examined what she was feeling in that moment.

She loved Carly Warner. That much she had known for a while. It made sense, in a way. Carly was her best friend. Ray didn't want to imagine life without her. She was happiest when they were together.

But was she *in love* with Carly Warner? Ray thought about that day on the beach with Carly and the panic attack. Though she had been trying hard not to dwell on it, she knew what had triggered her—thoughts of kissing Carly and the strange pull of arousal that the fantasy had conjured.

Ray let her mind play with that thought again, determined not to get upset. She remembered what it felt like to kiss Danny, then tried to imagine doing the same thing with Carly. Once upon a time Ray had absolutely loved kissing. The lips and tongue, the give and take. Carly's mouth would be softer than Danny's. So would her body. What would it be like to touch Carly's breasts?

Her heart was racing again, but this time fear wasn't the culprit. Ray's face burned. She was aroused, plain and simple. Carly's body had felt supple and inviting pressed against her own during their hug on the beach. What if Ray hadn't pulled away? What if instead she had brought her lips to Carly's? Would Carly have kissed her back?

The inevitable answer shattered Ray's fantasy. Why would Carly want to kiss her? Ray could barely go grocery shopping, let alone be a satisfactory sexual partner. Even if she could manage a relationship, she hardly knew how to please a woman. Her only lover had been her high-school boyfriend. "And let's face it," Ray said aloud, stomach churning, "Carly deserves the best."

No doubt Leeann's friend was a great kisser. Amazing in the

bedroom. Attractive, smart, funny, and above all, *normal*. As though Ray, with her gimp leg and psychological condition, could compete. Emotion rose in her throat again, and this time Ray let the sadness carry her away.

Leave it to her to fall in love with someone who could never love her back.

CHAPTER FOURTEEN

Carly pressed on the gas pedal, nudging her car's speed up another five miles per hour. She tightened her grip on the steering wheel, wary of taking the tight curves of Highway 1 so quickly. But she would risk it, if she could get to Ray's house any faster.

Three days. That's how long it had been since they spoke. Carly had called multiple times, left voice mails ranging from casual to concerned, and even broke down and sent two e-mails. And she received no response. Not even a one-word reply to let her know that Ray was all right.

Though they'd barely spoken since that day on the beach, at least before her date Ray returned her phone calls. They might have been trading voice mails, but at least she knew Ray was alive. Now it was as though Ray had simply vanished. She could understand one day of no contact. By the second day, she was mildly concerned. After three days, Carly had a hard time convincing herself that something wasn't very wrong.

Their last phone call hadn't gone well. Ray hadn't done a good job of hiding her reaction to the news of Carly's date, though Carly wasn't entirely certain what that reaction meant. Clearly Ray hadn't liked the idea, whether she didn't want to hear about Carly being with a woman or because she was jealous of someone else taking her attention. Either way, Carly didn't like it.

Jack sat in the passenger seat, and as always, she was grateful he was there to play the role of therapist. "I don't know what she wants me to do," Carly told him. "I have to start dating again at some point." It didn't help that she would have rather spent that evening with Ray.

Jessica from IT was nice, but she wasn't Ray McKenna. On the other hand, at least Jessica had the potential to return her feelings, if Carly ever developed any. Loving Ray was not only pointless, it was painful. And it had to end, no matter how impossible that seemed.

Of course, Ray's silence might have nothing to do with Carly's dating life. Maybe something had happened to her. Who would Ray have listed as an emergency contact if she had been in an accident? Or what if—God forbid—Ray had harmed herself? Things had been a little rough lately, but Ray had been improving tremendously. An icy shard of dread pierced her throat, making it hard to breathe.

Please don't let her have given up.

Carly floored the accelerator as hard as she dared, now less than a mile from Ray's house. If something had happened and she got there too late, she would never forgive herself.

When Carly pulled up to Ray's house and spotted her truck in the driveway, she felt relief. There hadn't been a car accident, at least. Carly exhaled, not realizing until that moment how intense that fear had been. After Nadia, unanswered phone calls seemed to hint at tragic consequences.

She parked quickly and called Jack out of the car behind her, anxious to knock on the door. Jack sprinted ahead to the porch, looking like she felt. Desperate to get inside, to see his friends.

Carly stepped onto the front porch, noting a slight movement through the front window. A shadow, probably in the den, too tall to be Jagger. Relief surged through Carly's veins, followed by a dose of anger.

So Ray was alive. Why was she avoiding Carly's calls?

Carly banged on the front door. "Ray?"

The shadow went still.

When Ray made no move to approach the door, Carly knocked again. "Ray, I know you're in there. Please open up." Carly's anger dissipated in a flash and sad confusion took its place, filling her eyes with tears. "I don't know what I did to deserve this, but please let's talk about it."

After a moment, the shadow disappeared from her line of sight. Carly tilted her head, listening for footsteps. She heard the jingling of Jagger's tags first, then the clomping of his enormous paws.

Straightening up, Carly wiped her eyes, not wanting Ray to see her cry. She was pathetic enough, being in love with a straight woman. She needed to be strong. If Ray didn't want to be her friend anymore, she couldn't do anything about it.

Ray opened the door and fixed her with an emotionless gaze. Jack went crazy with excitement, circling Ray and sniffing her hand, then he moved to greet Jagger in the same fashion. Ray patted his side but said nothing. She wore track pants and a sleeveless army green T-shirt. Her toned arms were slick with sweat, and she was breathing hard. Carly guessed she had been working out, and her anger flared up again.

Three days of silence, and Ray answered the door perfectly healthy and so sexy that Carly ached. Worse, she was staring at Carly like she barely recognized her.

"Hey." Carly controlled her tone, wanting to give Ray the benefit of the doubt. "You're alive."

Ray smiled tightly. "I am. Sorry I haven't had a chance to call you back."

Carly put her hands on her hips and bit her lip to quell the frustration that raged inside her. "I was worried about you."

Sorrow flickered across Ray's face, quickly replaced by a stoic mask. "I'm okay. I just needed some time alone."

"Oh." Carly looked down at her feet, unsure how much she should press the issue. Ray was dealing with a lot, after all. Maybe this was normal for her. Maybe Carly needed not to expect the same things from Ray that she would expect from other friends. After all, Ray wasn't like anyone else she knew. "I was concerned I did something to upset you." Searching Ray's eyes for confirmation, she said, "It seemed like everything was okay until I told you about my date."

Ray stiffened. "Sometimes I just need time alone. To think."

But this wasn't just about alone time. Carly could hear it in Ray's voice. "You couldn't just tell me you needed some space? You've been avoiding me. I was worried about you." Ray betrayed no reaction to her words, and Carly's heart sank. "I thought we were closer than this."

"We are close." Ray's voice wavered, and she finally broke eye contact. "You know that."

"I don't feel very close to you right now." Carly yearned to reach out and touch Ray's arm but wasn't sure that would be a good idea.

She craved some confirmation that she hadn't imagined how close she thought they had become. "I feel like I did something wrong and you won't tell me what it is."

Ray's jaw tightened. "You didn't do anything wrong."

"Is this about me being a lesbian?" Carly's heart rate picked up. That was the question she needed to ask, but she feared the answer. She didn't know how they would move forward if Ray couldn't accept her sexuality. "I know you said you were cool with it, but that was before I actually went on a date."

"I'm fine with you being a lesbian." Ray gave her a pained smile. "Really."

"Then what is it?" Carly knew she was coming dangerously close to pleading for an answer, but she didn't care. She hurt when Ray wasn't in her life. Though the implications of that fact were far too terrifying to explore, it was true. If Ray was prepared to end their friendship, she at least wanted to know why. "Just tell me, Ray. If you care about me at all, tell me what's going on."

Ray lowered her hand so it rested on Jagger's back, a sign that Ray was stressed, and so Carly exhaled, trying to calm herself. Propelling Ray into a panic attack wouldn't help anything.

"I'm sorry," Carly said softly. "I'm sorry if I'm pushing you too hard. And I'm sorry if I upset or disappointed you. That was never my intention." She met Ray's eyes. "If me dating does make you uncomfortable, I'm sorry about that too. But I can't postpone my love life indefinitely."

Ray flinched as though she had been struck. "I know that." She braced herself against the door frame and stared into Carly's eyes, obviously struggling with what to say next. "I was jealous."

Carly felt the confession in the pit of her stomach, though she wasn't entirely certain how she should interpret it. "Why?"

"Because—" Ray's voice broke and she closed her mouth.

Carly held her breath as she waited for more. "You can talk to me, Ray. Please talk to me."

"I was jealous because—" Visibly shaking, Ray curled a hand around the back of Carly's neck. Before Carly could process what was happening, Ray gave her the sweetest kiss she had ever received.

Carly didn't react. She felt frozen in place, terrified of somehow misinterpreting this gesture. Ray's lips were soft and tasted faintly of salt, and she panted heavily, nervous or excited or possibly both. Carly's legs trembled, and she put a hand on Ray's bare arm to steady herself. When Ray didn't retreat, but instead curled her other arm around Carly's waist, enfolding her, a dam broke inside Carly.

She traced Ray's lower lip with her tongue, unable to believe this was really happening. Ray parted her lips and found the tip of Carly's tongue with her own. Carly moaned against her will, no longer in control of her body.

Ray tightened her hand on the back of Carly's neck and pulled her inside the doorway, pressing her against the foyer wall. She kept Carly close, smashing their breasts together as she deepened the kiss. She traced the side of Carly's face with her free hand, as though trying to memorize its shape.

Carly had never imagined this side of Ray, which was breathtaking. Ray was probably acting on pure instinct. She cradled Ray's face in her hands, afraid that the kiss would be over too soon and Ray would regain her senses. What if Ray realized that she didn't enjoy kissing women?

Ray broke away with a gasp and stepped back, leaving Carly cold where their bodies had touched. "I'm so sorry," Ray said, red-faced. "I didn't mean to…I'm sorry."

Carly managed a weak laugh. Light-headed, she sagged against the wall where Ray had placed her. "That's not what I like to hear after a kiss like that."

"Maybe I'm not *sorry*, exactly. Just a little confused."

"So am I." Taking a chance, Carly put her hand on Ray's arm again. She tried not to shiver when solid muscle flexed beneath her fingers. "But I'm not unhappy."

Ray swayed on her feet. "Do you want to come in and sit down?"

"I think I'd better."

❖

Ray led Carly to the den, hardly able to believe that her legs functioned. Never in her life had she felt something so intense as that kiss. It made her kisses with Danny, as sweet as they were, seem like two kids playacting at being in love. This was the real thing, and it was with a woman.

Ray collapsed on one end of the couch, wishing she'd had time to shower. Carly had caught her lifting weights, her standard escape when she was stressed out. Three days of trying to stay away from Carly had been beyond stressful, and even the weights didn't help. Only seeing Carly, then feeling her, eased the pain of separation.

Carly sat on the middle cushion, close without touching. She played with her fingernails as though she didn't know what to do with her hands. She looked vulnerable and very young. "So what does this mean?"

Ray had never seen her like this and felt protective, even though she was the source of Carly's uncertainty. "I don't know what it means. I'm sorry for dropping this on you all at once."

"No apologies." Carly raised a trembling hand. "Not for that kiss."

Ray searched for some way to explain how she had gained the courage to make such a move, but she barely understood it. "I can't believe I did that."

"Do you wish you hadn't?"

Ray could hear the worry in her voice. "No. I'm just surprised."

Carly chuckled. "Understatement."

"I'm sorry for not returning your calls." Cutting off contact had been nearly impossible, but at the time Ray thought she needed to do it. "I needed time to think. And I was scared to see you again."

"Why?"

"I was upset when you told me Leeann set you up on a date. Jealous. At first I believed I didn't like sharing your time and attention, but it was more than that. I didn't like the idea of someone else kissing you." Ray's cheeks burned. She never thought she would be having such an intimate conversation with someone again. "When I realized I wanted to be the one kissing you, I didn't know what to do."

"A couple months ago you nearly walked out of my house when I told you I was a lesbian. This is a big change." Carly kept her voice gentle, but Ray could tell this was a real concern. To go from borderline homophobia to kissing another woman so quickly was quite a leap.

"I know. That was a knee-jerk reaction and I felt like a complete asshole. I didn't understand your intentions."

"Still, this must really surprise you." Carly looked away shyly. "Being attracted to a woman."

"Yes." Ray wanted to be as honest as possible. "And I wouldn't admit that I was until you told me about your date. Then I couldn't think about anything else."

Carly ran a hand through her hair, and Ray's throat went dry as she remembered how those strawberry-blond locks felt wrapped around her fingers. She stared at Carly's throat and imagined pressing her lips there, finding Carly's pulse with her tongue. Blinking, Ray looked away with effort. After almost two years with no sex drive, she didn't know what to make of the feelings Carly had unleashed.

"I've been attracted to you since we met." Carly's voice was so quiet Ray had to lean forward to hear. "But I never wanted you to know. I thought it would scare you away. That you could never feel the same way."

Ray inhaled. Though Carly had made it clear that she enjoyed their kiss, it meant everything to hear that she had been struggling with the same doubts. "I didn't know. It didn't occur to me that I had anything to offer you."

Carly shifted closer and traced her finger over the length of Ray's bare arm, leaving goose bumps in her wake. "It's time to stop saying that. Okay?"

Ray nodded. "But you need to understand something. I really don't know what I can offer you, or when. Till recently I would have told you I'm not ready for a relationship."

"And now?" The question was full of hope, tinged with what sounded like fear. "I know you're dealing with a lot. Do you think you're ready?"

Ray wasn't about to say no. Not when it felt better to be with Carly than not. "I want to try. If you can be patient with me."

Carly smiled. "I'm pretty patient."

"I know. You've put up with me this long." Ray hesitated, then took Carly's hand and held it between hers. As much as she hated talking about her past, there were things she needed to say. "A lot of stuff happened to me in Iraq. Stuff that changed me. Some of it you know already, and some of it I'm not sure I'll ever want to talk about. I came back a different person."

"I've only known this Ray," Carly said. "And I like her a lot."

"I'm so glad." Ray squeezed Carly's hand. "But I'm still figuring out what this new me is capable of."

"I understand."

As embarrassing as it was, Ray needed to lay everything on the table. If she couldn't be honest about what Carly would be getting into with her, they were doomed. She cleared her throat. "Since Iraq, my libido has been…nonexistent. It's like my body just shut down when I was over there."

"I have to imagine that's common with something like PTSD." Carly's eyes shone with unspoken questions, and Ray felt a tendril of fear that Carly would ask her to rehash things she had no interest in reliving. "Were you and Danny sexually active?"

"Yes. Very." Ray blushed as she remembered Michigan summer nights in the bed of Danny's pickup truck, lying naked beneath the stars. "I used to like sex, actually. A lot."

Nostrils flaring, Carly looked away. "Well, that sounds promising."

Ray recognized desire in Carly's voice, and a surge of pleasure skittered down her spine. "I'd be lying if I said I haven't experienced a bit of an awakening lately. And thank you for that, by the way."

"You're quite welcome."

"I just don't know when I'll be ready…for that part. Or what it will be like for me."

"We just had our first kiss, Ray. I won't push you to take things any further before you're ready." Carly met her gaze, clearly searching. "I just want you to be sure you feel comfortable being with a woman. Eventually."

Ray understood Carly's worry, because she had wondered the same thing. Loving someone and wanting to make love with them were different. Luckily three days had been plenty of time for Ray to examine her life. "I've realized that I've been attracted to women in the past. A couple times in particular. I told myself I admired those women or wanted to be their friend, but I see now that sexual attraction was there, too."

"Had you ever questioned your sexuality before?"

"No. But I never thought it was an option." Ray had known she would join the military from the time she was old enough to start hearing stories about her father's service in Vietnam. She would never have done anything to jeopardize that goal. "Besides, I had Danny. I loved him very much."

"I'm sorry things didn't work out between you." Carly put her hand on Ray's knee. "To lose your childhood sweetheart on top of everything else must have been devastating."

Ray shook her head. Losing Danny had been hard, but she had made that choice. "Our time had passed. He'll always be important to me, but the Danny and Ray who came back from Iraq weren't meant to be together."

"It's hard to lose your first true love." Carly sounded wistful, and Ray knew she was thinking about Nadia. "I don't think it's something you ever really get over."

Ray couldn't imagine what it would be like to lose a partner whom you loved deeply, and with her your unborn child. "I should be asking you how you feel about all this," she said, gesturing between them. "I know you've barely started dating again."

"I would never want to risk losing our friendship, but now that I know how you feel, I can't imagine not giving this a chance." Carly shifted closer, watching Ray's eyes. "I haven't felt anything even close to this since Nadia died. I never thought I would again."

Ray took Carly's willingness to entrust her with a still-healing heart very seriously. She wanted nothing more than to extend that same trust to Carly, to believe that she would take things as slowly as Ray needed. But it would entail more than trust for this to work. After everything she had seen and done, she wasn't sure she was worthy of Carly. Was there anything in her for Carly to love?

As though reading her thoughts, Carly said, "You're worth the risk, Ray."

"Even with all my issues?" Ray tried to hide her anxiety with a smile. "I'm trying to get better, but I'm not there yet."

"Who is?" Carly squeezed Ray's knee. "I'm not perfect either."

The warmth of Carly's hand through her track pants distracted Ray. She had so much more to say, but suddenly none of it seemed important. Her attention moved to Carly's lips, and she shivered at the memory of Carly's tongue in her mouth. "I think you're beautiful."

Carly's gaze drifted downward. "So are you."

"May I kiss you again?"

Shifting until she sat almost in Ray's lap, Carly planted a gentle kiss on the corner of her mouth. Ray closed her eyes, overwhelmed. She snaked her hands through Carly's hair but didn't try to deepen the kiss. Staying perfectly still, she let Carly trail a string of feather-soft kisses over her bottom lip, then the top. As much as she wanted to taste Carly again, Ray hated for the exquisite teasing to end. She waited it out, growing more and more aroused as Carly got closer to kissing her full on the lips.

"You're killing me." Ray groaned. "Don't stop."

"Never." Carly's breath was hot against Ray's mouth. She dragged the tip of her tongue over Ray's lower lip, then finally pressed inside.

Ray dropped her hands to hold Carly's hips, tugging her even closer. Carly gripped her arms, then slid her hands inside the cuffs of Ray's sleeveless shirt, touching her bare back. As much as Ray wanted to take things slow, it felt so good to touch Carly. That she could be this close to anyone was a miracle.

Used to a hard chest and muscled arms, Ray found Carly's curves entirely foreign. Her hands moved almost unconsciously in exploration, to the small of Carly's back, then inside her shirt, around to trace the soft skin of her belly. As Ray caressed every new inch of skin, her breathing grew more ragged. Carly panted into her mouth, biting gently on her lip when Ray grazed the underside of one breast.

Feeling the firm flesh, Ray drew back, shocked by her own boldness. She gasped when they broke apart, desperate for air. She hadn't meant to take things so far. Carly felt so incredible, Ray found it easy to get carried away.

"No apologies." Carly sounded like she was having trouble catching her own breath. "Please."

"None offered." Ray took a moment to recover, then said, "By the way?"

"Yeah?"

"I am definitely comfortable being with a woman."

Carly's laughter was tinged with arousal, and throatier than Ray had ever heard it. "You're also an amazing kisser."

Ray's chest filled with pride. "So are you."

"Thank you." Carly looked as though she were weighing what she was about to say. "Could I take you out on a date sometime?"

Swallowing, Ray said, "A date?" That sounded like it might require interaction with other people. Still, if it made Carly happy, Ray would try. "Like what?"

"How about dinner?" Carly watched Ray's face, and Ray knew she was trying to read an honest reaction. Carly never pushed her too far past her comfort zone. "I know this tiny little restaurant. Very intimate. Private."

"That sounds good." Ray put on her bravest face, determined to go along to the best of her ability. Carly deserved a normal, functional girlfriend, and even though Ray didn't fit the bill, she'd try her hardest to pretend. "When do you want to go?"

"How about tomorrow night?"

Ray's stomach turned over. Twenty-four hours wasn't a lot of time to mentally prepare, but at least she wouldn't have to deal with nerves for too long. "I'd love to go on a date with you."

Carly's look of pleasure made all the stress about going to a restaurant worthwhile. "Thank you," she said. "I'll even order for you. You don't have to do any talking if you don't want."

"I appreciate that."

"I want you to be as comfortable as possible. And I get that going out is a big deal. It means everything that you would do it for me."

Ray knew it was good for her to push herself. Carly was the worthiest incentive possible. "This is me trying to get better."

Carly gathered her into another hug. Burying her face in Carly's neck, Ray inhaled deeply, greedy for her scent. For that moment, all her fears disappeared. Not since she returned to the United States had she felt so at home.

CHAPTER FIFTEEN

Carly's cell phone rang twenty minutes before she was due to pick up Ray for their first date. She considered ignoring the call, but when she saw Leeann's number she answered. Though she hated to stomp on Leeann's dreams of having performed the ultimate fix-up, they had to have this conversation eventually. They hadn't spoken since the blind date, and Leeann had to be dying of curiosity.

Leeann's greeting confirmed her suspicion. "How'd it go?"

"It was nice." Dinner had been delicious, conversation easy, and Jessica most likely would have agreed to a second date. In a world without Ray, Carly probably would have asked. "Jessica's a really nice girl."

"Uh-oh." Leeann sounded disappointed. "That bad?"

"No, not bad at all." Carly burned to tell Leeann about what had happened with Ray. She usually shared everything with Leeann, but she wasn't ready to share this. The whole thing was still too new, too fragile. Better to see how things went before she admitted to Leeann that she was flirting with a potentially dangerous situation. "We had a good time. Jessica's very funny."

"And cute, right?"

"Totally cute," Carly said. And she was. Jessica was perfectly cute and genuinely funny. She just wasn't Ray. "I don't think we'll see each other again, though."

Leeann sighed. "I had such high hopes."

"I know you did." Carly checked her hair in the mirror, then grabbed her sweater. Patting Jack on the head, she walked to the door.

"It's okay, Lee. I had a lot of fun. Hopefully she did, too. I just don't think there's any future for us."

"I wasn't expecting you to get married or anything."

"I know." Carly locked the door behind her and hurried to her car. The sun hung low in the sky, painting the clouds in shades of pink and red. A cool breeze blew in from the ocean, carrying the distant noise of sea birds. "I'll be all right."

"Of course you will." Leeann was clearly bummed out. "I was just hoping to find someone to help take your mind off other things."

Like Ray. "I appreciate that. But don't worry about me, okay? Seriously, I'm doing great."

"Okay." Leeann didn't sound convinced. "What are you up to tonight?"

Carly cringed. "I'm having dinner with Ray."

"Carly—"

"I know, I know." Carly started her car and transferred the call to her wireless headset. "I told you I'm okay. Trust me, please?"

Leeann sighed. "I trust you."

"No more one-sided feelings for straight women," Carly said. Technically it was the truth. Her feelings no longer seemed to be one-sided, and Ray was definitely not what she would consider 100 percent straight. "I promise."

"It's that easy?"

"I love you, Leeann. Thanks for looking out for me." Carly was done talking about this for now, so she said, "I need to let you go. Talk to you later?"

"Yeah. Bye."

Carly disconnected the call and shifted into reverse. She didn't want to defend her decisions to Leeann right now. Especially not when she was worrying about them herself. Though she couldn't imagine not taking a chance on Ray, she was scared of all the ways it could go wrong. Already she was losing her heart to Ray McKenna, and she had no idea if a real relationship would be possible. Not only because Ray had so much to overcome, but also because this was her own first try at caring for someone since Nadia's death.

Carly was torn between the bone-deep need to love and be loved, and the paralyzing fear of having her heart broken again just as it was starting to heal. Though Carly felt ready to give love another try, Ray

McKenna was most likely a terrible risk. She had never been with a woman. She struggled to perform many of life's everyday tasks, and she was prone to panic attacks. On top of it all, she was apparently coping with some degree of sexual dysfunction.

Despite all the negatives, Carly had to see this through. Ray might be a mess, but she was a beautiful, compassionate, funny mess with a lot of shared interests and a body that made Carly want to weep. All Carly could do was hang on tight and hope for the best. She couldn't turn back now.

"Please," Carly murmured. "Please let this work out."

❖

Ray glanced at the clock in the lower right corner of her computer screen. Carly would be arriving to pick her up in fifteen minutes. It wasn't much time for an impromptu therapy session, but it would have to do. So much had happened in the week since she'd last spoken to Dr. Evans that Ray needed to talk about. Preferably before the big date. Though she was already scheduled for tomorrow morning, Ray had broken down earlier that evening and left a message for Dr. Evans that she had an emergency. Within two hours, Dr. Evans returned her call and asked her to log in to the computer.

Seeing her therapist in the video chat window wearing what looked like pajamas, Ray felt ashamed to be intruding so late. But she needed a last-minute pep talk. "Thank you so much, Dr. Evans. I'm very sorry to have bothered you at home."

"It's fine, Ray. This is the first time you've ever called with an emergency. Is everything all right?"

"I think so. Yes. I kissed Carly," Ray blurted out. Feeling clumsy with her words, she added, "She kissed me back."

Dr. Evans's smile suggested that she was trying to hold back the full scope of her reaction. "Yes, I don't suppose this could wait for tomorrow."

"I would have called last night when it happened, but she didn't go home until late."

Dr. Evans's eyebrow popped. "Really?"

"We didn't sleep together," Ray said quickly. "We just talked for a while. And kissed some more." She cursed the heat in her face. She never used to feel so embarrassed talking about this stuff. One of the things she missed most about the old Ray was the ability to see sex as something fun and exciting. The new Ray couldn't seem to get over the almost unbearable intimacy and trust involved. "I told her I wasn't sure when I would be ready for more than that."

"This is a very big step," Dr. Evans said. "On a lot of levels. How do you feel about it?"

"We're going out to dinner tonight. So that's scary, but also kind of exciting. She makes me feel so safe. Like everything will be okay."

"And how do you feel about being with a woman? Not long ago you were defensive about being perceived as a lesbian."

"I know," Ray said. "When you and I talked about Carly the other day, I wasn't ready to accept my feelings. I know I got defensive, and I'm sorry."

"But now you can see yourself in a relationship with Carly?"

"As much as I can see myself in a relationship with anyone. I'm not sure what I can offer her, but I'm happy she's willing to take a chance on me. She's incredible."

"You've made tremendous progress since meeting Carly. This could be a great experience for you." Dr. Evans smiled. "Take things at a comfortable pace. Push yourself a little here and there to break out of old routines and habits, but leave yourself room to go as slow as you need."

Ray knew Dr. Evans was talking about being in a relationship as a whole, but she thought about sex again. "I really enjoyed kissing her. She's so soft. I never really thought about how beautiful women are. When she held me, it felt so good to be close to her. I liked it when she touched me."

"Physical intimacy can be an almost spiritual experience with the right person. It can also be very intense. A lot of feelings and emotions may come up as you're exploring that part of your relationship with Carly. Maintain good communication and be true to your limits, and you'll find that a loving touch can be quite healing."

Ray checked the clock again. "She's due any minute. I should sign out."

Dr. Evans nodded. "You have a good time, Ray. Be gentle with yourself. This is all new for you and it may take some adjusting."

"Thanks, Dr. Evans."

"I'll talk to you soon."

Ray closed their chat window and stood up. She grabbed Jagger's service vest and he walked to her side, waiting patiently as she slipped it on. Her cell phone sat on the desk beside her and she picked it up, surprised to see the icon that indicated she had a voice mail. For a moment she feared that Carly had called to cancel their date, having thought better of the whole thing.

"Stop it," Ray murmured to herself as she pushed the button to dial her voice mail. "No negative predictions."

It wasn't Carly. Ray stood and listened to the message, icy dread prickling her skin as she took in its meaning.

"Hello. My name is Karen Jackson, and I'm trying to reach Ray McKenna. I'm writing a book about female soldiers fighting in Iraq and Afghanistan. Obviously I think you've got an amazing story and no doubt have a very interesting perspective on the role of women in the military, their participation in combat, and the issue of acceptance by your male counterparts. I'd love to interview you for the book, if you're willing. I know you haven't done any interviews before and I totally get that, but I want to assure you that I am taking on this project with the utmost respect for your service. My only goal is to illuminate the challenges women face in war and the roles women play."

Heart pounding, Ray deleted the message without taking down the phone number Karen Jackson left. She would not return her call. This was the first time someone had contacted her for an interview since she moved to Bodega Bay. How the hell had this woman gotten her cell-phone number? Ray kept it as private as possible, for exactly this reason.

Now a new fear gnawed at her gut. No matter how nervous she still was about going out in public, Ray had started to believe that interest in her story was waning. The initial onslaught of media coverage and recognition on the streets had diminished, and the national attention span being what it was, it seemed as though she might be able to live out the rest of her life in obscurity. Logically Ray knew that one author contacting her was hardly a sign of widespread interest, but emotionally, she all of a sudden felt in the spotlight again.

Right when she was finally moving on with her life and inviting someone else into it. Ray pocketed her cell phone, sick to her stomach. When she heard a knock on her door, she exhaled shakily. The last thing she wanted right now was to leave her house.

Ray walked to the front door on legs that felt disconnected, as though she weren't in control of them anymore. Peering through the peephole, Ray relaxed when she saw Carly. As much as she didn't want to go out to dinner, she was glad to have Carly here. She didn't want to be alone with her fears.

"Hey." Carly's radiant smile faded when she saw Ray's face. "Is everything okay?"

Carly wore a cable-knit cardigan over a form-fitting top, and for a moment a warm wash of arousal distracted Ray from her worries. She was staring at Carly's breasts, but she couldn't help it. Now that she had noticed them, she couldn't look away. She remembered grazing the firm flesh with her hand the evening before and shivered.

Carly put a hand under her chin and lifted Ray's face so their eyes met. She was biting her lip, clearly holding back laughter.

"I'm sorry," Ray said. "You look amazing."

"Keep staring at me like that and we won't make it to dinner."

Ray wished like hell they could just stay in and make out. Even the prospect of taking their physical relationship farther made her less nervous than going to the restaurant. "Would that be such a bad thing?"

Carly closed the distance between them, kissing Ray softly. "Not bad at all. But I'd love to go out, if you're up for it."

Dizzy from the feeling of Carly's lips against hers, Ray was ready to agree to anything. "Sure."

"I called ahead and told them we would be bringing Jagger. They've got patio seating with outdoor heaters, so we figured that would work best."

This would be Jagger's first time at a restaurant. Relieved that Carly had thought to clear everything in advance, Ray said, "Thank you."

Carly stepped back and took Ray's hand. Looking her up and down, Carly murmured, "You look pretty amazing as well, by the way."

Ray blushed. She didn't own anything dressy, so her jeans and sweater were just shy of casual. But Carly was being sincere, and Ray recognized the desire in her eyes. "You're very easily impressed."

Carly squeezed her hand. "Enough."

Ray knew she needed to work on her confidence. Self-deprecation wasn't attractive. "No, you're right," she said. "I'm pretty damn hot, if I do say so myself."

"That's more like it. You guys ready?"

Ray grabbed Jagger's leash off the peg just inside the door and steeled her nerve. Ready or not, she was committed to doing this. For Carly. "Let's go."

Chapter Sixteen

Carly was right: the restaurant was small and intimate, and their table was private enough that Ray was able to sit in the corner of the patio, out of sight of all but one other couple. That couple was a young man and a slightly older woman whose hands stayed clasped together even when the waiter took their order. Their gaze never strayed from each other, so the last thing they cared about was some ex-soldier and her service dog. It was a perfect, thoughtful setting for her first dinner out since coming home.

Why was she still so nervous? Ray eyed the waiter who brought drinks to the table next to them, keeping her guard up. He hadn't done anything to make her feel unsafe, but that hardly mattered. She was deep in a state of hypervigilance, so logic didn't penetrate her pervasive sense of foreboding.

"Ray?"

Blinking, Ray returned her attention to Carly. She had been talking, hadn't she? Ray searched her memory for some thread of what Carly had been saying, but came up blank. Shamed, she mustered a contrite smile.

"I'm sorry."

"Are you sure you're okay?"

Ray inhaled. *I am the master of my fate.* She could tell Carly what she was going through, but she didn't want to fall apart on their first date. Ray wanted so badly for things between them to work, and revealing the full extent of her anxiety might scare Carly away. She grinned with effort.

"It's just been a while since I've been in a situation like this." Ray picked up her glass of water and took a sip, then set it back down a little louder than she intended. This caught the attention of the man at the next table, who tore his eyes away from his date for an instant to look their direction. "This is a nice place."

"Good food, too." Carly gestured at the menu in front of Ray. "Do you know what you want yet?"

"What are you having?" In truth, Ray hadn't been able to focus on the menu. She barely remembered any of the choices. Glancing at the neighboring table again, she was relieved to see that the man had lost interest in her clumsy maneuvering.

"I was thinking about having the mac and cheese."

"Make that two." Ray forced herself to keep her eyes on Carly. If she could just focus on the reason she was pushing herself to be here, everything would be okay. "I told my therapist about us. She seemed really happy. She thinks you've been good for me so far."

"I hope I'm always good for you." Carly reached under the table and touched Ray's hand. "I promise to try my hardest to make you happy."

The waiter approached their table and Ray jerked her hand away from Carly's. Surprise registered on Carly's face and Ray shot her a contrite look, kicking herself for her reaction. It wasn't like anyone could see what they were doing under there.

"Good evening, ladies. Are you ready to order?"

Carly gave him a smile that immediately had him grinning back, intent on her. Ray watched as she ordered, envying the ease with which she conversed with the waiter. By the time he left the table they were both laughing. Carly returned her attention to Ray, any offense she might have felt at Ray's earlier retreat apparently forgotten.

"I'm flattered you told your therapist about me. I know this is all such new territory for you," Carly said. "So how was it? Coming out, or however you're thinking of it."

"It was good." Ray checked her watch. "It happened about an hour ago, actually."

"Right before our date?"

"I needed to tell someone."

"I get that." Carly folded her hands on the table. "Leeann called me as I was leaving to pick you up. She wanted to know how the date with Jessica went."

"Oh." At the mention of Leeann's name, Ray's throat went dry. Though she had just confessed needing to tell Dr. Evans about their new relationship, she wasn't thrilled with the idea of Leeann finding out. That wasn't exactly fair to Carly, but it had nothing to do with being fair. After learning that someone had discovered her cell number, she considered everything a violation of her privacy. "What did you say?"

"I told her that Jessica was a really sweet girl, but I didn't think we had a future."

"Did you tell her why?"

Carly watched her eyes. "No. I wasn't ready to tell her about us yet."

Ray relaxed. "Oh."

"You seem relieved."

"A little." Ray smiled, hoping to take any sting out of her words. "You know I'm a very private person."

"I know. But I do hope you'll understand that I'll want to tell her eventually. She's my closest friend, besides you."

"Of course. But if you wouldn't mind, I'd appreciate it if we kept this between us for a bit. Until we get more comfortable with it ourselves."

"I understand." Carly touched Ray's foot with her own, then retreated. "This is new for you. I get it."

"Thank you." From the corner of her eye, Ray saw the man at the next table lean across their bread basket to give the woman a kiss.

Carly followed Ray's line of sight. "They look like they're very much in love."

"Yeah." Ray dragged her attention back to Carly, embarrassed to have been caught looking. "Definitely seems that way."

"I think it's sweet. Then again, I'm feeling much more charitable toward romance these days." Carly smiled over the rim of her water glass. "Now that I've found some of my own."

Ray couldn't help but return her smile, charmed by the way Carly could shrink the world down to only the two of them with just a few words. She stared at Carly's mouth, lost in the memory of her other talents. Gazing at Carly's throat, she then drifted to the top of her breasts. What she wouldn't give to have Carly back on her couch right now.

Their waiter appeared at the table, breaking Ray out of her reverie. Face red, she looked at the floor as he set a dinner salad in front of her. She echoed Carly's thanks, then watched him walk back toward the kitchen with relief. Catching a glimpse of the couple at the next table, she wasn't surprised to find them caressing each other's arms on the tabletop.

Were she and Carly that obvious? They weren't making out in front of the entire restaurant like those two, but she was staring at Carly with just as much desire as that man had for his date. Did their waiter know she and Carly were a couple? And more importantly, did he have any idea who she was?

Ray turned Karen Jackson's message over in her head. Yet another interview request. For a while it had seemed like everyone wanted an interview, to the point where she stopped answering the phone completely. The fascination with her story had been intense, personal, and a violation that she had no choice but to suffer again and again. She could only imagine the interest a same-sex relationship would ignite.

War hero and her lesbian lover. Ray could see the story now. She picked up her salad fork, trying to choke down the bile that rose in her throat. No way could she go through that now. Looking across the table at Carly, she offered a weak grin. Carly smiled back, concern shining in her eyes. She would never put Carly through that kind of scrutiny, either. Ray endured it only because she had no choice. Carly would have choices, and Ray was terrified of where that would inevitably leave them.

"You're sure everything's okay?" Carly said quietly. "We can leave if this is too much."

Ray shook her head, determined to make it through dinner. After tonight she would be more careful about what she agreed to do, but she had promised Carly at least one real date. If Ray could give her nothing else, she would give her this.

"I'm okay," Ray said. "Let's eat."

CHAPTER SEVENTEEN

As much as Carly enjoyed taking Ray out to dinner on their first date, the second was a lot more fun. They kept it simple with pizza and a movie at home, which meant Ray got to relax. And relax she did. They held hands during the entire film, and twice Ray stole kisses that ended up turning into full-blown makeout sessions. By the time the credits rolled, Carly doubted that she had retained more than twenty minutes of the plot. Not that it mattered. It wasn't about the movie; it was about being close to Ray.

Ray picked up the remote and clicked the television off. "That was good."

"Was it?" Carly traced her fingertip over Ray's jaw, then touched her lower lip. "I was a little too distracted to pay attention."

Kissing her finger, Ray murmured, "Me, too. I wasn't talking about the movie."

Their eyes met and they shifted closer to one another as though drawn by an invisible force. Carly had been waiting almost the entire evening for this moment, when they could touch each another freely without feeling they should be engaged in a more respectable activity.

Carly waited for Ray to make the first move. Though she wanted to press Ray down onto the couch and kiss the hell out of her, she would play it safe and let Ray get them started. So far Carly had been cautious bordering on old-fashioned, not wanting to do anything to scare Ray from their burgeoning sexual relationship. While she was definitely willing to wait as long as Ray needed and would never push for more than she was ready to give, Carly yearned to take that final step and become lovers.

Ray wrapped her arms around Carly and tugged her into a close embrace. "You're driving me crazy, you know."

"Am I?" Carly kissed the side of Ray's neck, thrilling in the shiver she elicited. "I like the sound of that."

"I'm pretty fond of being driven crazy, myself." Ray put her mouth on Carly's throat, sucking gently. She moaned, then whispered, "God, Carly, I can't believe how badly I want you."

Carly closed her eyes when Ray's hands found the hem of her T-shirt and slipped inside. No matter how strongly she believed in taking things as slow as Ray needed, this was torture, plain and simple. Still, the last thing she wanted to do was discourage Ray from exploring the physical side of their relationship. Not when it might shatter her fledgling confidence. So Carly endured the sweetest agony she had ever experienced with a smile on her face.

Ray kissed her deeply, and once again Carly marveled at the skill with which Ray's mouth seduced her. Her kisses were tender yet passionate, curling Carly's toes and unleashing a flood of wetness between her legs. Ray's hands were just as skilled, caressing her stomach and back in a way that made Carly grateful she was already sitting down.

When Ray's fingers drifted close to the underside of Carly's breasts, just barely brushing the cups of her bra, Carly held her breath in anticipation. Then Ray retreated, tearing loose a groan from Carly's throat. Every time they made out Ray flirted with the idea of touching Carly's breasts, and every time she backed off. Carly knew Ray wanted nothing more than to run her hands over them, but apparently she was still working up the nerve. The buildup was so intense that Carly worried she would orgasm the moment Ray finally found the courage to breach that barrier.

Breaking away from their kiss, Ray rested her forehead on Carly's shoulder. From the way her body trembled and her breathing hitched, she was obviously trying to calm down. Carly rubbed her hands up and down Ray's muscular back, then kissed her temple. "I should probably go," Carly whispered. "It's late."

"Please stay." Ray lifted her head and met Carly's eyes. "I want you to stay."

Carly swallowed, unsure exactly what she meant. "Are you sure?"

"I don't like the idea of you driving home in the dark." Ray touched Carly's throat, then curled her hand around the back of her neck, pulling her in for another kiss. She murmured against Carly's lips, "It's too dangerous."

Returning Ray's kisses, Carly said, "Staying here could be dangerous, too. If you know what I mean."

Ray nodded and slipped her tongue into Carly's mouth. Her hands found Carly's hips and squeezed, sending a pulse of intense pleasure straight to Carly's pussy. Inhaling sharply, Carly broke their kiss with effort.

"I'm sorry." Ray dragged the back of her hand over her swollen mouth, staring at Carly with slightly unfocused eyes. "I honestly don't know if I'm ready to do more than this, but I don't want you to leave."

Fair enough. Knowing she was likely setting herself up for a long night in which she would crave to masturbate but not be able to, Carly said, "Okay."

"Okay?" Ray said. The excitement on her face made all Carly's sexual frustration worth it. "Really?"

Ignoring her desire to straddle Ray's lap and guide her tentative hands to all the right places, Carly said, "I can sleep on the couch."

Disappointment flashed in Ray's eyes. "Oh. I was actually hoping you'd sleep in my bed. With me."

Carly exhaled shakily. Of course. "Okay."

"You're sure?" Ray took her hand.

Interlacing their fingers, Carly brought their joined hands to her lips and kissed Ray's knuckles. "I would love for you to be the first thing I see tomorrow morning."

Ray's gaze searched her own. "Exactly what I was thinking."

Carly used her free hand to brush Ray's short hair away from her forehead. "You sure you feel comfortable having me in your bed?"

"I'm not sure *comfortable* is the word I'd use." Ray's cheeks glowed a lovely pink, most likely a combination of arousal and embarrassment. "But I want you beside me."

The quiet confession made Carly's pussy contract, and she gritted her teeth against the need to show Ray just how turned on she was.

"Hey, Carly?" Ray squeezed her hand. "I know this isn't easy for you, and I'm so sorry. To be honest, it's not easy for me either. I had no idea I would find it this difficult to keep my hands off you."

"That's quite the compliment." It was actually a hell of a relief. Initially she had worried that Ray was mistaking best friendship with sexual attraction. That clearly wasn't the case.

"I just want you to know that I don't mean to tease you."

"You're not." Though Carly had lately fallen into bed quickly with new lovers, she would be lying if she said she wasn't enjoying the slow burn of their growing intimacy. "It's about the journey, not the destination. And believe me, I'm loving every second of this trip."

Ray stood and pulled Carly up by her hands. "On that note, maybe we can fool around in bed a little?"

Carly laughed. "I figured we would." She glanced at the extra-large dog bed Ray kept next to the couch and giggled. Jagger lay stretched out across the pillow, and Jack slept curled in a ball against Jagger's chest. "Look at those two."

"I think they'll approve of this sleepover. We can take that pillow to the bedroom for them to use."

Carly whistled for the dogs to join her at the back door, and she let them out in the yard while Ray carried their pillow away. Watching Jagger sniff around for the perfect place, Carly tried to mentally prepare herself for what was about to happen. They might end up making love tonight. Even if they didn't, they would likely go further than ever.

Jagger loped inside and Jack followed. Carly shut the back door and flipped off the outside light, then turned around to find Ray standing behind her, smiling nervously.

"They're all squared away?" The dogs ran to Ray as though they hadn't seen her in ages, and she patted them both. "Ready for bed, good boys?"

"They're ready." Carly closed the distance between them on shaking legs. "So am I."

"Me too." Ray took Carly's hand and led her down the hallway.

Carly studied the pictures on the walls as she passed. Ray's father in Vietnam with another soldier, arms around each other's backs. One of Ray at about ten years old, holding a soccer trophy next to her father, who sat in a wheelchair and beamed with pride. The picture just outside her bedroom was of Ray and three other women, probably her mother and two sisters.

Ray stepped inside her bedroom and released Carly's hand. This was her first time in Ray's private domain, so Carly took in the room with interest. The bed was made neatly, corners tucked tight. Ray had placed the dog pillow at the foot of the bed, in front of a relatively small LCD television that sat on a modest entertainment center. There were no pictures on the walls in here, only shelves full of books.

"This is lovely," Carly said. The room didn't look very lived in, and she suspected Ray spent most of her time in the common areas. "I've never made a bed that well in my life."

"Those nice people in the military taught me." Ray smiled faintly. "Probably the best thing I learned."

Jack and Jagger leapt onto the bed, one after the other. Jagger immediately lay down while Jack circled him with a doggy grin on his face.

"Sorry, Jagger usually sleeps with me." Ray snapped her fingers and pointed. "Off."

"Eh-eh," Carly echoed, gesturing Jack down as well. "Yeah, Jack, too."

"Sorry, buddy." Ray stroked Jack's head as he passed on the way to the dog pillow. "She's all mine tonight."

Carly's nipples tightened. "Will you be okay without Jagger next to you?"

"I think so. He'll be close if I need him."

Nodding, Carly looked at the bed. For the first time it occurred to her that she didn't have any pajamas. The shirt she was wearing was cute, but probably not ideal for sleeping. "Do you have something I could wear?"

Ray blinked and then dragged her gaze over Carly's body. "Oh, yeah. Of course." She opened a dresser drawer and rummaged for a moment, then offered Carly a gray T-shirt that said *Army* across the chest. "Would you like a pair of boxers? I don't have any pajama pants."

"Sure." Carly took the clothing with a shy nod. "Thanks."

"No problem. Why don't you change in my bathroom? I'll use the one down the hall."

"Thank you." Carly wished she had something more profound to say, but nerves were making her stupid. "See you in a minute."

"Yup."

Carly went into the bathroom and closed the door. This might be harder than she thought. She undressed, then held Ray's T-shirt to her nose and inhaled. It smelled like Ray, and Carly's Pavlovian response was to get wet again. Grabbing toilet paper, she wiped herself thoroughly, not wanting to stain Ray's boxers. That would be embarrassing.

When Carly dressed and opened the bathroom door, Ray was sitting on the bed. Ray jumped up as Carly approached, moving her gaze up and down Carly's body. Carly took the opportunity to sneak a lingering look at Ray's toned arms and bare legs. Wearing a sleeveless T-shirt and boxer shorts, Ray was showing more skin than Carly had ever seen.

"You are so beautiful," Carly said. Ray was a fascinating study in contrasts. Well-muscled with delicious curves, both hard and soft, she was everything Carly found sexy in a woman. And then some.

Ray looked bashful. "I'm nervous."

Worried that she had given the wrong impression with her compliment, Carly said, "We don't need to do anything except sleep."

"Not about that."

"Then what?"

"Sometimes I have nightmares."

"Oh," Carly said quietly. That made sense. If she had experienced the things Ray had, she would probably have nightmares, too. "Don't be nervous."

Ray met her eyes. "I don't have them like I used to, but I want to warn you just in case. They're pretty intense for me, so I'm guessing they might be that way for a bystander, too."

"Can I do anything to help?"

"Just don't startle me or wake me up. Get out of bed if I get too active. I would never hurt you on purpose, but I've gotten pretty worked up before."

Carly felt a trickle of anxiety. She wanted to do right by Ray, and she hoped like hell that if something did happen, she reacted appropriately. "Understood."

"I'll probably be fine." Ray gave her a careful smile. "I really don't have them very much since I moved here."

"It's okay." Carly closed the distance between them. "Everything will be all right. You'll see."

"I hope so."

"Even if you have a nightmare, it's no big deal. We'll handle it. I'll be there for you."

Ray held out her arms and Carly stepped into her embrace. Kissing her hair, Ray said, "Want to lie down?"

"Yes." It was probably best now that Carly's bare thighs were pressed against Ray's, the soft, unrestrained breasts touching her own. "Good idea."

Ray pulled back the covers with shaking hands, and Carly climbed into bed as Ray got under the comforter next to her. Picking up a remote, Ray turned off the overhead light with the push of a button. The room stayed dimly lit by a night-light next to Ray's side of the bed and another near the closed bedroom door.

Carly turned on her side to face Ray. "Hi," she whispered, as though the darkness demanded she be quiet.

"Hi." Ray mirrored her pose. "Is it bad if we kiss now?"

Laughing, Carly murmured, "It's not bad at all. It is a slippery slope, though."

Ray scooted closer. "I'm willing to take my chances."

This time Carly initiated their kiss. Moaning in response, Ray snaked her arms around Carly's waist and pulled her close. Carly entangled their legs and put a hand on Ray's hip, then waited for some indication that she had crossed a line, but Ray just tightened her embrace.

Carly felt drunk on their kisses, dizzy with love and desire. This was Ray she was holding, shy, gorgeous Ray who made her heart ache and her knees tremble. These were Ray's hands touching the small of her back, then slipping inside her shirt. That was Ray's fingertip stroking the bare skin of her side, igniting a need so fierce Carly felt like she might lose control.

Ray drew back. "It was never like this with Danny," she murmured.

"Because he was a man?" Carly held her breath as Ray's hands moved over her stomach, so close to the underside of her breasts.

"I don't know. Maybe just because he wasn't you."

Carly needed more. She craved as much of Ray as she could get, so when Ray's knuckles brushed lightly against the curve of her bare breasts, Carly said, "Touch them, Ray."

Ray went still, but her breathing grew heavy.

"Please." Carly shifted to lie on her back, then took one of Ray's hands in her own. "May I show you?"

"Yes." Ray's voice came out like a gasp.

"You're sure?" Don't be pushy, Carly scolded herself. She played with Ray's fingers, waiting for permission. "Only if you want."

"Are you kidding me? Yes." Without waiting for Carly to guide her, Ray slid her hand up so it covered Carly's breast. She cupped Carly gently, then flexed her fingers.

Carly moaned at the contact she had been craving for days. "That feels so good."

Ray used her thumb to stroke Carly's erect nipple. "You're so soft."

"You don't need to be that careful," Carly murmured. "If you don't want to." She enjoyed Ray's tenderness, but as turned on as she was, Carly was happy to take whatever Ray could give her.

Ray pinched Carly's nipple between her fingertips, still treating her like she might shatter. "I love your breasts." Ray's voice was strained, as though she was struggling to maintain control. "You are so fucking sexy. I want to—"

"What?" Carly tucked a lock of hair behind Ray's ear, then touched her cheek. She wanted so badly to slip her own hands inside Ray's shirt, but waited for Ray to say when. "What do you want to do, darling?"

Growling softly, Ray moved both hands to the hem of Carly's T-shirt and dragged it up the length of her torso, baring her stomach and her breasts. Carly whimpered as cool air hit her overheated skin, surprised and excited by Ray's boldness. Ray climbed on top of her, settling between Carly's thighs. Carly spread her legs wide, thrilled by the sensual weight of Ray's body.

Carly reached to bring Ray down for another kiss, but Ray grabbed her hands and pressed them to the mattress above her head. Then she lowered her face to Carly's, plundering her mouth with a passion that threatened to take Carly's breath away. Carly attempted to wiggle free, but Ray held her down even harder and thrust her hips into Carly's pussy.

Carly groaned into Ray's mouth. Ray was so forceful. To be exposed and have all control taken away made Carly incredibly hot. She squirmed, desperate for direct contact on her breasts or her clit. Either would be fine. Both would be best.

She tore her mouth from Ray's, turning her face to suck in much-needed air. "Please." She lifted her hips, grinding herself into Ray's pelvis. "Please, Ray."

Ray released Carly as though she had been burned. Rolling off, Ray sat on the edge of the bed and choked out what sounded like a sob. "Oh, my God."

Carly lay still for a moment, not sure what had just happened. Then she pulled her T-shirt down over her belly, raised up on her elbows, and touched Ray's back. "Ray?"

"I am so sorry." Ray's whole body trembled. "Please forgive me. I got carried away."

Concerned, Carly sat up. Ray had her back to her so Carly couldn't see her eyes, but she was clearly fighting tears. "Hey." Carly rubbed her hand in gentle circles over Ray's lower back. "There's no reason to be sorry."

"I got too rough."

"No, you didn't." Carly missed the warmth of Ray's body next to hers, so she tugged Ray's shirt. "Get back in here. You didn't hurt me."

Ray buried her face in her hands. Jagger had come to Ray's side of the bed at the sound of her distress. What a good boy. Ray took a deep breath, then put her hand on Jagger's head.

"I just got so excited," Ray said quietly. "I wasn't thinking when I held you down like that. I never wanted to scare you."

Carly gave Ray's hip a gentle pinch. "Listen. You didn't scare me." When Ray didn't say anything, Carly added, "You turned me on. I'm soaking wet, Ray. Because of you."

Ray shivered, then looked back at Carly. "I promise I would never hurt you."

"I know that." Carly tugged Ray's shirt again, and this time Ray allowed herself to be coaxed back into bed. "It never crossed my mind that you could or would hurt me."

Ray drew her knees up to her chest and wrapped her arms around her legs. She sat next to Carly, face turned away. Carly stroked her back silently, willing her to calm down.

Finally Ray whispered, "I'm sorry I freaked out."

"It's okay. We've been moving pretty fast. Maybe we should slow things down."

"Yeah." Ray looked at Carly, her eyes shining in the low light, filled with emotion. "A guy held me down like that once. Scared the hell out of me."

Carly felt the confession in the pit of her stomach. She had wondered but would never have dared ask. "In Iraq?"

Ray didn't answer for so long Carly thought she might have decided against talking about it. Finally Ray rocked back slightly, then said, "You know the soldier who was captured with me? Archer?"

The one who had been decapitated. "Yes."

"He assaulted me in the bathroom on base about a month before we were taken." Ray sounded like she was relating a boring news story, not an event that had clearly been traumatic. "It happens a lot. When I was over there I heard rumors about female soldiers dying of dehydration because they were too afraid to drink water late in the day. They didn't want to have to go to the bathroom at night." Shrugging, she said, "I like water."

"Oh, Ray." Carly kept her hand on Ray's back. "I'm sorry."

Ray's shoulders began to shake. Carly wrapped her arm around them, only to realize that Ray wasn't crying. She was laughing.

"It's not funny," Ray said, but giggled anyway. "I know it's not, I just—Archer cornered me in the bathroom. It was just the two of us. He asked me to give him a blow job. When I refused, he said he'd settle for a hand job. I said no again, and that's when he decided to just try and rape me."

Carly couldn't imagine why this story moved Ray to laughter, but she stayed quiet and listened. Emotions were strange that way, sometimes seemingly at odds with the events that inspired them.

"Well, he got me down on the floor—it was so disgusting, that floor, you wouldn't believe it—and he finally managed to get my pants down. I gave him the fight of his life. He had a black eye the next day. I got a split lip and a bloody nose. So anyway, he gets my pants off—" Ray's laughter grew more uncontrolled. "And immediately he comes all over my thighs. After all that. Didn't get close to raping me. Just took one look at my bare legs and shot his load."

Carly sat silently at Ray's side, holding her close. She couldn't join Ray's laughter, though she thought she understood where it came from. Some things were so horrific you almost had to find the humor in them, if you were going to cope at all.

"It's not funny," Ray repeated. Her giggles subsided. When she spoke again, her tone was sober. "He was supposed to be one of my guys. He was supposed to have my back."

"Did you report him?"

"No. I mean, nothing really happened. It wasn't worth the grief. The military doesn't encourage those types of reports."

"Don't ever play it down like it was nothing." Carly captured Ray's hand and pulled it into her lap. "Something happened."

Ray nodded. "Dr. Evans told me the same thing."

"She's right."

"It just seems silly to dwell on something like that when I spent two months being held hostage. They may not have raped me, but it was a hell of a lot worse."

"They were both traumatic experiences. I don't think you can compare them."

"No, I guess you can't," Ray said quietly. "They were both scary. The worst part about being captive was waiting. And knowing I would die."

"But you didn't," Carly said. She brought Ray's hand to her lips and kissed her knuckles. "You're alive and you're here with me right now. And you're safe."

Ray met Carly's gaze. "I never realized how much that thing with Archer affected me until now."

"It makes sense that it would come up when we were getting intimate." Carly slowly kissed Ray on the cheek. Proof that she was still here. That Ray hadn't scared her away.

"I wanted to be inside you so badly," Ray whispered when Carly pulled back. "I never knew touching another woman could be so intense, that I would want you so badly. I just…lost myself for a moment." She shifted so that their bodies no longer touched, as though ashamed by the admission. "I wanted to make love to you, but I also wanted to fuck you. It scared me."

"You're not like him." Carly touched Ray's face, encouraging her to make eye contact. "What just happened between us was nothing like what he did to you. That was about power and control, not desire. Just now, that was desire. You touched me and I responded, and you got excited. I didn't say no. I didn't push you away. I have no doubt that if I did, you would listen."

"You're right. I know that."

Ray's voice sounded so full of sorrow. "Please don't be sad," Carly said. "You didn't do anything wrong."

"When I imagined making love with you, I thought it would be soft and slow and gentle." Ray laid her face on her knees and shrugged. "I couldn't even do that right."

"You were perfect. Soft is great, but so is hard. What's important is that we both enjoy what we're doing. Trust me, I loved every second of it."

Ray sighed. "You're way too good for me."

Though she sounded like she was trying to keep the comment light, Carly sensed that Ray meant exactly what she said. "I hope you don't really believe that."

"I try not to, but I feel so damaged sometimes. The things I saw over there, what I did, they make me feel dirty. Fucked up. Like I don't deserve someone as wonderful as you."

"I'm hardly perfect." Carly laughed nervously. The last thing she needed was to be put on a pedestal when she felt just as damaged. She might not have gone through the same kind of trauma, but she had her fair share of baggage from the past. "I'm bound to disappoint you if you think I am. Consider it fair warning."

"Point taken." Ray picked up Carly's hand and very gently traced the shape of each finger. "But you are really special. Beautiful. It seems like I'd have to force you or trick you into being with me, because if you knew who I really was—what I'm really like—you wouldn't want me."

"That's bullshit," Carly said. Ray blinked, obviously surprised by her word choice, but Carly continued. "So you have some battle scars. So do I. Nadia's death broke me. Even though I've had some time to heal, I still carry those scars. They may fade with time, but they'll never go away completely. Neither will yours. They don't define who you are, Ray. Just where you've been."

Ray didn't move, and for a moment Carly worried about relating her own tragedy to Ray's. But Ray pulled her into a tight hug.

"That's one reason I was so drawn to you," Ray whispered into her ear. "You can understand me, in some crazy way."

Carly put her hand on the back of Ray's neck. "I could never understand exactly what you've seen and done, but I'll always listen, and I'll never judge."

Ray drew back and nodded. "Should we try to lie down again?"

"Sure." Carly lay back against her pillow, then turned on her side to face Ray. Like before, Ray mirrored her pose. For a long time she was quiet, and Carly wondered if she was done talking. As soon as Carly considered closing her eyes, Ray spoke.

"I've never told anyone about Archer. Except Dr. Evans, of course." Ray eased her foot over to Carly's side of the bed, and Carly trapped it between her calves. She welcomed the connection, however tenuous. "After they killed him it didn't seem right to say anything, you know?"

"That must have been horrifying." Carly had heard the details of the execution video that surfaced on the Internet, but no amount of money would have convinced her to seek it out. She didn't need to see some things. "Watching him be murdered like that."

"I had a lot of guilt for a long time." Ray's hand crossed the empty space between them, finding Carly's hip and settling there. She made no move to touch Carly further. "After he attacked me, at times I wished he would die. So I wouldn't have to worry about him waiting for me again some night. He didn't deserve to die like he did—nobody deserves that—but when it happened a part of me was glad it was him and not one of the other guys."

"That's understandable."

"No, it's terrible. For a while I was afraid it was my fault, which is ridiculous. I wanted him gone, and less than a month later…he was."

"Thinking something doesn't make it your fault," Carly murmured. How many times had she consoled herself with that idea in the months after Nadia's death? "No matter what you felt after the assault, you didn't murder him. You didn't make that happen."

"I know that logically. But logic doesn't touch a lot of my guilt."

"I get it." Carly felt around under the covers for Ray's other hand and grasped it. "After Nadia called to tell me she was pregnant, I had this moment of sheer terror. I mean, I was excited, sure, but I was so scared. Maybe I wasn't ready to be a parent. Maybe we'd made a mistake. If I really wasn't ready, what would I do?" Carly shuddered. "Two hours later I got a call from the hospital. She and the baby were dead."

"I bet all prospective parents have those moments of doubt," Ray said. "Having a kid is a huge deal. I can't imagine not worrying about it."

"I wrestled with a lot of guilt, though." For months she had secretly feared that her doubts had somehow materialized and slammed into Nadia's car. "Logically I knew I never wanted to lose them, that thinking we made a mistake had nothing to do with what happened. But when you have gut-wrenching fear and the source of your fear suddenly vanishes, it's hard not to feel like you caused it."

"You're right," Ray murmured. "That kind of guilt doesn't make a lot of sense."

"Easier to see that from the outside, isn't it?"

"Yes." Ray rubbed her thumb over Carly's lower lip. "You're really good at making me feel better. That's one of the things I love most about you."

Carly's heart stuttered at Ray's declaration, but Ray's lazy smile showed that she didn't realize the full scope of what she had just said. "I try."

Ray put a hand on her shoulder. "Turn over. I want to hold you."

Carly rolled so her back was to Ray, then murmured her approval when Ray wrapped an arm around her middle and pulled her close. "Is this okay?"

"This is perfect."

"Thanks for sleeping over, Carly." Ray kissed her shoulder. "And for being so understanding about…before."

Carly closed her eyes, remembering how Ray's hand felt on her bare breast. "Of course," she whispered. God, she hoped they could try that again soon. "Good night."

Ray squeezed her gently. "I'll see you in the morning."

Chapter Eighteen

R ay woke up with a smile on her face and a cramp in her leg. Opening her eyes, she surveyed the scene around her. Carly's head lay on her breast, and one arm curled around Ray's waist. Their lower bodies were pressed together because at some point during the night, both dogs had snuck up onto the bed with them. With two adult bodies, a shepherd mix, and an almost two-hundred-pound Great Dane, real estate on the queen-sized mattress was scarce.

Desperate to stretch her legs, Ray started to wake Carly up. Then she stopped, gazing down at the crown of Carly's head, loath to disturb her. Carly's face rested directly on her nipple, which hardened when Ray marveled at their proximity. This situation could make her feel claustrophobic, trapped, but it didn't. She felt surrounded by love.

Last night had been surreal—both her intense arousal with Carly in bed and her ability to talk openly about things she never expected to share with anyone except in therapy. The emotional highs and lows of the previous evening were extreme, but in the amber glow of morning, Ray felt lighter. Maybe even cleansed.

She hadn't been able to reconcile what had happened to trigger her panic attack. That would take time, and she needed Dr. Evans's perspective. Carly's calm acceptance didn't stop Ray from being disturbed that she had lost control and also that she had enjoyed taking control from Carly.

Despite that new issue, this morning she felt optimistic. Carly was still there, wrapped in her arms. They would slow things down and work through this together.

"Ouch," Carly mumbled. Her mouth moved against Ray's breast, sending a jolt of surprised pleasure to the tips of Ray's toes. "I think your dog is lying on my foot."

Ray winced in sympathy. "Jagger, off."

"You too, Jack." Carly clung to Ray when both dogs jostled them as they clambered off the bed. "I'm not sure I'll be able to walk anymore. I can't feel anything below my knee."

"If you had to become incapacitated somewhere, I'm grateful it was in my bed." Ray kissed Carly's hair.

Carly looked at Jagger, who sat staring at them from the foot of the bed. "Did she promise you a cookie for doing that? I told you not to let her use you as a pawn in her nefarious misdeeds."

Ray laughed, and when Carly looked up at her grinning, she gave her a soft kiss on the mouth. "Good morning."

"Good morning to you," Carly murmured against her lips. "Did you have sweet dreams?"

Ray couldn't remember her dreams. That alone was sweet. "The sweetest."

"I'm glad." Carly lay on her pillow, but kept her arm around Ray's waist. "It's nice waking up with you."

"Very nice." Ray put her hand on Carly's side and found a strip of bare skin with her fingertips but fought the impulse to touch Carly's breasts. The contact would be welcome, but Carly was right that they should slow things down. Ray wasn't ready to make love yet and had no interest in driving them both crazy.

"What are your plans today?" Carly raised her hands above her head and stretched. "Anything exciting?"

"That depends."

"On?"

"What are your plans?"

Carly's face lit up. "Well, I'm not working today. So I was hoping they would include you."

"Perfect. Maybe we can go to your house and play video games or something." Carly always complained that it was hard to find women her age to game with. Ray was happy to learn if she could spend time with Carly.

"That would be awesome." Carly stroked the side of Ray's face. "I was also thinking about calling Tanya at ADI. They have another litter of puppies so we could get some puppy playtime in."

Shit. As much as Ray had enjoyed the puppy petting, she and Carly hadn't been lovers then. Or nearly lovers. Surely Tanya would see that something had changed between them. Hell, anyone who saw her with Carly would know exactly how she felt. It wasn't easy to hide being stupid in love.

"Maybe." Ray scrambled for an excuse. She didn't want Carly to know that she didn't want their relationship found out. That would hurt Carly—how could it not? And this was Ray's problem. It had nothing to do with Carly. "I'm not feeling very well, though. I'd prefer to stick close to home."

The concern in Carly's eyes made Ray feel like a fool. "What's wrong, darling? Are you okay?"

"Yeah. My stomach is bothering me a little. Maybe that pizza last night?" The only thing upsetting her stomach was the lie, but now that it was out there, Ray was committed to it.

"You sure you're up for video games? If you need some rest, I can find something else to do."

"No." The last thing Ray wanted was to chase Carly away. "I'll be fine. I just don't want to be far from home. Just in case."

"I understand." Carly sat up and peeked at the doorway, where both dogs now sat patiently. "I think they're trying to tell us something."

"Looks like it." Ray touched Carly's back. "You want to take the first shower?"

"You'll take care of the dogs?"

"Sure. I'll run Jack through the agility course before my shower. Then we can feed them."

"Hey, I'd love to see you take him through it sometime today, if you don't mind." Carly squeezed Ray's arm. "I'm really curious about how he's doing with the weave poles."

"Oh, he's awesome." Pride filled Ray's chest at the thought of Jack's steady progress. "Better every day."

"Do you think he'll be ready to compete in June?"

Ray's stomach clenched. Only six weeks away, the agility trial was a looming goal that both she and Jack had been working so hard toward. Jack was ready, but she wasn't certain about herself. Granted, she wouldn't have to get up in front of everyone and run him through the course. Carly would be happy to take on that role. Ray desperately wanted to see the result of their many hours of hard work from the sidelines. Before she and Carly got together, she might have been able to do it. Now she wasn't sure.

As though sensing her thoughts, Jack whined at the door. He just wanted to be let out, but the sound jarred her out of her fears. Of course she would go to the agility trial. No matter how scary it was. She owed it to Jack, and to herself.

"He's ready," Ray said, determined. For her own sake, she damn well better be ready, too.

❖

Usually when Dr. Evans started a session by asking Ray what she wanted to focus on that day, she struggled to come up with a topic. Three days after her first night in bed with Carly, Ray knew exactly what she wanted to talk about.

"Sex."

Dr. Evans raised an eyebrow. "I thought this might come up soon."

"Like you said, being with Carly…physically…is stirring up a lot of emotions. Some that I'm not sure how to deal with." Ray twisted her hands in her lap, face hot with embarrassment. Though they had mentioned her sexuality in the past, they had never focused on it in their sessions. They had discussed her lack of sex drive after Iraq, but that was it. She had built a great deal of trust with Dr. Evans, but it was still strange to talk about sex with anyone. "We haven't actually had sex yet, but we came close."

"Tell me what happened."

Ray told Dr. Evans about their evening on the couch, necking like teenagers instead of watching the movie. "Then I asked her to spend the night. In my bed."

"Did you intend to have sex?"

"No," Ray said, but she wasn't entirely honest. "Well, maybe. I mean, I thought that maybe we would. I was pretty scared, but I think I hoped we would."

"But you didn't."

Ray averted her eyes from the monitor, too humiliated to meet Dr. Evans's gaze even through the camera lens. "We started kissing and she told me I could touch her breasts. So I did, and I got so excited I kind of got carried away."

"Carried away how?"

Ray closed her eyes altogether, ashamed. "I pulled up her shirt so I could see her breasts, then all of a sudden I was on top of her. Holding her down and kissing her."

"Was she uncomfortable?"

Ray shook her head, glancing furtively at the monitor. "She said she wasn't. But I was. I had a brief flashback. Of Archer. I almost had a full-fledged panic attack, but luckily Jagger was there to help snap me out of it."

"Look at me, Ray." Dr. Evans had this amazing way of sounding patient and sympathetic, like she was incapable of passing judgment. Relaxing, Ray looked back at the webcam. "You are not Sergeant Archer."

"I know," Ray said. "But maybe I could be."

"You might hold Carly down and hit her in the face? Force her to have sex against her will?"

Ray flinched. "Of course not."

"Okay, then. You are not Sergeant Archer. Let's unpack this. There's a lot going on here. Think about how you felt when you got on top of Carly. How your body felt. What was happening in your mind?"

"I…" Ray tried to go back to that moment. Carly's breast was so soft, so perfect. For years Ray had lived with breasts of her own, never realizing how incredible they could be. She remembered baring Carly's chest, then feeling the blood surge through her veins when she saw tight pink nipples. Needing to be on top of Carly, inside her. "I was so aroused. I wanted her. Completely."

"That's perfectly normal with someone you're attracted to. Especially if romantic feelings go along with that desire. And friendship on top of that?" Dr. Evans chuckled. "We're talking major, major passion, Ray."

Ray frowned. "Does that explain the way I wanted to be in control, though? It wasn't even a conscious desire. All of a sudden I had her hands above her head and was kissing the hell out of her. The whole situation, including the control, excited me. When she moved like she was trying to pull away I pressed her wrists down harder."

"What did she do then?"

Ray shivered. "She pulled away from our kiss." She remembered Carly's murmured pleas, which Ray had interpreted as begging her to stop. "She said 'please' a couple times, and I freaked out when I realized what I was doing. But—"

"What?"

"She told me she was enjoying it. That…" Ray's face was on fire. "I made her wet. And when I think back on it, the way she moved beneath me definitely didn't feel like she was scared or upset."

"Sounds like Carly was getting off on you taking control." Dr. Evans smiled. "You two could have a great sexual dynamic. That is, if you can get comfortable enough to let it play out."

Ray shifted in her office chair. "I don't know if I will ever feel okay about taking over like that."

"If the activity is consensual and Carly enjoys it as much as you do, why not? Listen, there is nothing abnormal or sinister about enjoying the feeling of being in control during sexual situations. Plenty of people find it a turn-on. And others enjoy the opposite—surrendering control."

"You think that's what Carly likes? Surrendering control?"

"I don't know. You two should probably talk about it. But I will say this: I don't find it surprising that you would find issues of control, and specifically being in control, arousing. You've experienced two serious traumas in which you were made to feel powerless. In a situation like this one with Carly, when you're in a safe place with someone you trust, it makes absolute sense that you would be interested in exploring power dynamics."

"So there's nothing wrong with me?" Ray kept a straight face, but she felt an intense wave of relief. She hadn't known what to make of her behavior. It had never come up with Danny. That Dr. Evans felt it was healthy and even made some kind of sense was a huge weight off her shoulders. "I mean, at least in that regard?"

"You sound perfectly fine to me. But you and Carly need to keep the lines of communication open. Can you talk to her about sex?"

Shrugging shyly, Ray said, "I don't know. I think so." She sighed and put her hands on her face, cursing the heat in her cheeks. "To be honest, I'm not even a hundred percent sure what we'll do in bed. I mean, I can guess. I think. But it's still a bit of a mystery. I'm not sure I'd know how to talk about it."

"Do you ever touch yourself, Ray?"

Dr. Evans was so straightforward. Ray studied the pattern on Jagger's collar, anything to avoid eye contact. "Not really anymore, no." She had thought about it. Even tried for a moment in bed the other night. But she hadn't masturbated in so long that it felt foreign to do so, and she was scared. What if she couldn't feel pleasure like she used to? "It makes me a little nervous."

"About the emotions it may bring up?"

"That, and I'm worried it won't work." Ray's eyes filled with tears, blurring Jagger's collar into his gray fur. "What if I'm broken?"

"If you're frightened about whether you're capable of experiencing sexual pleasure, that's all the more reason to spend some time exploring it on your own. Better to confront whatever fears you can before you and Carly are in that situation again. Come to peace with your body and your desires. Then sharing yourself with Carly will become much easier."

"That's a good idea."

"The things you do to make yourself feel good would probably also feel good to Carly. And if you're still uncertain about what you two would do together, talking it out could not only answer some questions for you, but it might also be exciting."

Just imagining talking frankly about sex—their sex—with Carly made Ray's blood pressure rise. "I'll try to work up the nerve to bring it up."

"You'll be just fine. Maybe the first step before going any further with Carly is to simply adjust to having these feelings again. This is a lot, Ray. Not only are you just recovering your drive, but you're also thinking about making love with a woman for the first time."

Ray groaned. "This is definitely a lot."

"I happen to think you're up to the task." Dr. Evans paused. "Speaking of tasks you're up to, how are you doing with getting out into the world?"

Ray's relief vanished. This was the really difficult topic, and the one she was ashamed to talk about. "I'm doing okay." Did that sound as weak to Dr. Evans as it did to her?

"You don't sound very sure of that."

"Carly and I went out to dinner for our first date," Ray reminded Dr. Evans. "That was a pretty big step."

"Yes, it was. Have you gone anywhere since?"

Ray looked down at her hands. "Not yet."

"For a while you were doing really well. Things seem to have slowed down a bit since you and Carly became a couple."

"I don't know if that's true," Ray lied. She hated that her newfound confidence was slipping away, but she found it difficult to admit to Dr. Evans that it was. "I have a harder time with datelike things, like restaurants. Or going to the movies."

"Is that because of what you're actually doing, or because you're on a date?"

"Maybe a little of both?" Ray ran a hand through her hair, then tugged at a fistful until her scalp sang. "It's just new for me, doing that stuff with someone else. I'm sure I'll get used to it soon."

"Not if you don't practice. Tell me why you find it so difficult to do things with Carly all of a sudden. Before you were lovers, Carly was able to actually encourage you to try new things. Like spending time with that litter of puppies."

"That was fun," Ray murmured. She sighed. Better to just come clean. "She asked me if I wanted to go again last weekend to see another litter of puppies. And I totally did want to go, but I told her no. I just couldn't get over my fears."

"Tell me about those fears."

"Well, you know." Ray wished Dr. Evans could fill in the blanks. "I mean, everyone will be able to see that I'm totally in love with her."

"And what if they do?" Dr. Evans sat up straighter, and Ray knew she was excited to have hit upon the real issue. "Many people wouldn't notice you two at all. Some may assume you're best friends or even sisters. A certain number of people will notice you casually and guess that you're lovers. What about that frightens you?"

"Come on, Dr. Evans. You saw all the news coverage when I was captured. And then after I was released? It's died down a lot, but you and I both know that if someone figures out I'm with a woman now, that's one hell of a curiosity. The media wouldn't hesitate to make that a story."

"Whoa." Dr. Evans held up a hand. "Slow down. You're making a lot of negative predictions. You don't have to take things to that place. Sure, someone might recognize you. Even if they do, the chances that it would translate into a media feeding frenzy are pretty low."

"You don't know that. All it takes is one person who wants to break a big story or tip off a news source. And once someone mentions it, the story will spread."

"You need to tell yourself that even if people see you together, they will not know the nature of your relationship. And even if they do figure it out, that doesn't mean it will become a big story. But you know what, Ray, even if it did? You would deal with it."

Ray shook her head. Her heart hammered at the memory of what it had been like in the spotlight. "I can't deal with it again. I really can't. Especially not something so personal." She imagined Danny finding out by reading some news story, or her mother watching CNN only to discover that her middle child was now a lesbian.

"What are you thinking about, Ray? Where did you just go?"

From the concern in Dr. Evans's voice, Ray knew she wasn't doing a good job of hiding her neuroses. "I was thinking about my family finding out through the media that I'm seeing a woman."

"Have you thought about calling them and telling them yourself?"

A new seed of anxiety took root in the pit of Ray's stomach. "Not really. I haven't been talking to them about much of anything lately."

"Maybe it's time. Do you think they'll be upset that you're with a woman?"

Ray considered the question for a long time. Her mother and her sisters were all socially liberal, and she had never heard any of them make derogatory comments about gay people. Still, who knew how they would react if the gay person was her? "I don't know," Ray said finally. "I don't think so, but I don't know."

"You may find it empowering to tell them, to let them know on your own terms."

"Yeah." Ray put her hands on her head, wishing she could chase away the pain that throbbed in her temples. "I guess I just figured that if I'm careful about where I'm seen, it won't have to be an issue. I'm telling you, I don't think I can do it again."

"Listen, you're stronger now. You're not giving yourself nearly enough credit. And you've got Carly. If something did happen, you wouldn't have to go through it alone."

Ray swiped angrily at the tears that escaped her eyes. "But I don't want Carly to have to go through that with me. I doubt she would want to stick around for it in any event."

"Have you told Carly about your fears?"

Ray shook her head. "I've been making excuses to not go out. Basically."

"Carly sounds like a smart woman. She'll figure out that something's going on." Dr. Evans got that expression on her face that Ray had come to associate with being told that she would have to do something she didn't want to. "You need to talk to her. Keep her in the loop. Let her know what's going on and allow her to help you work through it."

Though Ray nodded because the advice was solid, she couldn't admit the depth of her fear of being found out to Carly. It could only hurt Carly's feelings.

"I'll try," Ray whispered.

"You'll do great. Keep the lines of communication open with Carly and everything will be just fine. You'll see."

Ray nodded miserably. She wished she could be so certain.

Chapter Nineteen

Leeann had impeccable timing. She called when Carly was a half mile away from Ray's house, just in time to force her into a lie. As much as she hated lying to Leeann, she had no choice. Ray still wasn't comfortable with anyone knowing about their relationship, and as long as Leeann thought Ray was unattainable, Carly wasn't about to tell her where she was spending all her time.

Carly activated her wireless headset and braced herself for the conversation. "Hey, Leeann."

"Hey, yourself. How are things up in the north country?"

Amazing. Overwhelming. "Things are okay."

"Keeping busy?"

That was an understatement. When she wasn't at work, she was with Ray. "For the most part."

"Any plans tonight? Maybe we could meet in Corte Madera for dinner. Or Larkspur. Whatever you want."

Carly felt a twinge of disappointment. She wanted to spend the evening with Ray, of course, but dinner out sounded nice. She probably wouldn't be able to talk Ray into going somewhere. "I'm so sorry. I'm working late tonight, filling in at the emergency clinic."

The lie tore her apart. She had never hidden her relationships before. When her parents came to visit her at college one weekend shortly after she and Leeann got together, Carly outed herself to them rather than pretend she didn't have a girlfriend. Luckily her parents had taken it well, which had set the tone for the rest of Carly's life thus far. It was easy to be out and proud in the San Francisco Bay Area, but she couldn't imagine living her life any other way. Lying felt unnatural. Hopefully Ray wouldn't expect her to do it for long.

"Oh, that's a bummer. I thought we could go to the Melting Pot and gorge ourselves on fondue."

"I'll definitely take a rain check on that one." Carly turned into Ray's driveway, setting Jack's tail thumping hard against the car door. "That sounds like fun."

"I miss you." Leeann's voice verged on petulant, and Carly smiled.

"I miss you, too." Carly put the car into park and waved as Ray stepped out onto her front porch with Jagger. She held up a finger to indicate that she would end the call as soon as she could. "Actually, I got an e-mail reminder this morning for a veterinary conference that I signed up to attend forever ago. It's next Thursday and I'll be spending the night in the city. If you're free, we should get together."

"Totally," Leeann said. "We could hit the club. Maybe even get you laid."

"I don't know about that." Carly hoped her chuckle sounded nonchalant. Ray sat on the porch swing grinning, and Carly flashed on a memory of how it felt to have that lean, muscled body on top of hers. "I'd love to see you, though."

"Where are you staying?"

"Oh, I reserved a hotel room. I'm covered."

"Don't be silly. You should crash with me. We can eat ice cream and watch scary movies. It'll be fun."

Tempting. Of course, she wouldn't have any privacy with Leeann, and no late-night phone calls to Ray. That was probably the only thing that would get her through being away for two days. Carly pinched the bridge of her nose. "I really appreciate the offer, but it would be easier if I kept my room. I'm staying where the conference is being held, and I need to get an early start on Friday morning, so—"

"Okay, I get it. That's fine. More ice cream for me, then."

Carly laughed. "Can I take a rain check on the slumber party, too?"

"Of course you can." Leeann sighed. "So, how are things with Ray?"

It figured she would ask a direct question. Hoping to get off the subject quickly, Carly said, "Fine. She's doing well. And Jack is doing great with the agility training she's giving him. He should be awesome at the trial in June."

"Uh-huh." Leeann couldn't make her lack of enthusiasm for dog-related conversation more obvious if she tried. "How are *you* doing with Ray?"

"I'm fine." Carly was getting very tired of this line of inquiry. Especially when she couldn't be honest about the fact that her unrequited crush wasn't so unrequited after all. "Trust me, okay? Everything is great. I'm wonderful."

"Good." Leeann sounded like she wasn't convinced, but was willing to let Carly off the hook. "So I'll see you next Thursday?"

"I'll call you," Carly said. Ray planted her feet and rocked the swing lazily, then folded her toned arms over her chest. She looked good enough to eat. "I actually need to let you go now, though. My shift is about to start."

"Have fun."

"I will." Carly disconnected their call and opened the car door, stepping aside to let Jack tear out behind her. "Hey," she shouted to Ray. "Sorry, that was Leeann."

"No problem." Ray beamed as Carly approached and patted the swing beside her. "How is she?"

"Great." Carly sat down and gave Ray a lingering kiss. She pulled away sooner than she would have liked, but she had promised herself not to let things escalate tonight. "We're planning to hang out when I'm in the city Thursday night."

"Oh, yeah." Ray gave her a brave smile, but Carly could see the disappointment in her eyes. "I keep forgetting you'll be out of town."

"I promise to call you before I go to bed that night," Carly said. "You can tuck me in over the phone."

"I'll miss you."

"I'll miss you, too." Carly put her arms around Ray and rested against her solid body. Ray kept them swinging with her legs and eased her arm around Carly's shoulders.

"This is nice," Ray said quietly. "I could definitely get used to it."

Carly squeezed Ray around the middle. The sun was setting and the light had taken on an amber hue. It bathed the green hills that surrounded Ray's house, making them almost seem to glow. Jack and Jagger lay on the end of the porch, side by side, ears perked and noses greedily taking in the salty air. For right now, at least, everything seemed perfect. Carly went still and tried hard to capture this moment in her memory.

She had once been so happy surrounded by the noise and energy of the city. It was hard to believe that this quiet, idyllic place existed a mere sixty-five miles from where she had lived that other life. She might as well have been on a different planet. Yet she felt just as happy now as she had then, no matter how different her life had turned out from what she had expected.

Fear slithered down Carly's spine. Losing this happiness had been devastating the first time. Could she survive a second loss? What if Ray wasn't really in this for the long run? What if she thought better of being with a woman?

"I can feel your mind working," Ray murmured, then kissed the top of Carly's head. "Want to tell me what you're thinking about?"

"That I don't want this to go away," Carly said. Drawing back, she met Ray's eyes with a shy smile. "Sorry. Occasionally I slip into a bit of melancholy. But I'm fine."

"I'm not planning to go anywhere." Ray's gaze penetrated her, deadly serious. "You mean everything to me."

Carly nodded, but no matter how sincere Ray's promise, anything could happen. Just when you thought you knew what life had in store for you, there could be a car accident. Or a change of heart. Anything.

"Likewise." Carly put her hand on Ray's upper chest and gave her a friendly pat. "What's for dinner, sweetheart? Are you up for going out? Or we could pack a picnic, bundle up, and eat on the beach."

A shadow passed over Ray's face. "Oh. I'm sorry, I already ordered Chinese."

"That sounds good." Carly wasn't surprised that Ray had taken care of dinner. This was becoming a pattern. At first Carly told herself she was imagining that Ray was making more excuses than normal not to leave the house, but now she was almost certain that something was going on. "Maybe we could go out to dinner again after I get back from San Francisco this weekend. I had fun on our first date. I'd love a second one."

"Yeah, maybe." Ray's smile looked like it took considerable effort. "We'll figure something out."

As much as Carly hated to pressure Ray into anything outside her comfort zone, she didn't want to ignore the obvious. If Ray's recovery was faltering, she wanted to know why. "It seems like you've been more hesitant to get out of the house lately. Is something going on?"

Ray flinched. "I haven't been more hesitant." Breaking eye contact, she said, "I was just craving Chinese. If I thought I could cancel the order I would, but they'll probably be here any minute."

"No, Chinese sounds fine." Carly took Ray's hand and squeezed. "I'm sorry, Ray. I just want to make sure you're okay."

"I'm great." Ray touched Carly's face. "Never better. Believe me."

Carly nodded. She wanted to believe Ray. She wanted to believe that the nearly empty cupboards and refrigerator she had noticed yesterday were now fully stocked, evidence that Ray had made it to the store. She wanted to believe that it was a coincidence that they hadn't been to the beach since Ray's breakdown. And she definitely wanted to believe that Ray would be willing to go out to dinner again one day, because that had been so nice, so wonderfully normal.

She also wanted to believe that Ray wasn't backsliding for some reason, even though she obviously was. But more than anything, Carly wanted to believe that she wasn't the reason Ray no longer pushed herself to face the outside world.

Unfortunately, she wasn't sure she could.

CHAPTER TWENTY

Ray lay in bed with her cordless phone on the nightstand beside her. She had a book in her hands, but had given up on actually reading it twenty minutes ago. She could look at the same paragraph only so many times without paying attention to the words. Besides, the book was the last thing on her mind.

She glanced at the phone's display to make sure the batteries hadn't died. Nope. Fully charged. Then she looked at the clock. It was after eleven. Carly had said she should be back to her hotel room by now and would call as soon as she got there.

Sighing, Ray marked her page and put her book down. Then she threw her arm over her eyes, disgusted by how pathetic this was. She couldn't remember needing another person so badly. And this wasn't even sexual need, though that was certainly part of it. She needed Carly like she needed to breathe. Life with Carly seemed brighter, more exciting. Happy, even.

Life without Carly was boring. And empty.

Ray let her mind wander as she waited for the phone to ring and thought about the advice Dr. Evans had given her about sex two weeks ago. It was reasonable that she should practice being comfortable with her body again without Carly. She just wasn't sure how to start.

That wasn't true. She knew exactly where to start but wasn't sure if she could bring herself to try.

Since when did masturbation seem so scary? She used to do this all the time. Even when she was a kid. How could something so familiar and so pleasurable frighten her now?

Ray let her hand rest on her stomach. She was a soldier, goddamn it. She had faced much scarier things than this and survived. This wasn't a big deal. Stay in the present. No negative predictions.

She pushed her T-shirt up just under her breasts and stroked the bare skin around her belly button. She had been so disconnected from her body since Iraq, it felt foreign to touch it like this. Like she was touching a stranger.

What if she had lost the ability to enjoy her body along with the old Ray, another of the many things—her sense of safety in her world, her innocence—she didn't know how to get back? She hadn't even tried. What if she was broken in ways too devastating to face?

But now that she had found Carly, she owed it to both of them to deal with her sexual issues head-on. It was evidently a very good sign that Carly aroused her and that she even wanted sex for the first time since Archer had held her down on that bathroom floor. If she still desired it, maybe she would be able to achieve orgasm. Right?

Ray took a deep breath and slid her hand under the elastic waistband of her panties. Without letting herself think, she found her clit and stroked it gently. It was sensitive to the touch, almost unbearably so.

Ray startled when the phone rang and tore her hand from her panties. Willing her heart rate to slow, she fumbled the handset when she picked it up. "Hello?"

"Hey, sweetheart. Hope I didn't wake you."

At the sound of Carly's voice, all the tension left Ray's body. She hadn't even realized how tightly wound she was until that moment. "Are you kidding me? I've been trying to stop staring at the phone and willing it to ring."

Carly laughed. "I've been looking forward to hearing your voice, too. How was your day?"

"Great," Ray said, though "adequate" was probably a fairer adjective. "I worked with Jack on agility for a while this afternoon, but it was pretty cold outside so we all decided to cuddle on the couch. We may have watched one too many Indiana Jones movies."

"That sounds wonderful."

"No day is wonderful without you. But it was pretty good." Ray wished she had been brave enough to accompany Carly to the city but knew Carly wasn't surprised that she hadn't. "How was your day?"

"Long. The lectures were interesting, but I get tired of sitting in auditorium seats. I had dinner with Leeann, which was nice. Then she insisted on dragging me to this noisy club, which wasn't as nice. My ears are still ringing." Carly sighed. "I'm getting old. I used to love to go dancing, and now all I can think about is whether they need to turn the music up that loud."

Ray laughed. "Thirty-two is hardly old."

"Older than you."

"Well, I don't like loud music, either." Who was Ray kidding? Even at twenty-five, the idea of being in a noisy dance club made her sick to her stomach. "Did you have fun, at least?"

"It was okay." Carly cleared her throat. "To be honest, I spent most of the evening dodging Leeann's attempts to hook me up with whatever available woman she could find."

Ray swallowed her immediate reaction to Leeann's obsession with getting Carly laid. It wasn't fair to be annoyed by Leeann when she had asked Carly to keep their relationship a secret. What Leeann was doing for Carly had nothing to do with Ray.

Carly murmured, "Anyway, I've been waiting for this moment all day. I've gotten so used to your good-night kisses that this hotel bed seems awfully empty right now."

"You're in bed?" Ray's frustration with Leeann melted away.

"Yeah. How about you?"

"I'm in bed, too." Ray closed her eyes and put her hand back on her bare stomach, pretending that Carly was touching her. "Missing you."

"I like the sound of that. Want to tell me more?"

Ray shivered at the arousal in Carly's voice. She still wasn't used to making Carly feel that way, and it was incredibly powerful. Ever since Dr. Evans asked if she was able to talk to Carly about sex, she'd imagined what it might be like. Maybe it would be easier over the phone.

"I'm sorry, I didn't mean to make you uncomfortable," Carly said, apparently taking Ray's silence as a sign that a line had been crossed. "I miss you, too."

"You didn't make me uncomfortable." Ray took a deep breath. "I was trying to work up the nerve to talk to you. About sex."

"Oh." Though Carly sounded cautious, her interest had obviously been piqued. "Something specific, or sex in general?"

Ray pulled her comforter over her head, embarrassed that this was so embarrassing. "Sex with you. With a woman. And me."

"Ah." Carly sounded like she might actually understand what Ray had just said. "You want to talk about what sex with a woman will be like?"

"Yes," Ray said. Thank God Carly was able to translate her gibberish. "I mean, I probably know. But I'm not totally sure. My therapist suggested I try to get used to talking about it with you, so I figured—"

"No, that's good. This is good." Carly cleared her throat, then laughed nervously. "Apparently I have stage fright."

"We don't have to talk about it. I was just…thinking about it before you called."

"I've been thinking about it, too." Ray heard some rustling on Carly's end of the phone. "Every time my mind wandered during that conference today, I was fantasizing about making love with you, actually."

"Like how?" Ray uncovered her face and took a deep breath of cool air. "I mean, what were you imagining?"

"Kissing you, of course. How it felt when you touched my breasts that night. You have amazing hands. So strong. When I first met you I thought your hands looked delicate, so I was surprised that they're so strong."

Ray's breathing picked up at the way Carly's voice got lower. Arousal dripped from every word, and it was contagious. "I can't wait to touch you again."

"You know what else I was imagining?"

"What?" Ray said breathlessly.

"How your mouth would feel on my breasts. I love having my nipples sucked, and you're such an incredible kisser. I can only imagine how your mouth will feel other places." Carly hesitated, then said, "Is this okay? Talking like this?"

"This is perfect." Ray knew what Carly was asking. "I feel very safe right now. And very horny."

Carly moaned. "I definitely like the sound of that."

"I like how it feels." And she did. Wanting Carly, no matter how scary, made her feel alive.

"So how does that sound?" Carly asked after a moment. "Do you want to suck on my nipples?"

Ray swallowed. Even when she and Danny were having regular sex, they had fucked far more than they talked about it. It was hard to believe that words could turn her on so much. "Yes. I've thought about that a lot," Ray whispered. "Your breasts are beautiful. So sexy."

"Would you enjoy having my mouth on your breasts?"

A jolt of pleasure rocked Ray's clit, taking her breath away. She gritted her teeth, surprised by her intense reaction. "Oh, yes."

"Are your nipples hard right now?"

Ray hesitated only a moment before she slid her hand into her T-shirt. She knew they were like granite before she touched them, as tight and painful as they were. But she wanted to close her fingertips around one, to pretend they were Carly's mouth instead of her own hand. "Yes."

"So are mine," Carly murmured. "I'm wearing just a T-shirt and panties, and my nipples are so hard right now they ache. I'd give anything to feel your warm tongue on them."

Another shock of pleasure rocketed through Ray's clit, and she slid her hand into her panties. She touched her swollen clit lightly, gasping at her response. Even more startling was the slick wetness that poured from her, all because of Carly's voice.

"I'm wet." It coated Ray's fingers, thick and hot. She drew a fingertip over her clit and shuddered. "Oh, my God. I'm so wet, Carly."

"So am I." Carly's voice shook. "Are you touching yourself right now?"

"A little." Ray stroked her clit again, relieved when pleasure rolled over her. She didn't feel broken. "Maybe."

"Don't stop," Carly breathed. "Close your eyes."

Done. It was almost easier that way. "They're closed."

"Those are my fingers, sweetheart. I'm touching you right now. Do you like it?"

Ray inhaled sharply. It wasn't difficult to pretend that Carly was the one rubbing lazy circles down over her labia, and her excitement ratcheted even higher. "You feel so good," she whispered.

"I want to touch you just like that. I hope you'll show me how you like to be touched."

"How do you like it?" Would Carly's pussy feel the same as hers?

Or would it be as foreign as Danny's body had been? "Tell me what you want me to do to you. Please."

Carly whimpered. "I want you to put your fingers inside me. One at first, then two."

Ray's heart threatened to pound out of her chest. She didn't need to worry about being unable to feel. She felt more than she imagined possible. The thought of sliding her fingers into Carly made her dizzy and weak. She might have loved sex before Iraq, but nothing she had experienced back then even came close to what she was feeling now. Touching Carly in that way seemed so natural and so sexy.

"Do you like it soft?" Ray asked. Pleasure began to build in the pit of her stomach, delicious pressure that would soon be released. It was no longer a question of if but when, and Ray didn't want to let go too soon. "Or hard?"

"Both. How about soft at first, then harder until I come on your fingers?"

Ray cried out as her pussy contracted slightly, sending a wave of sensation through her legs. She recognized the signs of impending orgasm and curled her toes, trying to stave it off. This felt so good. "I can do that."

"Will you let me lick you?" Carly sounded like she was trying hard to keep her breathing even, and failing. "Is that something you like?"

"I've only tried it twice." Danny hadn't been a big fan of doing that, which made Ray less than comfortable with it. But being licked had felt divine, and the idea that Carly would do that for her threatened to bring her off immediately. "I'd like to try again."

"Good. Because I've been thinking about it a lot and I don't want anything more than to taste you. I'm going to make you feel so good, Ray, I promise."

"You're making me feel good right now." Ray tensed her thighs and dug her heels into the mattress. Just a little more and she'd come. "Keep talking. Please."

"I want to suck your clit until you come in my mouth. Would you like that?"

Ray closed her eyes and arched her back as her body convulsed with pleasure. She felt like crying out but held back, not wanting to scream into the phone. Instead she gritted her teeth and tried to keep breathing. Her thighs shook and she slammed them closed on her hand, then turned her face into the pillow to muffle a groan.

Carly had stopped talking, but her heavy breathing was still audible. Slowly Ray eased her thighs apart, releasing her hand. Getting her voice back took more effort. She didn't trust herself to speak and didn't have the words to say what she felt.

"Did you come, sweetheart?" Carly finally asked. "You got pretty quiet there, but it sounded like—"

"Yeah." Ray's voice was hoarse, as though she had actually screamed her orgasm. "I definitely just came." Emotion grabbed her throat, squeezing painfully. Her eyes stung and she wrinkled her nose to try to stop her tears. When they flowed anyway, she gave herself over to her feelings. An incredible burden had been lifted. She had faced a fear and triumphed.

"You're beautiful," Carly said softly.

"I haven't had an orgasm in over two years." Ray pressed the heel of her hand against one eye, overcome with relief. "I wasn't sure I could anymore."

"Sounds like you didn't have any problem in that area. In fact, we managed to get you there pretty quickly."

Blushing, Ray said, "All credit to you."

"Give yourself some of that credit. It wasn't my hand." Carly chuckled. "Unfortunately."

"I hope it's your hand soon. Or your mouth," Ray said shyly. It would take some time to get used to flirting so blatantly, but it was nice to feel desirable again.

"Me, too," Carly said.

Ray bit her lip. "Did you come?"

"Oh." Carly giggled, sounding shy herself. "Well, no. I was trying to focus on you."

"But were you…touching yourself?"

"A little. Maybe."

Ray grinned. "Do you think you could finish?"

"Oh, uh." Carly cleared her throat, then laughed. "Yeah. Definitely."

"Will you?"

"Sure." When Carly spoke again, her voice was huskier. "This is nice. I wasn't expecting it tonight."

"Neither was I." Ray searched for something to say, some sexy comment that would help Carly climax, but she had gone blank. Apparently that orgasm had wiped out some of her brain cells. "I don't know if I can talk like you did. But I still want to hear you come."

"You don't have to talk." Carly's voice broke. "Just listen."

Ray stayed quiet as Carly's breathing grew heavy and she moaned occasionally, a sound of yearning so sensual Ray's clit twitched all over again. She heard Carly's own pleasure building and tensed in anticipation, desperate to hear Carly's release.

"This feels so good," Carly murmured. From the way she clipped her words, Ray guessed she was very close. "I want you so badly it hurts."

All of a sudden Ray knew exactly what to say. "I'm in love with you, Carly. I love you."

Carly cried out hoarsely. Holding her breath, Ray listened to Carly ride out what sounded like a shattering orgasm. The noises she made were almost spiritual in nature. Ray was afraid to speak, not wanting to break the spell.

When Carly finally fell silent, Ray whispered, "That was incredible."

"Yes, it was." She could hear strong emotion in Carly's voice. "Thank you."

"Are you okay?"

"I'm great. Wonderful." Carly hesitated, then said, "You're in love with me?"

Why would Carly sound so uncertain? Though Ray hadn't said the words before, she had been wearing her emotions on her sleeve. Surely Carly wasn't surprised that she had verbalized the obvious. "Of course I am."

"That's a big deal," Carly said in a quiet voice. "I mean, those words are a very big deal for me."

"I know," Ray said. "It's a very big deal for me, as well."

"I'm in love with you, too."

"You don't have to say that." Ray's heart swelled at the declaration. "I didn't tell you because I expected to hear it back. I was just feeling it, so I wanted you to know."

"But I do love you." Sniffing, Carly said, "I'm not sure I ever thought I'd say those words again, but God help me, I do."

"That's a good thing, right?" Ray's stomach knotted at the sorrow she could hear in Carly's voice. It made no sense. This should be a happy moment. "Why do you sound so sad?"

"I'm not sad." Carly's voice had brightened. "I'm sorry. I don't want you to think that. Not at all. Just a little overwhelmed."

"I get that. Make sure to breathe."

Carly laughed. "Good advice."

"I'm something of an expert, if you need any tips." Ray grinned, happy to be the one to provide strength for once. "Everything will be just fine, okay? I'm not going anywhere. I promise."

"Yeah." Carly yawned. "I hate to say this, but I should think about getting to bed. I've got a lecture on antiemetic therapy in dogs and cats at eight o'clock tomorrow morning."

"Sounds fascinating." What the hell was antiemetic?

"It should be pretty good, but not if I'm dead on my feet."

Ray smiled. She was in love with a woman who enjoyed dry veterinary lectures. Life certainly took some interesting turns. "Then I'll wish you sweet dreams. Have a great day tomorrow, and call me when you get back to Bodega Bay."

"Count on it. Maybe we can go out to dinner or something, like we talked about?"

Ray quit smiling. What was with the constant desire to go out? Carly knew she didn't like it. Ray needed to make more of an effort, but she wished Carly would back off. All she wanted was some time to get over the fear of exposure. Was that too much to ask?

"Maybe," Ray lied. "We'll do something fun, I promise." Her vote would be to stay in and try some of what they had talked about this evening.

"All right. Tell Jack I'll see him tomorrow night."

"Will do."

"And give Jagger a big kiss on the noggin."

"He'll appreciate that." A wave of fatigue swept over Ray, taking her by surprise. "Wow, I'm going to sleep like a baby tonight."

"Yeah," Carly murmured. "Me, too."

❖

Carly clicked off her cell phone and set it on the cheap wooden nightstand in her overpriced hotel room. Her hand wasn't shaking. From the outside, she probably looked calm. Hopefully she sounded that way when they were saying good-bye. She thought she had held it together rather well, which was surprising. After all, Ray had just shaken her universe to the core.

She had no idea why hearing Ray say *I love you* would make her feel like the world was crumbling around her. She should be happy. It wasn't like she wasn't deeply in love with Ray, too. Having those feelings returned was a good thing. So why, instead of feeling overjoyed, was she struggling not to descend into full-blown panic?

Those three words, now that they were out there, suddenly made everything very real. She was in love with a woman who wasn't Nadia. Even more alarming, she was giving her heart away again, now that it had finally healed. After all the pain she had suffered since losing Nadia, this was just crazy. Leeann thought Ray was a bad risk, and she just might be right. Even if Ray was sincere about her feelings, as Carly believed she was, Ray clearly wasn't all that comfortable being with a woman.

Hell, she wasn't even comfortable leaving the house.

Carly cringed at the direction of her thoughts. She'd known Ray had issues when they met. She'd known Ray would have to overcome challenges when they started their romantic relationship. And yet she'd moved forward anyway, accepting those facts. It didn't seem fair to freak out about all this now that both their hearts were invested. In fact, she felt downright shitty.

Shitty or not, she was afraid.

When they started their relationship, Ray was at least able to go to the grocery store. They walked on the beach regularly, and Ray even agreed to spend that wonderful afternoon at the Assistance Dog Institute. So yeah, Ray had problems, but there seemed to be a light at the end of the tunnel.

Now all Carly could see was darkness. Ever since their dinner date, Ray always had some reason they couldn't or shouldn't leave the house, and for a while Carly tried to write it off, but she wasn't stupid. Ray was uncomfortable being seen with her. She was afraid of being outed—to the point where she wouldn't even permit Carly to confide in her best friend.

This wouldn't work. They were on a path to disaster. The situation as it stood was untenable—for Carly, and for Ray. Did it matter that they loved each other if their relationship set Ray back? If she truly loved Ray, shouldn't Ray's welfare be her primary concern? It would be selfish for Carly to allow things to keep on like this while Ray continued to backslide.

Carly ran her hands over her face, then rolled onto her stomach. She hugged her pillow and tried to block out her negative thoughts before they ruined what had been such an amazing night. She really had thought of Ray all day. First at the conference, then at that club with Leeann. The loud music and writhing bodies on the dance floor hadn't made her feel old so much as lonely and frustrated. She'd come back to the hotel horny and ready to hear Ray's voice, and she had gotten so much more than she expected.

To experience that kind of intimacy with Ray had been a gift. It had taken Ray a great deal of courage to share herself so freely, and that meant more than Carly could ever appreciate. She wasn't sure she had ever been so turned on as she was when she heard Ray bring herself to orgasm. Not to mention honored. She loved Ray heart and soul, and even one day of being apart tore her up inside.

So why was she letting her brain step in and introduce all these doubts? Carly swore loudly, letting the pillow muffle her words. It had been so long since she'd last been in love, she'd forgotten how confusing it could be. Though she was pretty damn sure things with Nadia were never this confusing. Sometimes she would give anything to be new and shiny again. She used to take her optimism for granted, never realizing it could be snuffed out like a light, and now she missed it.

Carly rolled onto her back and closed her eyes. She really did need sleep. Maybe things would seem less scary in the morning. Maybe she would know what to do.

She hoped so, at least. Otherwise she might really fuck things up.

CHAPTER TWENTY-ONE

Morning brought few answers, but at least Carly had the long drive back from the city to help clear her head. She took Highway 1 north along the coast, grateful for the ocean view and the meandering pace. Usually she took the 101, but today she was in no hurry to get back to Bodega Bay. As much as she wanted to see Ray, to hold her tight and never let go, Carly was nervous.

Tonight she would ask Ray to go out one more time. It didn't really matter where—a restaurant, the beach, something. If Ray agreed, maybe Carly wouldn't be so anxious. But if she got another silly excuse, they needed to have a very serious talk. Unfortunately she knew what Ray's answer would be. Now she needed to figure out what she would say when she heard it.

It tore her heart out to consider abandoning Ray. But something needed to change. She could be patient, but she had her limits. No matter how much her life had slowed down since moving to Bodega Bay, she wasn't ready to enter self-imposed isolation. Not even for Ray.

But she wouldn't abandon her. This was about practicing tough love, for both their sakes. Maybe they should spend some time apart. Ray could decide whether she wanted to deal with being in a lesbian relationship. And maybe Carly could gain perspective. If her life seemed emptier without Ray, she would just have to endure it. For Ray's sake.

It was a solid plan, at least until she pulled into Ray's driveway. Then Ray strode out of her house wearing blue jeans that fit perfectly and a hooded gray sweatshirt that barely hugged her curves, and Carly immediately dismissed any notion of tough love. This woman was beautiful, she was intelligent, and she made Carly laugh. She also understood how much Carly loved dogs, which seemed like a small thing, but wasn't.

Carly opened her car door and smiled. "Hey, sweetheart."

Ray closed the distance between them and pulled Carly into a warm hug. "How was your drive?"

"Wonderful." Carly ran her hands over Ray's back, then down to her hips. It took everything she had not to slip them beneath Ray's sweatshirt. "I took the scenic route and it was gorgeous. It's a beautiful day."

"Yes, it is." Ray took a step back and traced a fingertip between Carly's breasts. "On that note, we should go inside."

Carly shivered at Ray's suggestive tone. "Okay."

Ray led her into the house, where they both braved an onslaught of affection. Jack ran straight to Carly, wiggling his back end and rubbing his face against her hands. Carly dropped to her knees and hugged him, then scratched Jagger's chest.

"You can see they've missed you as much as I have." Ray tugged lightly on Jagger's jowls. "We were a bunch of sad sacks waiting for you to get back."

"I missed you guys, too." Until this moment, she hadn't realized how much. Carly kissed Jack on the head, then Jagger, then she stood and embraced Ray again. Somehow over the past few months, these three had become her family. Carly's throat tightened and tears welled. Not wanting to explain what she was feeling, she kissed Ray instead.

This kiss was different from any they shared before. Carly felt it right away, though she couldn't put her finger on what had changed. Ray seemed more relaxed, perhaps more confident. One hand caressed Carly's face and the other settled on her hip like it was the most natural thing in the world. There was passion in her touch, but also love.

Carly pulled away with a shaky exhalation. "That was very nice."

"I've been thinking about doing that all day." Ray dropped her hand from Carly's face to her chest, touching just above the swell of her breast. "Among other things."

Carly's stomach fluttered with anticipation. She had wanted Ray for so long, and now, finally, was the chance to have her. The determination in Ray's eyes told her that if they went into the bedroom now, they would make love. The thought was so powerful it threatened to erase all Carly's worries.

At least until they were basking in the afterglow. Then what?

"We talked about maybe going out tonight." Carly heard the words coming out of her mouth before she realized she was saying them. When Ray's face darkened slightly, she was glad she had. They needed to sort this out before they consummated their relationship. No matter how badly Carly wanted to. "I'm hungry. Aren't you?"

"Not for food." Ray gave her a shockingly seductive smile, then whispered close to her ear. "But yes, I am hungry."

Carly stood paralyzed, warring with what to do. One part of her wanted to take Ray by the hand and drag her to the bedroom. At the same time, fear bloomed. If they made love, there was no turning back. Her heart would belong to Ray completely, and she would be at Ray's mercy.

"I need to use the bathroom." Carly needed to get away from Ray, to clear her head. How could she think with those gorgeous hazel eyes staring at her? "Just for a minute."

Ray nodded, but her disappointment was clear. "I'll wait for you in the bedroom?"

"Sure." Carly forced a smile. She didn't want Ray to sense her conflict until she'd had a chance to sort things out, but from the look on Ray's face, she wasn't doing a great job of hiding her unease. "I'll be right in."

"Is everything all right, babe?"

Carly's heart swelled at this first term of endearment from Ray. "It's fine. Just one minute."

"Okay. I'll let the dogs hang out in the backyard for a bit."

"That's fine." Carly tried not to think about what they would do in the bedroom all alone. "I'll be right there."

It took everything Carly had not to sprint to the bathroom. She shut the door behind her calmly, then slumped against it and closed her eyes. When she thought about asking Ray to go out tonight, she never imagined that her silly excuse would be the desire to stay in and make love instead. Honestly, that didn't seem very silly to Carly.

She wasn't even sure it was an excuse. They'd shared something powerful last night, and clearly it had affected Ray. She seemed more open, more comfortable in her own skin. The thought of turning this into a confrontation over leaving the house instead of honoring Ray's courage made her sick. But she couldn't in good conscience sleep with Ray when they needed to have this conversation first.

Carly took a deep breath and stepped out of the bathroom. When she glanced out the window and saw the dogs playing in the backyard, a sudden thought stopped her. Jagger was in the backyard. Apart from Ray. That Ray felt confident enough to be separated from him was astounding, a sign of progress. But if they had this talk, Ray would need him close.

When Carly walked into the bedroom with Jack and Jagger trailing her, Ray looked confused. She sat on the bed with the lights dimmed, a few lit candles on the nightstand. The atmosphere was simple but romantic, and Carly had to ball her hands into fists to work up the will to follow through with what she had planned. Falling into bed with Ray would be much easier. Not to mention more satisfying.

"Were the dogs upset about being outside?" Ray smiled when they approached her, but pointed at the dog beds on the floor. "Lay on your pillows, boys."

Feeling as though she were moving in slow motion, Carly sat next to Ray. She took Ray's hand and held it in her lap. No matter how important it was to have this talk, Carly couldn't shake the fear that she was about to do something very stupid.

"What's wrong?" Ray's voice was low and worried. "And please don't tell me nothing."

Carly put her other hand on Ray's face, encouraging her to make eye contact. "I just wanted to talk to you about something before we…" She nodded at the mattress. "You know."

"What do you want to talk about?"

She could hear the tension in Ray's voice, almost as though she had some idea where this might be going. "I love you, Ray. I want the best for you. I want you to be happy."

"I love you, too." Ray seemed to search Carly's eyes. "You make me very happy."

"I know." Carly squeezed her hand again. "I'm worried about you."

Ray frowned. "But I'm doing great. I mean, last night…" Her frown transformed into a shy grin. "Was incredible. That was a really big step for me. And you were wonderful."

"You are doing great," Carly said. The truth was, in almost every way except her agoraphobia, Ray *was* doing awesome. Even better than Carly could have imagined. After their first attempt at making love, Carly thought it might take months for Ray to work up the nerve to try again. But here she was weeks later, like a new woman. "I've seen so many changes in you since we met, and I am so, so proud of all your progress. It means everything to me because I know it means everything to you."

"It's amazing." Ray stroked Carly's knuckles. "I never thought I would feel the things you've made me feel. I don't think I'll ever be able to explain to you exactly how life-changing this has all been."

Carly nodded, feeling increasingly sick to her stomach. "I've noticed something, though. For a while you were doing so well with getting out of the house. You were buying groceries, and we were walking on the beach almost every day. But it seems like since our dinner date, you haven't wanted to go out anymore."

Ray's smile was gone. "I'm not sure that's true."

"Ray, you've been living on next to no groceries for two weeks now. We haven't walked on the beach since the day you had your panic attack. Every time I ask you to do something, you have some reason we should stay home instead."

"Maybe I want to be alone with you." Ray withdrew her hand from Carly's. "Is that abnormal? I've been falling in love with you and all I want is to spend time with you. The rest of the world be damned."

"It's not abnormal. But you know there's more to it than that. This isn't about wanting to be alone with me, is it? I think it's about not wanting to be seen with me. As your lover."

"You're wrong," Ray said, but she seemed to have suddenly found something interesting to look at on the floor. "I just…need a chance to adjust."

"When do you think you'll be okay with me telling Leeann about us?"

Ray's head snapped up. "You said you understood about that."

"I did. I do. But keeping our relationship secret makes me feel very alone. I don't like secrets. I can't live like that."

Ray shifted slightly, angling her body away from Carly. "I wasn't asking you to live like that forever. I just needed time."

"How much time?" Carly said quietly. "Because it seems like

things are getting worse instead of better. And I don't like feeling that our relationship is detrimental to your mental health."

Ray stood up and walked away from the bed. "You don't know anything about my mental health," she said, grinding the words out. She stood with her back to Carly, shoulders tense. "You have no idea how much better I'm doing now than when I first came home."

"You're right. But I do know that you were doing better three months ago than you are right now."

Ray spun around, eyes ablaze. "Bullshit. I might have been going to the grocery store and taking walks on the beach, but I wasn't *better* than I am right now."

"Maybe we just have different definitions of *better*." Carly tried to keep her voice calm, but she was having a hard time. She had never seen Ray so angry, and everything she said just made her angrier. "I'm not trying to piss you off, sweetheart. I just think we need to talk about this."

Ray closed her eyes and inhaled deeply, then exhaled. She turned away from Carly again and continued to breathe quietly. Carly stayed silent. When Ray turned around again, it looked like she had regained some control.

"Go ahead and tell Leeann about us. Do you trust her to be discreet?"

Carly's stomach sank. "She's my best friend. Of course I trust her."

"Fine, then. Tell her whatever you want. As long as she doesn't go around telling anyone else—"

"Who is she going to tell?" Carly's ire rose, both at Ray's distrust of Leeann as well as the idea that their relationship was some dirty little secret. "I appreciate having your permission to stop keeping this from Leeann, but it doesn't resolve anything if you still insist on us being totally closeted."

Ray's brow furrowed. "I don't know what to tell you. This is new for me. I need more time to get used to it, and I don't understand why you're pressuring me about this right now. Tonight, of all nights." Her voice cracked. "I thought we would have a special evening together, after last night, and now—" Folding her arms over her chest, Ray said, "I feel attacked."

"I need to know that things won't always be this way. I need to know that at some point in the relatively near future, we'll be able to go places together. I need to know that you're not going hungry because you're too afraid to buy groceries." Carly swallowed and shifted her gaze away from Ray. "I need to know that you're ready to be with me, and right now I don't think you are."

"What are you saying?" Ray's words were clipped, almost cold. "Are you breaking up with me?"

"No," Carly said, a little more loudly than she intended. "But maybe we should spend some time apart. Until you can be with me without backsliding on all the progress you've made."

Ray stared at her without speaking for what felt like forever. Carly met her gaze, willing herself not to cry. She could see pain and betrayal in Ray's eyes, even though it was obvious she was trying hard to keep her face impassive. Finally Ray walked to the nightstand and blew out the candles.

When she straightened, Ray said, "Get out."

"What?" Carly's heart twisted painfully.

"I said, get the fuck out of my house." Ray stalked to the bedroom door and opened it. "You want to leave? Then leave. That's your choice."

"I don't want to leave. I'm not breaking up with you, Ray. I just—"

"You just want to control everything, including my recovery. You want to force me into an openness I'm not ready to deal with." Ray's voice rose. "You want to make all the decisions for us, so I'm letting you. You think we should spend time apart? Fine. Then get the fuck out of here." She shouted the last bit, and Carly's heart rate picked up at Ray's barely concealed rage.

Jagger walked to Ray's side and nudged her hand. She touched his head, lips trembling. Jack paced anxiously next to the bed, whining. Carly could tell that the tension in the room was freaking him out, so she called him to her and stroked his side. Then she stood, trying to stay as calm as possible.

"Please don't push me away," Carly said. "I love you and I only want what's best for you."

"You're the one who's pushing me away." Ray wouldn't meet her eyes. "I was always honest with you about my limitations, and you told me I was worth the risk. You said you could be patient. But I guess that was before you actually had to deal with me."

Carly's legs threatened to buckle. She felt like someone had taken a knife and cut into her chest, like she was bleeding all over the floor. Her heart was breaking again. Everything she had feared was coming to pass, and it was all her fault.

"Fine," Carly said thickly. "I'll leave. But I'm not walking away from you. We can talk about it when you've had some time to think about what I'm saying."

Ray didn't say anything, but she seemed to lean against Jagger, who stood protectively at her side. Carly walked to the door and paused next to Ray so Ray could say good-bye to Jack. Ray dropped to her knees and hugged him like she would never see him again. A chill ran down Carly's spine. What if by walking out of this room, she lost Ray forever?

When Ray got to her feet after one last gentle tug on Jack's ear, Carly reached out to touch her hand. Ray jerked away sharply, hitting her elbow on the wall. Stung, Carly took a step backward.

"I'll call you." Carly's voice shook. "Please answer the phone when I do, okay?"

To her surprise, Ray finally made eye contact. Carly read nothing in her blank expression. "How about I call you? After all, I have no idea how long it'll take me to become the person you want to be with."

"You're already the person I want to be with. Just not at the expense of your health."

Ray gestured at the door again. "Drive safe."

Carly knew that if she kept talking, they would just go round and round about this. Maybe leaving was best. If Ray had time to think about Carly's concerns, maybe she would understand why Carly felt like she had to say something.

"Fine." Carly stepped out the bedroom door past Ray, calling Jack to her side. "I'll see you later."

Silence followed her to the front door.

CHAPTER TWENTY-TWO

R ay slumped to the floor when she heard the front door shut
behind Carly. She pressed her back to the wall and folded her
hands over her stomach, fighting not to lose her lunch. Jagger lay down
in front of her and maneuvered his head on to her lap. Grateful for his
closeness, she stroked his face and tried to calm down.

What a fucking idiot she was. All day she had been planning
to make love with Carly, blissfully unaware of the trouble brewing
between them. Though she had known that Carly was catching on to
her reluctance to be seen in public together, she had hoped to have more
time before Carly made a big deal about it.

Ray balled her hands into fists, overcome with the urge to strike
something. But she was pinned beneath Jagger's bulk and didn't want
to startle him by slamming into the wall, so she stayed still. She was
glad Jagger was there. If she were alone, she didn't know what she
would've done.

She couldn't decide who she was more angry with: Carly or
herself. On the one hand she felt like Carly had ambushed her when
she least expected it. That Carly had suggested they take a break was
a punch in the gut. On the other hand, she couldn't blame Carly for
wanting more than Ray could give. Normal people liked to leave the
house on occasion. And Carly was unashamed and unapologetic about
who she was, which was something Ray loved about her. Of course it
would be difficult for Carly to lie.

So what had she expected? That Carly would stand by silently
while Ray isolated them from the world? Even if Carly did love her,

that was a hell of a lot to ask of someone. Unfortunately, Ray didn't know what more she could give Carly.

Dr. Evans had told her to talk to Carly about her fears and she hadn't. From here on the floor, broken in two, she could see that she had been a coward. She hadn't wanted Carly to know how anxious the threat of exposure made her, or about the attention they could both receive if someone found out about their relationship. She was afraid Carly wouldn't stay with her.

That had worked out well. Ray's laugh came out harsh, like a sob. "Why did I ever think I could be with her?" Ray asked Jagger, who blinked in response. "I am so fucking *stupid*."

She wished there was beer in the house. Though she had never been much of a drinker before Iraq and stayed far away from alcohol after being diagnosed with PTSD, right now she desperately wanted a drink. Anything to numb her pain. It was either that or put her fist through a wall.

She needed to call Dr. Evans. Now.

With effort, Ray picked herself up off the floor. Jagger stood with her, staying close by her side. She walked to her cell phone as though she were in a dream, then watched her fingers navigate the contact list until she had Dr. Evans's number on-screen. She listened to the phone ring in a haze, waiting for the voice mail where she would leave her message.

After the beep, Ray said, "Dr. Evans, this is Ray McKenna. I need you to call me back as soon as you have a chance. I'm having a pretty bad day—" Her voice broke, and she closed her eyes. No point in lying. "I feel like I want to do something to hurt myself right now." Realizing how that might be interpreted, she hastily added, "Not like kill myself or anything. Just…I need to talk to you. I'm really upset. Thank you. Bye."

Ray hung up and stood motionless, unsure what to do next. She wasn't hungry. Television wouldn't hold her interest, nor would a book. She took the phone to her bed and lay down, inviting Jagger next to her. Her whole body felt numb. Carly had only been gone ten minutes, but it could have easily been ten years. She felt entirely alone.

Wrapping her arms around Jagger, Ray held him close. He groaned, bringing a smile to her face despite herself. No matter what, Jagger was here for her. It didn't matter how fucked up she was. He would stick by her in good times and bad, even if she had a setback. All he wanted was to be loved and cared for, and she could do that. At least she had one dependable relationship.

The phone rang in her hand. Ray checked the display then brought it to her ear. "Hi, Dr. Evans."

"I got your message, Ray. Can you sign on to your computer?"

"Sure." Ray sat up in bed.

"Are you all right? You haven't done anything to harm yourself, have you?"

"No." Ray kept her free hand on Jagger's back as she walked to her office. "I was cuddling with Jagger."

"That's a very good way to deal with strong emotions. Is this about Carly?"

Ray brought her computer to life, then clicked the chat program icon. "Is it that obvious?"

"Well, I would think that if it weren't about Carly, you might have called her. That may be an incorrect assumption, but it was my first thought."

"No, you're right. This is about Carly." Ray double-clicked on Dr. Evans's username, launching a video chat window.

"I see you calling. Let's hang up the phone now, okay?"

"Okay," Ray said, then disconnected their call. A moment later Dr. Evans appeared on-screen. Ray could see her deep concern. "Thanks for getting back to me so quickly, Dr. Evans."

"It's no problem. Your message worried me. I haven't heard you that upset for a very long time."

"I know. I haven't been."

"Can you tell me what happened?"

Ray opened her mouth to speak and was mortified when her jaw chattered. Angry at how her body betrayed her, she clamped her mouth shut. If she started crying now, she wasn't sure she would be able to stop.

"It's okay," Dr. Evans said. "This is hard. Your body is trying to release some of the emotion you're feeling. Go with it."

Ray made fists with her hands until her blunt fingernails cut into her palms. "Carly thinks we should spend some time apart. Take a break." Her eyes filled with tears and she blinked them back, pissed off. "Fuck, I don't want to cry."

"If you need to cry, it's better to just let it out. Did Carly say why she thinks you should spend time apart?"

"Because—" Ray's chin quivered and she tightened her jaw, desperate for control. "Because she thinks our relationship is detrimental to my mental health."

"Is it?"

Ray glared at the screen. "Of course not. I haven't been this happy in forever. I had an orgasm last night, for God's sake. I've seen more progress in the past few months with Carly than I did in the two years before."

"You had an orgasm?" Dr. Evans raised an eyebrow. "With Carly?"

"Sort of." Now that Ray thought about it, this was embarrassing to talk about. Still, she wanted Dr. Evans to know how well she was doing. "We were on the phone. Talking."

"Ah, okay. And that was last night?"

"Yeah, she was at a conference in San Francisco and called me before bed. We started talking about sex, and then…you know."

"Wonderful. That must have been a relief. I know you've been concerned about your ability to climax."

"It was incredible." Sorrow overwhelmed her, a crushing sense of loss. "Not that it matters now."

"It matters. I know how much courage it must have taken for you to share yourself with Carly in that way. Good for you." Dr. Evans gave her a reassuring smile. "Regardless of whatever else has happened, take some time to savor that victory. Okay?"

Ray nodded miserably. "I just feel so stupid now."

"Because of what happened tonight?"

"It came out of the blue. Like she ambushed me. Here I thought we were going to sleep together, maybe, tonight, but instead—"

"Why does Carly think your relationship is detrimental to your mental health?"

Ray looked down. "She's noticed that I'm having trouble leaving the house. Especially with her." She shrugged, embarrassed that she had let her fears lead them to this place. "She doesn't think I'm ready to be with her."

"When we talked about your anxiety around going out a while

ago, we discussed the importance of sharing your fears with Carly. Did you two ever have that conversation?"

Ray picked at a spot on the corner of her desk. "Not really."

"Not at all? Or just not extensively?"

"She brought it up once. Said she'd noticed that I seemed more reluctant to do stuff than I had before we were together, but I blew it off. I didn't want to admit that she was right." Ray's throat stung. "I didn't want her to know what I was afraid of. It was stupid."

"So all she knew was that when you two got into a relationship, all of a sudden you didn't want to go anywhere or be seen with her." Dr. Evans paused, then said, "Do you understand why she would be concerned?"

"I guess. But she knew I had problems from the beginning. I never lied to her."

"Knowing you have problems and seeing that they're getting worse after you enter a relationship are very different things. It sounds like she cares about you a great deal. And I have to imagine that it would be difficult for her to be isolated if it's not what she's used to."

"I get that." Ray touched Jagger's head. "But she said she would be patient with me. She knows this is new for me. We've only been together a couple months. She didn't give me a chance to get comfortable."

"Maybe you didn't give her the chance to be supportive by not letting her in on what you were going through," Dr. Evans said. "Let me know if this sounds right, okay? Carly tried to bring this up with you and you dismissed her concerns. Perhaps she felt the only way to get you to confront these issues honestly was to make you see that they were important enough to her to force a separation."

"You think she did the right thing? Leaving me like this?"

"I think she did what she thought was right."

"Well, she's wrong. She didn't have to leave to make her point." Ray felt her emotion rise again, and she took a deep breath.

"It sounds like you're angry at her. Do you think the suggestion to spend time apart came from somewhere other than a place of concern?"

"Maybe she's scared." The words seemed to come out of nowhere, but Ray knew there could be some truth to them. "Last night I told her I was in love with her for the first time. After I did, she seemed very emotional, not necessarily in a good way. She said she was overwhelmed."

Dr. Evans tilted her head. "It could be that she's afraid of getting too serious when you two still have so many fundamental issues to deal with."

It always came back to Ray and her fucked-up neuroses, didn't it? "So it's pretty much all my fault no matter how you look at it."

"I don't think it's necessary to assign blame. It takes two people to make a relationship work, or not. I do think you two need to focus on communication."

"What's the point? I know what she wants and I can't give it to her."

Dr. Evans raised her hand. "That sounds like a thought distortion. Why couldn't you give Carly what she wants?"

"Because she wants a normal girlfriend who will take her out to dinner and a movie and probably hold her hand on the street, and I can't imagine ever being able to do that." A powerful wash of grief swept over her, choking her up. "She deserves so much better than me."

"Do me a favor, okay?" Dr. Evans waited until Ray nodded, then said, "Take a moment and remember what you felt like when you first came home from Iraq."

Ray shuddered. Everything had been so painful and frightening back then: the night terrors, the sudden bouts of rage and grief and guilt, and the awful certainty that she was losing her mind.

"Don't let yourself get swept away by it," Dr. Evans said. "Just remember."

"I remember."

"Would you have ever imagined then that you would be where you are now?"

Where was she now? Aside from her fear of being in public, not in bad shape. The nightmares were infrequent and her moods were relatively stable. Most days she felt like she might come out the other side of this thing, if only she gave herself half a chance. Two years ago, she would never have dreamed that a relationship was even an option.

"No, I couldn't have imagined it," Ray said. "You're right."

"So don't you think it's likely that you will only continue to improve? Two years from now you may look back on this time and think the same thing—I never would have believed then that I could be where I am now."

The dam burst. Ray bent at the waist and folded her arms over her stomach, opening her mouth in a silent sob. Dr. Evans let her cry for what felt like hours. Ray didn't know what set her off, just that she didn't have any room to keep this emotion inside any longer.

"It's okay, Ray," Dr. Evans said when her sobs finally abated. "Everything is going to be okay. You're a survivor. You're a strong and capable woman, and you *will* become whoever you want to be."

"How?" Jagger rested his head on her arm and Ray hugged him close. "How the hell am I supposed to stop being afraid?"

"You told me before that one of your concerns about having your relationship with Carly made public was that your family would find out. Have you thought about talking to them about Carly on your own terms?"

Ray cringed. She hadn't even talked to her mom or sisters about the California weather. It was hard to imagine making the first phone call in months to chat about her sexuality. "I'm nervous."

"It can be extremely nerve-wracking for people to tell their families that they're in a same-sex relationship. How do you think yours will react?"

"Okay, but I don't know. I would probably tell my older sister Juliet first." Ray tried to imagine the conversation and her stomach knotted up. "She and I used to be close, but we haven't talked in a while. It seems weird to call her up and drop that bombshell."

"Maybe it would make you feel better. The anticipation is usually the worst part, regardless of the outcome. Keeping secrets is hard, and it takes a physical and emotional toll."

A flash of guilt stiffened her spine. That was what Carly had been trying to tell her, wasn't it? Too many secrets poisoned things. "I'll think about it. I promise."

"Do what you can. Carly would most likely be happy just to see some effort, if not a tidal change."

Ray pinched the bridge of her nose. Her head ached. "I really fucked things up."

"How did you two leave things tonight?"

The pain in her head intensified. "I yelled at Carly to get the fuck out of my house. So I was a complete asshole, and I'll be lucky if she ever speaks to me again."

"You don't think she will?"

"She said she would call me. That she wasn't going to abandon me." The thought was cold comfort. "But I don't know when I'll be ready to talk to her."

"Listen, you had a bad day. Tomorrow you have a chance to start making things better. You said Carly deserves better, right? Start taking steps to feel more confident about being in this relationship. That might mean talking to your family. It could also mean starting to challenge your negative predictions about what will likely happen if you go out in public with Carly. Once you get to a place where you feel you're worthy of Carly, you'll probably find that you're ready to talk to her."

"And what if I can't?"

Dr. Evans smiled. "You can."

CHAPTER TWENTY-THREE

Carly sewed one last suture, completing an uneventful neuter surgery on the six-month-old papillion puppy who was stretched out across the table. She handed the needle holder and scissors to Susan, who took them to be sterilized. Carly gently picked up the puppy and carried him to the kennel where he would recover. "All done, little guy."

"Beautiful work, Dr. Warner," Susan said. They walked out of the recovery room together, stripping off their caps and masks. "You make it look so easy."

Carly chuckled. "Only after a lot of practice, I assure you."

"I'll bet." Susan took off her surgical gloves and gestured for Carly to do the same. Throwing both pairs of gloves in the medical waste bin, she said, "You heading out to lunch now?"

"I was thinking about it. I'm sure Jack is dying to get out of my office for a bit."

Susan gave her a sidelong glance. "Your friend isn't watching him for you anymore, huh?"

Carly tried to keep her smile painted on, but faltered. She hadn't spoken to Ray in over a week, not for her lack of trying. Though she was careful not to flood Ray with phone calls, she had definitely made enough overtures to let Ray know she didn't intend to cut off contact. Unfortunately, Ray's silence sent a strong signal that she didn't want anything to do with Carly at the moment.

"No." Carly tried to sound casual. "She's got a lot going on, so Jack gets to hang out here for a while."

"Sorry, I wasn't trying to be nosy." Susan stopped in front of the restroom door so Carly also paused. "Or bring up a sensitive topic."

"Not at all." Carly knew from Susan's cautious tone that she had guessed the nature of her relationship with Ray. No matter how much Carly hated keeping it secret, she wanted to respect Ray's limits. "Nothing to be nosy about."

"Good." Susan put her hand on the bathroom door. "I've got to make a quick stop, so have a nice lunch."

"Thanks. Talk to you later."

Dr. Patterson poked his head out of his office down the hall. "Dr. Warner, did I hear that you're heading to lunch?"

"I sure am. Unless you need me to stick around?" She didn't mind. At lunch she had nothing to do but think about Ray. At least when she was working she could keep her thoughts focused on something other than her broken heart.

"Not for too long. But if you could spare a few minutes, I'd like to talk to you."

"Sure." Carly stepped into his office and shut the door behind them. She noted the ever-growing stacks of travel books on his desk with amusement. Now that the tallest pile leaned precariously to one side, it was probably silly not to say something about them. "Planning a vacation?"

Dr. Patterson grinned widely. "That's what I wanted to talk to you about."

"Okay." Carly read the spine of one of his books as she sat down. "I've heard Ireland is gorgeous. Have you been before?"

"I haven't." Dr. Patterson sat with a groan and a tired smile. "I've never been anywhere outside the country except Australia. A travesty I'm eager to put right."

Carly suspected where this conversation was going, and it sparked a heady mix of excitement and anticipation. "This will be a long trip, won't it?"

Dr. Patterson's smile became a toothy grin. "My wife has been begging me to retire for five years now. I've decided that she's probably smarter about these things than I am."

"Congratulations." Carly admired and respected Dr. Patterson, and she would be lying if she said she wouldn't miss him. But this could be an incredible opportunity for her, if she hadn't misread his desire for her to take over. "You've had a long and successful career. You deserve to enjoy everything else the world has to offer."

"I appreciate that. As much as I'm looking forward to globetrotting with my wife, I'll be sad to let this practice go." He raised a thick white eyebrow. "But it'll make it a heck of a lot easier if I know it's in good hands. I was hoping that you might consider taking it over when I leave. I'm prepared to offer it to you for a very reasonable price. That is, if you're interested in sticking around Bodega Bay."

For the first time since her fight with Ray, joy welled up in Carly. When she'd graduated from Davis, her goal was to one day own a private practice. To have her dream within reach was amazing. "I would like nothing more, Dr. Patterson. I love it here, and I love this practice."

"You're a very fine vet. I knew when I hired you that I could finally start thinking about retirement. I'm not sure I could bring myself to do it unless I knew someone like you would carry on for me."

"It means a lot to have your confidence. Thank you. And tell your wife that I'm happy for her."

Dr. Patterson snorted laughter. "Oh, she loves you for this. We should get together for dinner soon. Maybe you and I can spend the evening talking logistics about transferring the practice, then we can grab something to eat after."

"That sounds lovely." Eva Patterson was a sweet woman, and though seeing the two of them still deeply in love after thirty-five years of marriage inspired deep melancholy, Carly enjoyed their company. "Let me know when you two are free."

"I don't know if you have anyone in your life right now, but you're welcome to invite her along, too."

"Thank you," Carly said quietly. "It'll be just me, but I appreciate the offer."

"Ah. Well, in that case, Eva tells me that her friend's daughter recently moved back to the area and she's looking to meet people here. If you're interested, I can see if she wants to join us."

Now Dr. Patterson was trying to fix her up. Incredible. "I don't know if I'm up for that, but I'd love to have dinner with you and Eva."

Dr. Patterson patted her hand. "I promised Eva I would ask."

"I appreciate the offer, but I'm taking a break from my love life for a bit. Besides, I've got a new practice to tend to. That doesn't leave much time for a relationship." At least that's what she planned to tell herself. Dr. Patterson's retirement announcement couldn't have come at a better time. If she couldn't be with Ray, at least she would have plenty of work to bury herself in.

"I salute your work ethic. Just make sure to leave time for play. One day you'll find yourself done with work, and it's nice to have something else to look forward to."

Carly swallowed the grief that Dr. Patterson's gentle words elicited. "Point taken. Thank you."

"No." Dr. Patterson rose and she followed suit, shaking his hand firmly. "Thank you. From Eva and me."

Carly left Dr. Patterson's office feeling like she was floating. It was hard to process what had just happened. She looked around the back room silently, taking in the rows of kennels, the counters full of equipment, and the grooming tub. Matt clipped an excited mutt's nails, and Susan walked into an exam room with a chart in her hand. This would all be hers soon, a place where she could put down roots and build her career. Nadia's death had left her feeling aimless for so long, but with this one conversation, that lack of direction vanished. This was her life now.

It wasn't what she expected, not this place and not without Nadia, but she was happy. At least professionally. She burned to pick up the phone and tell Ray the good news, but she knew Ray wouldn't answer. Seeing a dream realized wasn't nearly as satisfying when you didn't have anyone to share the moment with.

Carly sighed and walked to her office. She might not have Ray, but at least she could call Leeann. And Leeann would be happy for her, even if it wasn't the same. Carly met Jack at her office door and clipped a leash to his collar, then pulled out her cell phone as they walked to the back door.

Leeann answered on the first ring. "Hey, girl."

"Hey." Carly walked to her car and got in. "I'm heading to lunch. You busy?"

"I can take a break. What's up?"

"I just got some exciting news." Carly pulled out of the lot and headed for the park down the street. Jack needed a walk more than she wanted food. "Dr. Patterson's planning to retire. He asked me to buy the practice and I accepted. We still need to work out the details, but it looks like I've got my own business."

Leeann whooped, making Carly grin. It wasn't a hug from Ray, but it was something. "That's awesome, honey. Just what you wanted."

"It does appear that things are falling into place." Carly quit smiling. *Some things, at least.*

"We need to celebrate. Let me buy you dinner." Leeann paused. "That is, if you're not planning to celebrate with Ray. You probably are. Just tell me when you're free and I'm there."

"Actually, I'm all yours tonight. How about I come to you?"

"Really? Is everything okay?"

Despite the concern in Leeann's voice, Carly didn't want to have this discussion. Not over the phone. "We can talk about it at dinner."

"Okay. But you're all right?"

"I'm fine," Carly said, though that wasn't true. "I can be down there by eight o'clock."

"Great. I'm taking you to Sutro's, if that sounds good to you."

"Perfect." Jack whined excitedly as they approached the park. Carly patted him on the head. "I've got a very anxious dog next to me who's expecting a brisk walk. I'll see you tonight?"

"Absolutely. And congratulations again. I'm so proud of you."

"Thanks." Carly pulled her keys from the ignition and relaxed against the seat. "I miss you. I'm glad we're having dinner."

"Me too. See you then."

Carly hung up and got out of the car. Jack hopped out after her and strained against his leash until she gave him a verbal correction, then reluctantly walked by her side. He had been stir-crazy without Ray and Jagger to keep him company while Carly was at work. Carly knew exactly how he felt. Life was a lot more boring without Ray in it.

❖

Leeann had secured a table near the window at Sutro's, giving them a gorgeous view of the white-topped Seal Rocks. The late-evening sun set the ocean on fire and bathed their tablecloth in warm light. Carly stared out the window, frustrated that all she could think about was how she wished Ray could see the spectacular sunset.

"You seem awfully down for someone who just got handed her own practice." Leeann sat with her hands folded on the table, staring at her cautiously. "Penny for your thoughts?"

Carly tore her gaze away from the ocean and shrugged half-heartedly. "It's been a rough week."

"I'm assuming it's not work that's been rough." When Carly shook her head, Leeann asked, "Is this about Ray?"

Though she technically had permission to tell Leeann about their relationship, Carly hesitated. Ray had caved to her request only under pressure, and despite Carly's conviction that she should have every right to talk to her best friend, she hated the circumstances under which she had gotten the okay.

"I'll take that as a yes," Leeann said. "What happened? Did she find out you had feelings for her?"

Carly put on a smile that threatened to shatter her face. No point to lie now. Leeann would see right through her. "Yeah, you could say that."

"Oh, no." Leeann reached across the table and took her hand. "I'm so sorry, honey. Was it bad?"

Carly shook her head as tears threatened to spill. "No. I found out that she had feelings for me first. When she kissed me."

Leeann blinked. "Okay, back up."

"I'm so sorry, Leeann. Ray didn't want me to tell you—"

"Wait a second. When did this happen?"

"A couple months ago."

Leeann collapsed back in her chair. "You're kidding me."

Carly shook her head. "No. We've been...well, I don't know if you'd call it dating. We've been together, I guess, for that long."

"Why didn't she want you to tell me?" Leeann sounded as hurt as Carly knew she would. They had shared the details of their romantic lives for so long that it was simply expected.

"She was nervous. She has trust issues. It has nothing to do with you personally, I promise. She wanted to keep the whole thing under wraps."

"So what happened?" Leeann took a sip of wine and rolled her eyes. "Based on your mood, I'm guessing there's trouble in paradise."

Carly gave Leeann a pleading look. The last thing she needed was sarcasm.

"Sorry," Leeann said. "I'm still trying to wrap my head around this. I can't believe I didn't know something was going on."

"I didn't like lying to you. I apologize for that. I don't like lying in general. Or being closeted."

"But that's the only way she feels comfortable being with a woman?"

Carly nodded. "At the moment, yes."

"That's rough. Especially for you." Leeann paused when their food arrived, then continued talking after their waiter walked away. "Did you guys have a fight?"

"Yeah." Carly took a bite of her dinner but had to choke it down. Her appetite had disappeared. "A bad one. She's become even more isolated since we got together. I was worried about her. And our relationship was getting serious, even though she apparently didn't want to be seen in public with me. So I told her I wasn't comfortable with all the secrets and suggested we take a break. Until she felt like she could be with me and still face the world."

"You broke up with her?" Leeann sounded incredulous.

"No." Carly bristled at the accusation. "I didn't break up with her. I suggested we spend some time apart. That was over a week ago. She hasn't been answering my calls, but I'm not giving up on making them."

"Wow. I mean, let's be honest. You and I both know I'm not convinced she's good for you. Especially after what you just told me. But I'm shocked that you ended things after only a couple months—"

"I didn't end things. We're taking a *break*."

"After all your talk about not being able to abandon her, not wanting to step back, why now? Don't get me wrong, I think it's probably for the best. But I can't believe you did it."

"Could you be with someone who wanted to keep your relationship secret from the rest of the world? No matter how much you loved them?"

"Of course not. But I wouldn't have gotten involved with Ray in the first place. That's not to say I'm right and you're wrong. The fact that you *would* be with her is one of the reasons I love you. You're a good, sweet person who gives people a chance, much more than I do. That's who you are at the core and it makes you beautiful."

"Well, even I have my limits." Carly took a hearty bite of food, barely tasting it.

"Do you think in this case, your limits have to do with Ray not turning into an out-and-proud lesbian in a couple months? Or is it maybe something else?"

Carly frowned. When Leeann laid it out there like that, it did seem a bit unreasonable to cut things off with Ray after only eight weeks. Hell, she had known going in that this was Ray's first relationship with a woman. Her first since Iraq. She knew Ray had issues. Hadn't she anticipated they wouldn't find their happily-ever-after without some struggle?

"It's not that I expected her to be out and proud." She had a logical reason for what she'd done. She just wished she could remember what it was. "I didn't like the way she lost all the gains she had made."

"I get that. I really do." Leeann set down her fork and stared at Carly so intently she squirmed. "Still, I can't help thinking that you're partially running away."

It stung because it had the ring of truth. "I would have expected you of all people to understand."

"I don't think you were wrong. You shouldn't have to be in a relationship that you can't even tell your best friend about. Most people wouldn't accept that. But it's interesting that you were steadfast until your relationship started to get serious. Then all of a sudden it became too much for you." Leeann shrugged.

"We were about to sleep together for the first time," Carly said in a low voice. "If I hadn't said something, I would've had to say it after we made love. That would be a huge betrayal. I didn't think that would be right."

"Listen, you know the situation better than me. I'm just surprised. I know how you felt about her."

"My feelings haven't changed." Carly put her fork down and pushed her plate away. No way would she get another bite down. "I love her, Leeann."

"I know."

"It scares me to death."

"I know it does."

"Maybe I am running away a little." Carly rubbed her eyes with the heels of her hands. "I don't know if I can take having my heart broken again."

"Life never offers any guarantees, honey. You know that." Leeann took Carly's hand and kissed it gently. "Granted, Ray is a huge unknown. But you'd most likely be scared even if she weren't dealing with these particular issues."

"You're probably right. I don't know how not to be scared, though."

"I'm not sure there's any way to turn off the fear. You know better than a lot of people what real loss feels like. And you don't want to experience it again. That's natural." Leeann squeezed her hand. "Part of healing is pushing past the fear so you can put yourself out there again. I don't think you'll be truly happy unless you do that."

"That's a gloomy thought." Sighing, Carly looked out the window again. A flock of sea birds circled the rocks that jutted out of the water, startling points of white in the darkening sky. "I wasn't unhappy before Ray came along."

"No, but you weren't all that happy. You *were* safe."

"I liked safe," Carly said. "I miss safe."

"How about Ray? Do you miss her?"

A tear escaped from Carly's eye and she caught it on her finger, wiping it away. "Desperately."

CHAPTER TWENTY-FOUR

Her hands are tied behind her back. The plastic cuffs chafe her wrists and warm blood drips down her fingers from her futile struggle to break loose. At least it distracts her from the shooting pain in her broken leg. Her cuffed feet rest in a large pool of blood, but it's not hers. They have her sitting in the same chair Archer was in when they cut off his head.

The guttural sounds of Arabic are being spoken behind the closed door of this windowless room. They plan to kill her. The video camera they used to record Archer's murder is pointed at her, watchful on its tripod. How does it feel to be decapitated? When will awareness end? Will she feel the knife slice across her throat?

Then the voices disappear. She isn't sure how she knows, but her captors are gone. They aren't coming back. She begins to struggle anew, but the restraints hold firm, digging deeper into her tender wrists. If she could just stand up and open the door, she can go home. She can go back to the way things used to be before, and she'll be able to put this place behind her forever.

Except she can't break free. And no one is coming to rescue her. The cuffs on her wrists grow tighter, and the horror of knowing that she will die here, after all, consumes her—

Ray's eyes snapped open and she inhaled sharply. Heart racing, she took in the broad stripe of early-morning light painted across the foot of her bed. Jagger's solid bulk pressed against her side, and as her breathing evened out, he gave her a sloppy kiss on the cheek. The slobbery gesture should have grossed her out, but all she felt was deep relief.

"I'm home." Ray rolled onto her side to clutch at Jagger. Burying her face in his broad neck, she murmured, "I'm home and I'm safe."

The mantra usually reassured her after a nightmare, but this morning it didn't ease her disquiet. She grasped at the rapidly fading details of the dream so she could remember why it had been so terrifying. Usually she tried to push her nightmares out of her head as soon as she woke, but this one was different. Her dreams of Iraq never carried any sense of hope, but this one had, if only for an instant. This time it was up to her to escape, to leave that room behind, and she hadn't been able to. That disturbed her even more than the dreams that ended with a knife to her throat.

If she had the power to save herself, she damn well wanted to.

Ray glanced at the digital clock on her nightstand. Seven in the morning. Carly was probably still sleeping—she loved to sleep in on Saturdays. Unless Jack had already woken her up to go potty. Ray smiled at the thought of Carly grumbling, still half asleep, as she let Jack outside.

She shifted her gaze to her cell phone and stopped smiling. Untangling herself from Jagger, she grabbed it off the nightstand and dialed the number of her voice mailbox. She punched in her passcode then pushed the button to play the message she'd saved last night before bed.

"Hey, Ray. It's Carly. Um, I don't really know what to say at this point. It's been over two weeks now, and I'm—I don't know how I am. Are you even listening to these voice mails? Or am I just making an ass of myself by continuing to leave them? I wish you'd answer my calls. I miss you and I love you very much. Please call me, okay? Let's talk about this. You don't have to go through this alone. I love you. Okay, bye."

Ray saved the message again and hung up. She ached to return Carly's call, but knew she wouldn't. At least not yet. Not when she had nothing to show for their time apart. She hadn't had any breakthroughs. Sure, she had gone to buy groceries, but that didn't mean a lot. Especially when she wasn't sure she would have gone if Carly had been with her.

Ray gave Jagger a pat on the back. "Ready to go outside, big boy?"

Jagger opened his mouth in a mighty yawn and lumbered off the bed, stretching until he nearly fell onto his stomach. Ray laughed at his clumsy attempt to start the day. She met him at the foot of the bed and they walked to the door together. He left the bedroom before her, sniffing a path to the back sliding door. Ray let them both into the backyard and soaked in the crisp morning breeze while Jagger took care of business.

Summer was nearly here. Though the ocean still sent cool air inland, the sun overhead bathed her with slight warmth even this early in the day. Ray had mixed feelings about the change of season. Though she enjoyed the weather, she mourned the passing of time. Tomorrow was the first day of June. In just over a week Jack's agility trial would happen. No matter how scared she had been to go out in public with Carly, she wouldn't have missed that. Not after she and Jack worked so hard to prepare.

"Too late now," Ray murmured. Disappointment sliced through her. No way would she make the kind of progress Dr. Evans had suggested in that time. Let alone feel like she was good enough to go back to Carly.

The dream came back to her in a flash. The helplessness of being tied to that chair, unable to escape. Experiencing a brief surge of hope, only to have it crushed when she realized she couldn't help herself. Ray tightened her hands into fists. She was so fucking tired of feeling helpless and hopeless. And she missed Carly like crazy.

Without letting herself second-guess what she was about to do, Ray walked back to her bedroom and grabbed her cell phone. She pulled up her contacts and navigated down the list until she found Juliet's number. It was ten o'clock in Boston and her older sister had never been a late sleeper, so it was probably safe to call. Besides, if she didn't do it now she wasn't sure when she would work up the courage again.

Ray walked back to the den listening to the phone ring. Part of her hoped Juliet wouldn't answer, but mostly she prayed she would. Dr. Evans was right. Anticipation was terrible. She just wanted to get this over with.

Juliet answered as Ray let Jagger back into the house. "Ray?"

Juliet's obvious surprise made her ashamed for taking so long to make this call. She had once been close to her sister, but they had barely spoken since she returned from Iraq. "Hey, Jules."

"Oh my God." Juliet sounded like she might cry. "How are you? It's so good to hear from you."

"I'm okay." It was true enough. "How are you? How's Tom?"

"We're great. We just finished remodeling our upstairs bathroom, so we're finally getting the house back in order." Juliet laughed. "But that's not really that interesting, right? Let me hear about you. How's California?"

"I like it. I've got a little house near the ocean, the weather is a hell of a lot better than Michigan—"

"Or Boston, probably."

"Probably." Ray sat down on the couch and rubbed a hand over her face. No matter how nervous she was to tell Juliet about Carly, she couldn't deny that it felt good to hear her voice. "I'm so sorry I didn't call you sooner."

"It's okay. I know you've had a lot on your plate."

"Yeah. I've been doing better, though. Did Mom tell you I got a therapy dog?"

"She mentioned that. She misses you, by the way. I bet she'd love to hear from you."

Ray's throat went dry. She could only worry about talking to one of them at a time. "I know. I'm…it's hard."

"She knows that. That's why she's been trying to give you space. We all have. She's just worried about you. You know how she is."

"Yeah." Ray cleared her throat. She could make small talk or try to get the hard part out of the way. Maybe if she could figure out how to bring up Carly, she would be able to relax and enjoy the rest of the conversation. "Danny called me a few months ago. Did you hear he's getting married?"

"I did," Juliet said cautiously. "How do you feel about that?"

"It's great. I mean, it's weird. But I'm glad he's doing well."

"Allison met his fiancée. She said she's nice."

Ray snorted at the thought of their outspoken younger sister sizing up Danny's new girlfriend. "I'm sure that was interesting."

"How about you?" Juliet's voice sounded cheerful, but had an undercurrent of resignation. Almost like she already knew the answer and was disappointed. "Have you met any hot California guys yet?"

This was it. Juliet had given her the perfect opening. All she needed to do now was speak up. Ray opened her mouth and hesitated, scared of what might happen after the words were out. What if Juliet thought she was disgusting and hung up? What if she told her husband, who told someone else?

"I'm sorry," Juliet said in a rush. "I wasn't trying to be insensitive. Forget I asked."

Ray took a calming breath. This was her sister, for God's sake. Juliet loved her and cared about her. The chances that she would hang up on her or otherwise betray her were slim. She had never given Ray any reason to think she would react with anything other than curiosity or even pleasure. Juliet wanted her to be happy, and since Carly made her happy, Juliet would most likely be okay with this revelation.

"No, I'm sorry." Ray closed her eyes and leapt. "I was trying to figure out how to tell you that I have met someone. She's a hot California girl, though."

Silence. Then delighted laughter. "You mean—"

"Her name is Carly. She's my dog's veterinarian."

"And you guys are—"

"Yeah." From Juliet's obvious mirth, it was clear that Ray hadn't needed to worry. "It surprised me, too."

"I'll bet. So tell me about her. What's she like?"

All the anxiety that had been coiled up in Ray's stomach dissipated as she launched into excited chatter. It felt great to confide in someone who wasn't her therapist, especially because Juliet was so receptive.

"She sounds wonderful," Juliet said finally. "I can't tell you how happy I am to know that you've got someone out there."

Ray felt her grin slip away as reality washed over her. It wasn't like she actually had Carly, at least not at the moment. But hopefully talking to Juliet was a good first step to finding her way back.

"She's helped me so much," Ray said. "And I haven't been the easiest person to deal with, to say the least."

"You're worth it. She's lucky to have you."

If only Ray could be so confident. "Thanks, Jules. For everything. I was so scared to tell you about all this, and you've been great. It's such a relief."

"You were scared? What did you think I would say?"

"I don't know. I wasn't sure how you would react. I'm still not sure how Mom and Allison will react."

"They love you, Ray. Just like I do. They'll be happy if you're happy. I promise."

Ray realized she was crying only when she felt tears streaming down her face. "I hope so."

"I promise. We're your family and we're so proud of you. Nothing you could do will change that."

Ray wiped her tears away. "Everything seems scary these days. I've been struggling with the idea of people finding out about Carly and me. I have these visions of magazine articles and my picture plastered all over the Internet—"

"Hey, the important part is that Carly loves you, your family loves you, and you're happy. That's it. I know it's probably trite to say this, but screw the rest of the world. Right?"

It was a little trite, but Ray appreciated the sentiment. "Right."

"This might be a good time to tell you that I slept with a girl in college."

"What?" Ray sputtered shocked laughter. "When did you have time with all those boyfriends you brought home?"

"I made time, believe me. It was a lot of fun, actually."

So her sister had more experience with lesbian sex than she did. That was about the last thing she'd expected to learn today. "I had no idea."

"I didn't want to tell you when you were in the military. I knew you were a little…put off by that whole topic."

"Yeah. Times have changed."

"Clearly." Juliet paused. "Thank you for calling, Ray. It was great talking to you. And I'm honored you told me about Carly. I'm so excited for you."

"Time to get off the phone?"

"Yeah, Tom and I are going hiking with another couple. If I don't get ready now, we'll be late."

"I don't want to make you late. I'll talk to you soon?"

"That would be wonderful. Could I call you tomorrow when I have more time?"

"Awesome. Looking forward to it."

"I love you, sis."

"I love you, too. Bye." Ray hung up smiling. Any remaining traces of her nightmare disappeared. She had her sister back.

When she'd picked up the phone she thought she was calling Juliet for Carly. To prove that she could make progress, that she wouldn't hide from everyone forever. But talking to Juliet had been as much for her as Carly. Just as finally talking to Danny had lifted a weight off her shoulders, reconnecting with her sister provided the unexpected thrill of feeling like the old Ray, even if just for a little while.

Ray brought her contacts list up again. She had a couple more phone calls to make.

CHAPTER TWENTY-FIVE

Carly accidentally found the video online. At first she almost didn't watch it, afraid she'd stumbled upon the record of Sergeant Robert Archer's murder. But the screen grab showed a grainy picture of Ray looking frightened and wearing a headscarf in front of a colorful tapestry, so she took a chance and clicked Play.

This was her first time watching Ray's hostage video, but Carly remembered hearing about the message the insurgents forced Ray to read. An anti-American, pro-Jihadist statement that some in the media had criticized her for reciting, even though a disembodied hand held a knife to her throat throughout the minute-long clip. Ray's voice was flat and unaffected, clearly disassociated from her words.

Carly shivered when the video ended. She had followed the news coverage during the hostage crisis, but since meeting Ray had only read dry facts on Wikipedia to refresh her memory. Seeing stills from this video years ago had been chilling, but now that she had held Ray in her arms, the images were horrifying. The fear in Ray's eyes, the sharp blade against her neck seared into Carly's brain, and she had to push her chair back from her computer and stand up to get away.

Shakily, Carly sat cross-legged on the floor next to Jack's pillow. He opened his eyes and lifted his head, always ready to wake from a nap for some excitement. Carly wrapped her arms around him, needing the comfort. He sighed and laid his head back down.

"She went through so much," Carly whispered. It helped to talk through her conflicted thoughts aloud, and Jack was the perfect audience. No judgment, the consummate listener. "I can't imagine how

I would have handled being in that situation. Let alone everything else that happened to her over there."

It was easy to know something without dwelling on what it really meant. Of course she was aware of the horror Ray had endured, but watching that video brought everything into focus in a way that left her shaken and slightly ashamed. It was a wonder Ray wasn't institutionalized. That her biggest issues centered around the ability to do things like go to the grocery store or walk on the beach was a miracle.

And she had given Ray a hard time because she wasn't ready to be out as a lesbian.

It was more complicated than that, but since dinner with Leeann, Carly had been beating herself up over her rush to put the brakes on her relationship with Ray. Her concerns were valid, but Leeann raised a good point. Maybe Carly had been too quick to step back when things started getting serious. Surely she could have addressed her worries with Ray in a more sensitive way.

It was scary to imagine losing another lover, but was even worse to think that she might have sabotaged a chance for true happiness. Perhaps if she had offered to stand by Ray while she dealt with her fears, or at the very least tried to talk through them with Ray instead of asking her to work them out on her own, things would be different now. She knew Ray wanted to get better. Leaving probably hadn't been the only or even the best option.

Carly glanced at the phone. How many unanswered calls had she made over the past few weeks? She had no way of knowing if Ray was listening to her messages, though she hoped she wasn't leaving them in vain. Knowing it was probably futile, she tried again. She owed Ray an apology, even if she couldn't do it in person.

Carly wasn't surprised when her call rang through to voice mail. She listened to the generic outgoing message, wishing that Ray had recorded something personal. She longed to hear Ray's voice, and even a canned greeting would be nice.

When the voice mail beeped, Carly closed her eyes. "Hey, Ray. Me again. I promise I'm not stalking you. I just need you to hear me out. I've been thinking a lot and—" Here went nothing. "I screwed up. We had issues we needed to work out, absolutely, but I was a coward to ask you to deal with them alone. It was unfair. And so I'm sorry. I know what it took for you to trust me in the first place, so maybe asking for another chance is really pushing my luck, but here I am, asking. I want to do right by you so badly. I promise never to leave you alone with your demons again, if you can find it in your heart to forgive me."

Carly paused. Surely Ray remembered that Jack's agility trial was tomorrow, and the last thing Carly wanted to do was pressure Ray by mentioning it. Though Ray had clearly wanted to go at one point, things were different now. And it wasn't worth making Ray feel as though anything hinged on her attendance. Still, Carly wanted to be sure that Ray knew where she would be, if she did try to call.

"I'm taking Jack to the agility trial in Santa Rosa tomorrow, so if you call and I don't answer, that's why. I love you, Ray. Please call me."

Carly disconnected and slipped the phone into the pocket of her pajama pants. Improbable as a return call might be, she didn't want to risk missing it. All she could do was hope that Ray really listened to what she had to say. The rest, unfortunately, was out of her hands.

CHAPTER TWENTY-SIX

Ray fiddled with her key chain as she replayed Carly's voice mail for the third time in a row. Because she had also listened five times before going to bed the night before, she knew the words by heart. That didn't make it any less important to hear them again now. Standing on her front porch with Jagger at her side, Ray was trying to work up the nerve to get in her truck. Jack's agility trial began in fifty minutes, so if she wanted to make it there on time, she needed to leave immediately.

Carly's apology sounded so sad. Apparently Ray's silence had led her to take all the responsibility for their separation, even as Ray came to a different conclusion. Though she appreciated Carly's promise never again to leave her alone with her demons, being away from Carly had forced her to deal with some issues she never imagined she could. Right or wrong, the possibility of losing Carly made Ray realize that if she wanted to be in a relationship with someone, she had to push herself even harder than she did when she was alone. Because it wasn't all about her anymore.

Ray closed her phone and tucked it into her pocket. She had wanted to go to the event before their separation, but she wasn't positive she would have. Now she didn't have a choice. Though Carly wouldn't hold it against her if she didn't, Ray needed to swallow her fear and go. For Jack, for Carly, for herself.

"Easier said than done," Ray said to Jagger. "Right?"

With his large yellow eyes and solemn face, Jagger always looked as though he were commiserating with whatever she said. Ray rubbed his ears, then exhaled.

"We can do this," she murmured under her breath. She could do anything, right? After coming out to both her sisters and her mother on the same exhilarating day, something like this shouldn't faze her. She just had to drive to Santa Rosa and sit in a crowd of spectators who would be paying more attention to the competing dogs than to her.

Piece of cake.

Ray snorted. This was anything but a piece of cake. But she would do it anyway. To prove to Carly and to herself that she could, and to show Carly that she would do absolutely anything to keep her.

Drawing up every ounce of her courage, Ray stepped off the porch with Jagger in tow. She buckled them into the car quickly, then turned the truck's engine over and pulled out of the driveway in one swift motion. If she didn't allow herself to hesitate, hopefully she would reach a point where it would be too late to back out. Because the last thing she wanted was to back out now.

She had considered returning Carly's call last night, but held back for the same reason she'd stayed silent for the past week. She didn't want to make any promises she couldn't keep, and she hadn't been sure she would be able to work up the nerve to go today. It had seemed easier to say nothing and hope for the best, even while reserving the right to fail miserably at this test of her new resolve. Going to the agility trial had taken on epic importance in her mind, and if she was going to chicken out she didn't want to disappoint Carly too.

What would Carly think if Ray managed to show up? Or, rather, *when* Ray showed up? She would be proud, no doubt. But would she be upset that Ray hadn't called first? Or even offered to ride with her? Carly had to be frustrated by Ray's failure to return her calls, even though she sounded more worried than irritated. Especially when Ray gave no indication that continuing to call was anything but a pointless waste of time.

And yet the calls kept coming, bless Carly's heart. Some part of her had been testing Carly, trying to determine whether she would cut and run at the first sign of trouble. These past few weeks weren't among Ray's finest moments, though she liked to think she had achieved some measure of grace here at the end. Being honest with her family about Carly, and having their relationship accepted, was huge. It got her ready to take the next step, which was to invite Carly back into her life.

Maybe now she could be worthy of Carly's love.

Ray took in a road sign with surprise. She hadn't even noticed when Bodega Highway turned into Highway 12. Like it or not, she was fast approaching her destination. This was the point of no return she had been hoping to reach. Resolved, she kept moving forward.

She had plugged the address into her GPS and now she started obeying the spoken directions, concentrating on the maze of streets she drove through rather than dwelling on what awaited her at the fairgrounds. She wore a baseball cap and her favorite pair of sunglasses, so she doubted anyone would recognize her. She had no reason to be nervous. Everyone was there to watch the dogs, not worry about who the shy woman with the Great Dane might be.

Ray kept up the internal pep talk as she drove into a large parking lot and found a spot near the back wall. She pulled into a space and turned off the truck quickly, so she wouldn't be tempted to back right out again. Putting her keys in her pocket, she sat with her hands on the steering wheel and closed her eyes.

"I am the captain of my soul." Ray gripped the wheel tight to stop the trembling of her hands. She thought of Carly's strawberry-blond hair and how soft it was against her face when they held one another. Then the way Carly's curves felt beneath her fingers. "I'm doing this, goddamn it. Right now."

She grabbed Jagger's leash and didn't look back.

People and dogs were everywhere. For a moment Ray forgot her nerves as she marveled at the bustling activity. This should make her nervous, so much movement, so many people, but the dogs kept her calm. They trotted next to their owners, all of them grinning and excited, and their enthusiasm was infectious. Even Jagger seemed to pick up on the positive energy, galumphing at her side happily as they made their way into the stands around the large dirt arena where the agility course was set up.

Ray saw a series of jumps, two tunnels, an A-frame and a dogwalk, and of course the dreaded weave poles. She smiled as she sat down with Jagger, taking in the entire course. She hadn't worked with Jack in weeks, unfortunately, but she knew he could handle everything that came at him today. Excitement built in the pit of her stomach, slowly replacing the fear she had been carrying around for days.

A surreptitious look around confirmed that, as she guessed, nobody was paying attention to her. One woman glanced at Jagger, grinned, then returned her focus to the agility course at a comment from the man sitting next to her. Everyone seemed similarly involved in their own conversations and private thoughts, hardly a look spared in her direction.

Not bad. She was just another face in the crowd, nobody worth noticing. All her worries began to seem a little silly, maybe even self-centered. Obviously she wasn't nearly as interesting to these people as their dogs or the competition about to begin.

With a sigh of relief, Ray returned her attention to the course. Her stomach clenched when her gaze landed on Carly, who stood beside the dirt ring with Jack on a nylon lead. Carly didn't seem to notice Ray, but she scanned the stands intently, and Ray knew that eye contact was inevitable. Ray braced herself not to react, but couldn't stop the tidal wave of emotion that swept her away when Carly looked directly at her, then put a hand on a metal railing as though steadying herself.

Ray was glad she was wearing sunglasses to hide the tears that filled her eyes. Carly's face showed a mixture of love, heartache, and wonder that kicked Ray's heart rate up a notch. Feeling like somebody else was controlling her body, Ray got to her feet and walked down to meet Carly beside the ring. Now that their eyes had met, Ray couldn't wait another minute to break their weeks-long silence.

When Jack spotted Ray, he wagged his tail and whined excitedly. Carly took a step forward then stopped, glancing around at the people who surrounded them. Ray could see the conflict in Carly's eyes, the desire to greet her warring with concern about how to do so in public. Ray closed the distance between them and bent to scratch Jack behind the ears, never taking her eyes off Carly's face.

"I'm sorry," Ray said. "I didn't mean to get him all amped up right before you guys go out there."

Carly blinked as though she had expected Ray to say something else. "Oh. No, it's okay. Hi."

"Hi." Ray straightened and managed a weak smile when Carly greeted Jagger with a pat on the side. "You look beautiful."

Carly kept a straight face, but her cheeks flushed. "I wasn't expecting to see you here. Thank you for coming."

"I couldn't miss it. Not after all the time I spent practicing with Jack." Ray lowered her gaze, not that Carly could see behind her sunglasses. "Not when I could show you that I'm getting better."

Carly twisted Jack's leash in her hand. "Did you get my voice mail?"

"All of them. I'm sorry I haven't called. There's no excuse."

Carly shook her head. "I'm the one who said we should spend time apart." She spoke so quietly Ray could barely hear her above the crowd.

Ray opened her mouth to respond, but an announcement over the loudspeaker cut her off. Carly tilted her head to listen. "We're almost up," she said. "Can you hold Jack while I go listen to the judge's briefing?"

"Sure." Ray took his leash and gave Carly a cautious smile. "You'll do great."

"I'll be back to get him in a few minutes. He's one of the first dogs out, so you won't have to wait long to see him."

Ray nodded. She would stay until Carly was ready to leave, regardless of when Jack finished his run. They desperately needed to talk, and Ray wanted to do it as soon as possible. Being this close to Carly with no privacy was excruciating. All she wanted was to take Carly into her arms and kiss her silly. She had missed her, but until this moment she had no idea how badly.

"We'll be sitting over there." Ray nodded toward the stands. Carly jogged over to a woman holding a clipboard who stood in front of a group of about ten other handlers. Casual in a T-shirt and track pants, with her hair gathered into a loose ponytail, Carly made Ray's hands itch to touch her.

Carly glanced back and beamed, then turned her attention to the judge. Certain that she was being overly obvious about how in love she was, Ray tore her eyes away. At her side, Jack and Jagger were going nuts greeting one another, licking each other's faces and stumbling over each other's paws in their attempts to get closer. Three weeks was clearly a hell of a long time for dogs.

Who was she kidding? If it hadn't been totally improper, Carly would have gotten approximately the same greeting from her.

Ray sat down and waited for Carly to return, which only took five minutes. She offered Jack's leash, expecting Carly to take it and leave for the ring, but was surprised when Carly settled down next to her instead.

"We're sixth." Carly grabbed Jack's leash and kissed him on top of his head, avoiding Ray's eyes. "Do you mind if we sit with you for a few minutes before we line up?"

"Of course not."

Carly glanced around at the crowd, then tentatively met Ray's gaze. "How are you doing with this?"

"Not too bad." Ray joined Carly's scan of the people surrounding them. "Better than I expected. Nobody's paying me any attention."

"Good." Carly clasped her hands in her lap. "I'm really proud of you. This is big, coming here."

"Thank you." Taking a deep breath, Ray covered Carly's hands with one of her own, giving her a brief squeeze. "I've had a lot of time to think. Maybe when this is over we can go home and talk."

"I'd like that," Carly whispered. Eyes shiny with unshed tears, she gave Ray a pained smile. "We have a lot to talk about."

"I know." Ray looked away. "I'm sorry I yelled at you."

"We were both very emotional that day. It's forgotten."

"No, it's not. But I appreciate your forgiveness."

"Always." Carly looked at the agility course, and for the first time Ray realized that a dog and its handler were running through the obstacles. "Jack and I need to get to our spot now. We're up soon."

"You guys will do great." Ray looked at Jack, who wagged his tail madly at the attention. Scratching up and down his sides, she told him, "You can do it, buddy."

"You'll be here when we finish?" Carly looked scared to walk away, like Ray might disappear if she did.

"Of course."

Nodding, Carly stood. "Then wish us luck."

"You won't need it. But good luck anyway."

"Thanks." Carly trotted off with Jack following energetically.

Ray wrapped her arm around Jagger and pulled him close to her side. He laid his head against her shoulder and groaned, seemingly content to cuddle up and watch the other dogs quietly. The border collie who flew through the obstacles in front of them was Jagger's polar opposite, all controlled energy and fluid movement. Jagger had many skills, but he moved like a clumsy elephant most of the time. He was the right color, too.

"That's okay," Ray murmured as she took in the pure athleticism of the smaller dog. "I happen to love baby elephants."

Though she remained aware of the crowd, Ray found it fairly easy to concentrate on the action on the agility course. Occasionally she would feel eyes on her back, but every time she glanced around she found no one watching. When Carly and Jack finally stepped into the ring, everything else faded away.

Carly looked both nervous and excited. Pretty much exactly what Ray was feeling. She led Jack to the starting spot and slipped off his collar, tossing his leash behind her. He sat still in front of her, vibrating with energy. Ray grinned. It took a lot for Jack to rein in his natural exuberance, and he was showing admirable restraint in not tearing across the field.

A bell sounded and Carly took off jogging toward the first obstacle, a low jump. Jack followed at her command, completing the jump easily. Carly stayed five feet in front of him, directing him to three more jumps, then a tunnel, then over the dogwalk. Ray's heart lodged in her throat as she followed his progress around the course. So far, so good. Beyond one brief moment where he threatened to lose focus, he was running through the obstacles like a champ.

Ray held her breath as Jack approached the weave poles. She had no idea if Carly had practiced with him during their time apart, and this was by far his weakest obstacle. Shoulders tense, she watched as he slipped between the first two poles, then deftly weaved in and out of the line of ten poles. Not the fastest dog, certainly, but he did it.

Even from across the ring, Ray could see the joy on Carly's face when Jack emerged from the poles. With a hand gesture and a brief shout, she directed him toward the last two low jumps, then to the designated finish line. Carly whooped out loud when he got there, and Jack hopped around her legs excitedly. Ray's face hurt from a grin she couldn't suppress, watching the two of them celebrate their victory.

Carly slipped Jack's collar back on and exited the ring. She stopped to say something to a woman holding a clipboard near the judge's table, then jogged to the stands.

Carly's excitement was so infectious that Ray stood and immediately swept her into a tight hug. Brushing her lips against Carly's cheek, she said, "That was awesome! You guys did so well."

"Thanks," Carly said breathlessly. Her hands landed on Ray's back. "I was really geeked when he did those weave poles."

Ray pulled back slightly, too excited to care about how long she was lingering in Carly's arms. They hadn't been this close in weeks, and it was hard not to kiss Carly.

"You did a wonderful job teaching him, Ray. Congratulations." Carly squeezed Ray's biceps lightly, eyes sparkling. "Are you up for sticking around for the rest of the trial with me?"

"Sure." Ray stepped away from Carly, glancing back at the stands. Even with the show she and Carly had just put on, they weren't drawing any attention. She was both embarrassed and relieved. Her overwhelming fear of being out in public had almost certainly been overblown. Sure, anything could happen. But that didn't mean it would.

"Want to sit down?" Carly asked.

"Please." Jack had his head on her thigh as soon as she was seated. Ray rubbed his ears and grinned.

"I still can't believe you came." Carly scratched Jack's chest, grazing Ray's arm.

"I love you," Ray whispered. "I wanted to show you I could."

"I'm sorry if I made you feel like you needed to prove something to me. It would have been okay if you hadn't made it today, you know. It wouldn't have changed how I feel about you."

"But it may have changed how I feel about myself. I'm tired of being helpless."

Carly bit her lip. "We need to stay for the ribbons ceremony, but do you want to get out of here after that?"

Ray nodded. All she wanted was to get Carly alone. They had a lot to talk about, but she felt ready to work things out. "Yes."

Exhaling, Carly turned her attention to the arena. "I'll try to think about dogs in the meantime."

Ray chuckled. At the moment, that was easier to say than to do.

CHAPTER TWENTY-SEVEN

After the ceremony in which Jack was awarded a ribbon and a squeaky toy for his performance, Carly followed Ray's truck back to Bodega Bay. Unfortunately for both of them, Carly had forgotten her cell phone and so it would be a long, silent fifty minutes before they could begin to hash out the last few weeks. Riding separately was torture when all Carly wanted was to be with Ray. Their brief hug at the fairgrounds had triggered a deep, physical need that Carly had been trying hard to suppress. Now that it had surfaced, it wouldn't be easy to shut down again.

When they finally pulled into Ray's driveway, Carly threw open the car door and called for Jack to follow. Ray hopped out of her truck and helped Jagger out the passenger side, then they both hurried to the front door. Carly's breath caught when Ray pulled off her sunglasses, revealing the hazel eyes she had so missed gazing into.

"I'm sorry the place is a bit of a mess," Ray said as she unlocked the door.

"I doubt it is." Carly had learned that Ray's idea of messy was roughly equivalent to her own concept of sparkling clean. When they stepped into the house, Carly laughed. "My house hasn't looked like this since I moved in."

Ray smiled shyly. "Well, I've got some dishes in the sink."

"Let's just avoid the kitchen, then."

"Probably best." Ray hesitated, then took Carly's hand and silently led her to the couch in the den. Releasing Carly, she sagged against the cushions. "Now that I've got you here, I'm nervous."

"Why?"

"Because of the way we left things last time." Ray's jaw tightened. "Because of the way I behaved."

"I don't blame you for getting upset." Carly took Ray's hand again, needing the contact. "I made a mistake, telling you that we should spend time apart. I'm sorry."

"No, you were right. I asked you for impossible things. You deserve better than someone who doesn't want to be seen with you."

Carly's chest ached. What Ray said was true, but Carly should have asked for what she needed in a more sensitive way. "And you deserve someone who understands that recovery takes time and that sometimes there are setbacks. I'm sorry I wasn't that person."

Ray looked down at their joined hands and lifted the corner of her mouth. "How about we both say we hope we can be better in the future?" She met Carly's eyes tentatively. "We do have a future, right?"

"I hope so." Carly blinked back tears at the thought of life without Ray. "I want to try for one."

"Me too."

Carly thought she had sabotaged things between them, and now she felt boneless with relief. "I was scared. I saw all the ways that loving you could lead to heartbreak, and I acted out of fear and pushed you away. Only to realize that being scared is better than the alternative."

"You also acted out of concern. I was having trouble coping with the idea of people knowing I was with a woman, and I should have talked to you about it. Instead I tried to hide it, and you did what you thought was right. I get that. I didn't at the time, but I do now."

"I was concerned. I am concerned. I don't want to see everything you've worked so hard to achieve slip away because of me." Carly shifted closer to Ray. "You are so strong, and so brave, and I want you to be happy. I know it can't be easy, any of it, and being in a relationship like this certainly doesn't make things any easier."

"I was afraid of becoming a media story again. Scared that my family would find out I was with a woman by watching the news." Ray flushed. "I should have talked to you so you could understand what I was thinking. But I worried that knowing you could be trotted out for public consumption would scare you away."

"Nah." Carly had no doubt it wouldn't be fun, but three weeks without Ray had shown her there were far worse fates. "I can handle it."

"I hope you won't have to."

"Me too." Carly smiled and touched Ray's face. "For both our sakes."

Ray returned her smile. "I told my mom and my sisters about you. Found out my sister Juliet slept with a girl in college. I'm not sure I'll ever shake that image, but it was worth it."

Shocked, Carly said, "You told them? Everything?"

"Well, not the sordid details. But I told them I've fallen for a veterinarian named Carly, who is a wonderful woman. They were all really happy for me. And obviously quite relieved. It was good to talk to them."

"Wow." That Ray had somehow found the courage to come out to her family filled Carly with hope that everything would indeed be okay.

Ray wrapped an arm around Carly and pulled her close. "Thank you. For some reason I'd been avoiding talking to them, but I feel so much better now. And not only telling them about us, you know? Just talking to my family again. I've missed them."

Carly put both arms around Ray and rested her chin on a strong shoulder. She closed her eyes, savoring Ray's heartbeat against her chest. "That's amazing, Ray. I never expected that so soon. But I'm really happy for you."

"Well, you were right. I was insisting on total secrecy, and a relationship can't thrive under those conditions."

Carly could tell that Ray had been talking to her therapist. That was a good sign. "Just so you know, I don't expect to hold hands and kiss on the street. That's not what I was asking."

"I know. Doesn't mean that's not something to work toward. One day."

"Wow." That was probably the last thing Carly had expected to hear. Whether or not Carly had been right to suggest time apart, it appeared to have done Ray a lot of good. "Well, for now I'd settle for the easy stuff."

"None of it's easy."

Carly had a flash of Ray in that headscarf, knife pressed to her throat. "No, you're right. I'm sure it's not."

"All I can do is promise that I will try my hardest. Always."

"That's all I can ask."

"And all I ask is that you give me a chance. Even if I stumble."

Carly blushed, ashamed that Ray even had to appeal for such a thing. "You were right, you know. I did tell you I would be patient, and I knew perfectly well what I was getting into with you. I should have helped you work through your fears. It wasn't fair to run away like I did."

"I appreciate that. A lot. Thank you."

"Let's promise each other something," Carly said. "In the future we'll talk about our fears instead of just reacting to them."

"I promise."

"Good. Me, too." Carly stared into Ray's eyes, something stirring deep in her belly. "I love you, Ray. I don't want to lose you."

"I'm not going anywhere."

Carly felt a twinge of fear. That wasn't a promise anyone could make. But it was the best Ray could do. And it would have to be enough. "I'm going to kiss you now, okay?"

"Okay." Ray's voice caught and she gripped Carly's arms, drawing her closer. "I love you so much."

Knowing that words could never come close to expressing what she felt, Carly pressed her lips to Ray's and almost burst into tears at how much this felt like coming home. Ray inhaled sharply when Carly pressed her tongue inside, then clutched her as though frightened she would draw away.

Though they hadn't kissed in weeks, there was nothing tentative about their joining. Ray pressed Carly back against the sofa cushions, easing on top of her with a newfound confidence that set Carly on fire. Carly wrapped her legs around Ray and used her hands to trace the contours of Ray's face as they kissed. She groaned at the sheer decadence of Ray's heavy weight on her and the knowledge that they had no place else to be tonight.

Ray broke their kiss first. "You taste so good." She skimmed her hand over Carly's stomach, then settled lightly on her breast. "I want to make love to you badly, Carly. I know we've barely had a chance to talk, but—"

Carly shook her head. They were beyond words now. "We can talk later. Right now I want to show you how I feel."

CHAPTER TWENTY-EIGHT

Ray's legs shook as she led Carly to her bedroom. Some of it was nerves, but mostly it was pure arousal. Blood surged through her veins and her heart pounded in her ears. The sensation reminded her of the adrenaline rush she used to experience in combat, but this time fear played a very minor role in what she was feeling.

She took Carly's hand when they reached the bedroom door and pulled her inside.

"I can't believe we're really going to do this." Ray's face heated as soon as the words left her mouth. Could she be any more of a dork? "I mean, I've been thinking about it for so long."

"Me too." Carly shifted on her feet and glanced at the bed. "I hate to tell you this, but I think we're going to mess up your rack."

Carly sounded so cute when she spouted military jargon. "I hope so." Pulling Carly into a gentle embrace, Ray kissed the corner of her mouth. Unsure how to initiate their lovemaking, she searched Carly's eyes for guidance. Her own nervousness reflected back at her. "You okay?"

Carly exhaled, sliding her hands up Ray's back. "I'm shaking."

"Have you been with anyone...since...?" Ray avoided saying Nadia's name, not wanting to do anything to ruin the mood. But she had always wondered, and it might explain Carly's nerves.

"Yes," Carly said quietly. "But nobody important. Not until now."

Ray felt strangely relieved. It took some of the pressure off not to be the first. "Is that why you're scared? Because it means something?"

"That, and I want to make this so good for you."

"Me, too." Her biggest fear was that she wouldn't be able to please Carly. She didn't want Carly to regret being with someone who had never slept with a woman. "Give me lots of guidance, okay?"

"You, too." Carly put her hands on Ray's shoulders. "You look very hot today, by the way."

Ray blushed. "Thanks." To her surprise, Carly stepped back and pulled her T-shirt over her head. Ray gazed at the pale flesh that rose above the cups of her white bra, and her breathing hitched. "So do you."

"Thank you." Blushing, Carly took Ray's hand and walked backward until her thighs hit the edge of the bed. "I'm not sure how to start."

Ray licked her lips and eyed Carly's cleavage. "Oh, I think you're doing a fine job."

Carly snaked her arms around Ray's neck and drew her in for a slow, wet kiss. When she pulled away she murmured, "You make me feel very sexy."

Ray's heart felt like it would explode. She squeezed Carly's hips, then ran her hands up over the soft skin of her back until she found the clasp of Carly's bra. Taking a deep breath, she managed to unhook it without fumbling too badly.

"Very smooth." Carly shrugged the bra off her shoulders and tossed it to the floor. Her breasts bounced slightly, reducing Ray to a state of mindless lust. Dark pink nipples contracted under her hot gaze, begging to be touched. "I'm impressed."

No longer capable of speaking, Ray captured Carly's mouth in a passionate kiss. She pulled Carly close to her chest with one arm around her back, then cupped her bare breast in her other hand. Carly's heart beat madly against her fingertips, wrenching a groan from Ray. When Carly wobbled as though her legs were giving out, Ray tightened her embrace.

"I won't let you fall." Ray trailed kisses over Carly's neck, then ran her thumb over Carly's stiff nipple. "Just hang on to me."

Carly inhaled sharply and gripped Ray's upper arms. "Please don't let me go."

"I promise." Ray's chest filled with such intense desire that it was hard to breathe. She brought her mouth back to Carly's and they kissed again.

Carly's hands found the hem of Ray's shirt. "May I take this off?"

Ray released Carly long enough to allow her to tug the shirt over her head, then pulled Carly close again, flinching when the bare skin of Carly's stomach pressed against her sensitive flesh. Her legs threatened to buckle at the delicious intimacy of skin on skin, and she gritted her teeth as she fought to keep her balance.

"You okay?" Carly found the clasp of Ray's bra and hesitated. "May I?"

Ray shivered at the thought of Carly's bare breasts touching her own. "Yes."

Carly unhooked her bra with a great deal more fumbling than Ray. "Damn it," she whispered when she finally worked the clasp open, pulling the straps down Ray's arms. "I've never been good at that."

"I'll help you practice." A twinge of self-consciousness shot through Ray as the cool air hit her breasts, tightening her nipples into hard points.

Carly's gaze dropped and her eyes were full of desire. "You're gorgeous, Ray."

Ray glanced down at the body that had felt like a stranger's for so long. Though she would probably never see what Carly did, knowing that someone saw more than the physical and emotional scars she carried made her stand taller. She took Carly's hand and put it on her breast, then touched her forehead to Carly's and breathed deeply. It felt good to trust someone again.

"I don't think I've ever wanted someone as much as I want you." Carly brought her other hand up and covered both of Ray's breasts, brushing the nipples with her palms. Then she moved her hands around to Ray's back and kissed her again.

When Carly's breasts touched hers, Ray's knees weakened. She could never have imagined something so exquisite. This was totally different from being with Danny, affecting her so deeply she could barely think. She groaned into Carly's mouth, lost in their embrace.

Carly's fingers stroked up and down her bare back, leaving goosebumps in their wake, when they suddenly stilled. Embarrassed, Ray realized that Carly was touching one of the large scars the insurgents had left on her body, the result of a beating she never understood. Ray broke their kiss, ashamed.

"We should lay down." Carly's eyes shone with emotion. Her fingertips played along the sensitive length of the scar, not shying away. "I'm so turned on my legs are about to stop working."

"Mine, too." Ray lowered Carly onto the bed and eased on top of her. Her thigh slipped naturally between Carly's, and a surge of arousal took her breath away. Gasping, she buried her face in Carly's neck and struggled to maintain control.

Carly rubbed Ray's upper back soothingly. "Don't be nervous. You won't do anything I don't want."

Remembering how it made her feel to hold Carly down, Ray whispered, "You'll tell me if I do?"

"Yes, but I want everything you can give me. It won't be too much."

Ray lifted her head and kissed Carly again. Raising her thigh, Carly provided Ray with delicious pressure that she ground against unconsciously. She could come like this, rocking back and forth against Carly's body, but that wasn't her foremost objective. More than anything, she wanted to bring Carly pleasure.

Shifting to the side, Ray put a hand on Carly's bare stomach. She desperately wanted to take Carly's track pants off and met Carly's gaze with a pleading look. Carly nodded. Taking a deep breath, Ray curled her fingers beneath the elastic waistband and tugged Carly's pants down her legs and off.

The sight of so much bare skin made Ray's hands tremble. Carly wore light blue cotton panties with a dark wet spot staining them already. Ray put her hand on Carly's calf, caressing the outside of her thigh as she ascended Carly's body to capture her mouth in a languorous kiss. The kiss gave way to smaller kisses and finally to Ray stringing light licks and nibbles over Carly's throat to her breasts.

Ray flashed on Carly's sultry words the night they had phone sex, and she lowered her mouth to carefully lick around an erect nipple. Encouraged by the way Carly's stomach muscles tightened beneath her hand, she sucked the nipple between her teeth, nibbling gently. Carly moaned and ran her fingers through Ray's hair, holding her in place.

"You're a ringer." Carly's voice was strained. "There is no way you haven't done that before."

Ray smiled around Carly's nipple, encouraged by the praise. She opened her mouth wider and took more of Carly's breast inside, tracing large circles with her tongue. Her hand crept from Carly's stomach to the waistband of her panties, and she ran a fingertip along the length of the elastic over Carly's hip.

"Touch me." Carly sounded tortured, like she was barely holding on. "Please, Ray, with your hand."

Inflamed by Carly's passionate plea, Ray nonetheless froze, all too aware that she wasn't sure what to do next. She lifted her head, drawing a disappointed groan from Carly, and managed a sheepish grin.

"Want me to show you?" Carly asked.

Ray nodded, then gasped when Carly took her hand and guided it to rest directly on her damp panties. "Wow." Ray flexed her fingers. The small spot of wetness seemed to have grown exponentially.

"Feel what you do to me?"

Ray nodded again, then swallowed. She had never felt so powerful. Bolstered by the reaction to her touch, she cupped Carly and squeezed lightly.

"Help me take them off." Carly lifted her hips and gave Ray a reassuring smile.

Not trusting herself to speak, Ray slipped the panties down Carly's shapely legs, trying hard not to stare at her dark curls. Her gaze kept straying between Carly's thighs anyway, and she caught a flash of glistening, swollen flesh both intimately familiar and wholly foreign. Her hand drifted toward Carly's inner thigh as though disconnected from her body, tentatively caressing the silky skin.

"You're even more beautiful than I imagined," Ray murmured. Overtaken by awe, she forgot to be nervous and let her fingers comb through the damp, kinky hair that covered Carly's pussy. At Carly's shaky exhalation, she tore her eyes away and met Carly's gaze. Raw desire lanced through her at the need on Carly's face, sending her scrambling to take Carly's mouth in a hard kiss.

Groaning, Carly put her hand on top of Ray's and guided her fingers down until they found impossibly hot, wet flesh. Ray closed her eyes, shaken by the almost unbearable lust the touch ignited, and broke their kiss with a gasp.

"Let me show you." Carly began to move Ray's hand slowly, dragging her fingers over the length of her swollen clit, then along her labia. As she stroked herself using Ray's fingers, Carly's breathing picked up. "It feels so good when you touch me like this."

Carly released her hand and Ray continued stroking her as she had been shown. She lowered her face and took Carly's nipple in her mouth, sucking a little harder than before. Carly moaned loudly, so Ray used her teeth to apply slightly more pressure to the turgid flesh. When Carly's hand landed on her head and gripped her hair, holding her in place, Ray grinned broadly.

"Keep doing that and you're going to make me come." Carly's voice had taken on a raspy quality that made Ray shiver. "You are so *fucking* good at that."

This was the first time Ray had ever heard Carly use that particular word, and it sent a surprise spark of pleasure straight to her own pussy. Hearing such coarse language come out of Carly's mouth made Ray feel as though they were sharing something very private and terribly intimate. She curled her fingers slightly, slipping deeper into Carly's wetness until she found her tight opening.

Ray felt like she was about to burst into flames. Any remaining traces of shyness or uncertainty melted away as the powerful need to possess Carly consumed her. Lifting her head, she stared into Carly's eyes. "Want me to fuck you?"

A fresh flood of wetness soaked the fingers that probed at Carly's opening. Though that was really all the confirmation Ray needed, she was excited when Carly nodded and ground out, "Please. Now."

Ray pushed inside slowly with one finger, not wanting to hurt Carly with this first clumsy attempt. Carly slipped a hand around the back of Ray's neck and stared into her eyes, pleasure written all over her face.

"Does that feel good?" Ray wiggled her finger around slowly, amazed by the intricate folds that surrounded her.

"Incredible. Give me another finger."

Ray slipped a second finger inside, delighting in the much snugger fit. Carly's pussy tightened around her, and Ray groaned. "I love being inside you." That was an understatement. Ray couldn't remember ever enjoying sex as much as she did in this moment, with this act.

"I love you." Carly's eyes welled up, and she pulled Ray down for a long, slow kiss that said far more than words ever could. Ray pumped her fingers in and out of Carly gently, belying the crudeness of her earlier words. She made love to Carly with her hand and her mouth, putting everything she had into showing the woman she loved just what she meant to her.

Instinctively, Ray moved her thumb to rub Carly's clit in time with her thrusts. Carly whimpered into her mouth and grabbed her forearm tightly, rocking her hips to meet Ray's strokes. Carly's pussy gradually tightened around her fingers, and her clit hardened, no doubt extraordinarily sensitive to the touch. When Carly's thighs trembled and quaked next to Ray's arm, intoxicating power surged through Ray at Carly's loss of control.

Ray kissed down Carly's neck and scraped her teeth over her throat, growling her lust. "Come for me, baby."

Carly arched her back and cried out loudly, a high-pitched whimper that stole Ray's breath. Her pussy contracted around Ray's fingers, again and again, and Ray moaned sympathetically. There was something incredibly satisfying about knowing exactly what that rhythmic tightening meant, how Carly's orgasm rolled through her body in waves.

When Carly's orgasm subsided, Ray collapsed at her side, fingers still buried deep inside. She trembled, overwhelmed by the enormity of what just happened. For so long she had doubted she would ever feel anything again, certainly not with another person, and that fear had just been shattered. She might not be whole again, but she was damn sure on her way.

"I'm serious, darling." Carly snaked an arm around Ray's back. "That was incredible. If you were worried about being with a woman—"

"I was."

"There was no need. That was one of the most intense orgasms I've ever had. Honestly."

Ray beamed, wiggling her fingers carefully. Maybe Carly was ready to do that again. Carly stiffened slightly and gasped, then slammed her thighs shut on Ray's hand.

"Not yet?" Ray said.

"Give me a few minutes." Carly opened her thighs, allowing Ray to withdraw. She gathered Ray into a tight hug, kissing the side of her neck. "Seriously, I won't need long."

"I hope not." Now that she was over her nerves, Ray couldn't wait to make Carly come again. And again. "That's officially my new favorite thing."

"Lucky me." Carly scratched her blunt fingernails down Ray's bare back, then tugged gently on the waistband of the jeans Ray suddenly realized she was still wearing. "How are you feeling?"

Wet. Horny. Desperate to be touched. Ray unbuttoned her jeans, then pushed them off, kicking them over the side of the bed. There was no place for modesty now, not when she ached for release. Hesitating only a moment, she slipped off her panties, then lay back down beside Carly.

Carly got up on her elbow and gazed down the length of Ray's body. Ray squirmed under the scrutiny, even as she enjoyed the way Carly's eyes darkened and her breathing seemed to quicken.

"I'm a very lucky woman." Carly dragged her gaze up to meet Ray's. She shifted until she hovered over Ray's body, but didn't settle on top of her. "I want to feel your skin against mine."

She was asking permission. Ray put her hands on Carly's back and applied light pressure until Carly settled fully on top of her with a groan that Ray echoed. Spreading her legs so Carly could slip her thigh between them, Ray grinned shyly at the feeling of her wetness painting Carly's smooth skin. She rocked her hips against Carly and shuddered at the resulting wave of pleasure.

"I can't believe how wet you are." Carly smiled and tucked a lock of hair behind Ray's ear, then traced her tongue over the lobe. "I'd love to have a taste, if you'd let me."

Ray's pussy contracted sharply and she gasped, frightened that she would come right then. She was determined to draw this out as long as possible, or at the very least until Carly had a chance to really touch her. It was almost hard to believe that Carly wanted to lick her, having never been with someone who genuinely enjoyed that act. But Carly was offering and Ray could only assume she was sincere.

Ray pushed down any lingering hesitation. "I'd love that." Her voice cracked and her face warmed. "I don't have a lot of experience with it, though."

"I don't want to make you uncomfortable."

"Oh, no," Ray said quickly. "I wasn't the one who was uncomfortable with it." Her face burned now. "I want you to do it."

Carly gave her a gentle kiss on the mouth. "Don't be afraid to tell me what to do," she murmured, then kissed her way down Ray's throat, to her breasts.

Ray tangled her fingers in Carly's hair, tightening her grip when Carly's mouth closed over a painfully erect nipple. Hypersensitive, she could feel the tip of Carly's tongue trace gentle circles over her areola, soothing and inflaming. Carly kissed over to her other breast and gave it the same treatment, and Ray surprised herself by moaning. Carly's stomach was against her pussy and Ray thrust against her, greedy for contact on her swollen clit.

Carly released her nipple, eyes sparkling. "Are you trying to tell me something?"

Ray gritted her teeth. "I need you."

Carly blinked and her face softened. "I need you, too." She kissed her way down Ray's stomach and finally fit her shoulders between Ray's trembling thighs, then lowered her face to gently kiss Ray's pubic mound.

Ray's body tensed with anticipation. Would Carly really enjoy this? Would she? Would it feel different from the last time, better with a woman? Closing her eyes, she caressed Carly's face with a shaking hand.

When Carly touched the tip of her tongue to her labia, Ray cried out in surprise. That single, whisper-soft lick sent a bolt of pleasure ricocheting through her body, so intense her thighs quaked in reaction. Carly followed with another lick, tracing her tongue down to Ray's opening, then back up to play over her labia again. She took her time, avoiding Ray's clit entirely, in a patient worship beyond anything Ray had ever imagined.

Ray's hands found their way back to Carly's head, and she combed her fingers through Carly's hair, pulling her close. Seemingly encouraged, Carly increased the pressure of her tongue, then used her whole mouth to suck gently on Ray's pussy, driving all conscious thought from her mind.

Ray held Carly's head and thrust her pussy into her mouth, feeling powerful, though powerless to do anything but lie there in the pure bliss of being made love to. Her orgasm built, and she craved to draw things out but would probably come soon.

In Carly's mouth.

That stray thought sealed her fate. No longer able to hold back,

Ray pumped her hips against Carly and came hard, screaming as her orgasm ripped through her. She could hear Carly moaning, could feel the vibrations against her pussy, which only intensified the pleasure. Flexing her toes until her feet began to cramp, she released Carly's head so she could claw at the sheets, needing to hold on to something lest she fly apart at the seams.

Without stopping the motion of her tongue, Carly grabbed one of Ray's hands, squeezing it tight. Grateful for the tether, Ray rode out the end of the orgasm until she couldn't bear another second of it. "Stop," Ray gasped, and Carly immediately pulled back.

Ray tugged Carly up until they were face-to-face and wrapped her in a bear hug. She held on tight, too overwhelmed to speak. Carly returned her embrace and kissed her lightly. Ray deepened the kiss, whimpering at the taste of her own juices on Carly's lips.

Carly drew back first. "You okay?"

"I don't think you need to worry about me enjoying sex with a woman. That was…"

Carly rested her head on Ray's chest. "Yeah, it was."

Ray scraped her fingernails down the length of Carly's back, delighting in the shiver she elicited. "Ready for more?"

Carly lifted her head, eyebrow arched. "Are you?"

Ray held on to Carly and rolled them over so that she was on top. Carly opened her legs and Ray settled between them with a contented sigh. "Buckle up, sweetheart. I feel like I could go all night."

"Promise?" Carly looped her arms around Ray's neck.

"I'll try my best." Ray slid out from under Carly's arms, eager for round two. Mouth watering, she pressed a wet string of kisses down Carly's stomach. She knew exactly where she wanted to start.

CHAPTER TWENTY-NINE

Carly woke in the middle of the night to find Ray's side of the bed empty. She hadn't heard Ray get up, but she had been dead asleep, exhausted after their marathon lovemaking session that stretched from late afternoon into the deepest part of the night. Carly had finally passed out after her ninth or tenth orgasm, when not even the urgent need to make Ray come just one more time could keep her going. She had been unconscious for a few hours at least, judging by the uncomfortable burn of her very full bladder.

No doubt Ray had gotten up with the same need. Unable to work up the energy to get out of bed, Carly decided to wait until Ray came back before she forced her own legs to work. No matter how badly she needed to pee, she wasn't sure she was ready to move. It had been a long time since she'd had so much sex in so few hours.

Aches and pains aside, Ray's sexual appetite was a glorious revelation. Though Carly had certainly seen hints that Ray was full of passion just waiting to be unleashed, she never dreamed what an amazing lover Ray would turn out to be. Especially for their first time together. Carly shivered at the memory of Ray's fingers inside her and the first tentative touch of Ray's tongue against her clit. That Ray managed to be better at licking pussy than nearly any of her past lovers was surprising, and extremely exciting.

Incredibly, Carly felt the stirrings of arousal in the pit of her stomach once more. She groaned as the need to pee increased with her ardor, then propped herself up on her elbows with effort, glancing at the bathroom door. It was wide open and the lights were off. Carly sat up in bed, ignoring the protest from her weary muscles.

"Ray?"

No answer. Carly crawled to the foot of the bed and looked down at Jagger's empty pillow. A few feet away, Jack was curled into a tight ball on his own bed, but his ears were perked and his eyes followed her movement. When Carly stood up, he sprang to his feet and rushed to the bedroom door.

"Sorry, Jack." Carly dashed into the bathroom just in time. As much as she wanted to find Ray, she had priorities. "False alarm."

When Carly finished she walked back into the bedroom. The digital alarm clock on Ray's nightstand told her it was after four. Where could Ray be so early in the morning? Had she woken up and panicked about what they had done? Carly took a deep breath, willing herself to calm down. Ray wouldn't run away after all they'd been through.

Jack whined at the door. At least one of them was thinking clearly. If she wanted to know where Ray was, they would go find her. Simple as that. Carly put on a pair of pajama pants and a long-sleeved T-shirt she found in Ray's chest of drawers, then followed Jack.

He led them to the front door, where he sat and whined again. Curious, Carly opened the door and poked her head outside, not sure what to expect.

"Hey," Ray said quietly, startling Carly. She sat on the porch swing with Jagger at her side. He stared out at the road with watchful eyes, as though standing guard. "What are you doing up?"

Carly stepped out of the house into the brisk night air and shivered. "Had to pee. You were gone so I decided to make sure everything was okay."

Ray smiled and held out a hand. "Everything's great. Come sit down."

Wrapping her arms around her stomach, Carly tiptoed to the swing, wishing she had put on some socks. "It's chilly out here."

"A little, yeah." Ray bent and pulled off her slippers, handing them to Carly after she sat down. "Put these on."

"I would refuse, but I really, really need them." Carly slipped them on and sighed as the downy insides immediately began to thaw her frozen toes. "Thank you."

"My pleasure." Ray eased her arm around Carly's shoulders and pulled her close. "Let me help."

Carly snuggled into Ray gratefully. She had no idea how Ray

could still be so warm after sitting out here, but she was glad. "So what brings you out into the arctic?"

Ray laughed. "It's not that cold."

"I guess you're made of tougher stuff than me." Carly knew that was true on many levels. She cuddled closer to Ray, kissing her on the cheek. "You sure everything's all right?"

"Yeah, I wanted to let you sleep. I didn't think I'd be able to if I stayed in bed."

Carly's chest swelled. "Really?"

"Are you kidding? I could barely keep my hands off you. I want you constantly."

The naked desire in Ray's voice made Carly's clit twitch. The muscles in her thighs ached and her pussy was sore from overuse, but she might be ready to go again. It was worth a try, at least. "You are so sexy, you know that?"

Even in the dark, she swore she could see Ray blush. "So you tell me."

Carly put a hand on Ray's face, marveling at the heat suffusing her cheek. Was it evil that she liked making Ray squirm? "And I love how you lick my pussy."

Ray groaned. "Maybe we should go back inside."

"I like the way you think." Carly sat up. She would need to drink some water to replace some of the fluids she had lost over the past twelve hours, but she was more than ready to pick up where they left off. She might be older than she used to be, but she wasn't dead yet. "I'm not sure I'll be able to walk tomorrow, but it'll be worth it."

Ray's hand landed on her arm just as Carly was about to stand, stopping her. "Carly?"

Sensing a shift in Ray's tone, Carly looked into Ray's eyes. "Yeah?"

"I'm sorry I've put you through everything I have. I know I accused you of not being patient enough, but you've been more than patient. Most people wouldn't be able to take on all my baggage. I get that."

"Neither of us has been perfect," Carly said softly. "But we're trying. We're not giving up. No more apologies, okay?"

Ray nodded. "I just want you to know that even though I'm still scared of a lot of things, being with you isn't one of them."

Carly covered Ray's hand with her own. She would be lying if she said the same thing. "It's okay to be scared, you know. Loving someone can be scary." Terrifying, even.

"The idea of not loving you is even scarier."

Carly touched the side of Ray's neck and found her pulse, strong and steady. Nothing frightened Carly more than the possibility of losing Ray. She still didn't know whether she would be able to survive another heartbreak of that magnitude. But after being separated for the last few weeks, she would do anything to be with Ray. Even risk her own happiness.

"To be honest, I'm still afraid," Carly said. "But you're worth it, Ray. All the fear, even the possibility of pain. You're worth everything. And I will always be here for you, no matter what."

Unshed tears made Ray's eyes glitter in the early morning gloom. "I'm going to try and make you so happy."

"You do." Carly couldn't imagine Ray making her any happier. Sure, there were things like going to restaurants and hanging out in the city. Or even doing something with Leeann. But those things would come eventually. Ray was capable of anything. And Carly was more than willing to wait. "You make me very happy."

"Well, I plan to get better at it."

Trying to lighten the mood, Carly drew a finger down the center of Ray's chest, between her breasts. "Better might just kill me, darling."

Ray shivered, and it had nothing to do with the cold. "Oh, no. I can definitely get better. But I'll need practice. Lots and lots of practice."

"Want to go practice now?"

Ray stood, pulling Carly to her feet and into a tight embrace. "I'd love that."

EPILOGUE

Ray sat down at the computer in her office and double-clicked her video chat icon. She was three minutes late for her appointment with Dr. Evans. Unacceptably tardy. Ray was used to military precision and usually paid attention to detail. Not so much these days, though. A lot was going on in her life, so many things competing for her focus.

And it felt great.

The chat window opened onscreen and Ray immediately offered Dr. Evans a sheepish grin. "I am so sorry. Time just got away from me."

"Not a problem, Ray. Things are pretty busy around there, huh?"

"Oh, yeah. We've got so much going on right now, it's crazy. If I stop to think about it all, I'll probably get overwhelmed. But it's good. Great, even."

"I'm glad to hear that. Tell me about 'great.' You had mentioned going back to school. You were planning to do some research on programs in the area. Anything come of that?"

"Actually, yeah." Ray clicked on a minimized browser window, eager to bring up the Web site for the Bergin University of Canine Studies. Instead, she got an eyeful of something entirely inappropriate for the middle of a therapy appointment: the Good Vibrations online catalog, still displaying the strap-on harness she and Carly had purchased just the night before. She blushed as though Dr. Evans could see what she was looking at, then closed it quickly. Finding the correct window with another click, she cleared her throat. "I've applied to an assistance dog education program. It's an associate's degree, and it'll prepare me for a career as a professional dog trainer."

"Sounds perfect. When will you find out whether you've been accepted?"

"The semester starts at the end of August, so pretty soon." Ray was able to think about attending classes with only slight anxiety, which was a good sign. The anxiety would grow upon learning that she had been accepted and would peak right before her first day of class, but Carly would be there to help her through it. And Jagger. "I'm nervous, but also excited. I like the idea of working with dogs."

"I'm so pleased for you." Dr. Evans grinned broadly, looking like she might cry. "You have no idea how proud I am, Ray."

"I think I might." Ray glanced at Jagger, who sat next to her chair. It seemed like everyone was telling her that these days. Every time she pushed herself or stepped outside her comfort zone, Carly nearly burst with pride. Her mom and sisters met every piece of news, including this school thing, with tremendous delight. Sometimes she even thought she saw respect in Leeann's eyes, despite their rocky start. "I'm feeling good."

"Well, you should." Dr. Evans's grin grew more watery, if that was possible. "Your sister is visiting soon, isn't she? That will be exciting."

"Yeah, Juliet will be here in a week and a half. Carly and I are probably crazy for doing the move right before she gets here, but we can't stand it anymore."

Dr. Evans raised an eyebrow. "The move?"

Ray searched her memory. She could have sworn she'd told Dr. Evans about this the last time they spoke. Then again, it had been a spontaneous decision. "Yeah, Carly's moving her stuff into my place. Our place, I mean. I know it's only been six months, but it didn't make sense to keep both houses when we only ever spend time at one or the other."

"Wow, congratulations. So I take it this means things are going well with Carly."

"Oh, yes." That was an understatement. "She's incredible. I can't wait for Juliet to meet her."

As though summoned by the sound of her name, Carly tottered into the office carrying a large Rock Band 2 box. "What do you say we set this up, sweetheart, and I school you—" She halted abruptly when she saw the video chat window on the computer. "Oh, my God, I am so sorry. I totally forgot. I'll leave you—"

Ray motioned to Dr. Evans, then jumped up and took the large box from Carly's arms. "Let me get that for you."

"Thanks." Carly mouthed "I'm sorry" again. "It's heavier than it looks."

Ray set the box down with a smile. It was nice being the physically stronger one. She felt like she could take care of Carly in a tangible way, just like Carly did for her. "Stay for a minute, if you don't mind. I'd love to introduce you to Dr. Evans."

From the computer speakers, Dr. Evans said, "That would be lovely. It'd be great to put a face with all the wonderful things I've heard."

Ray gave Carly a shy smile, then took her hand and led her to the desk chair. She sat down first, then pulled Carly onto her lap. Carly wrapped her arm around Ray's shoulders and smiled into the webcam.

"It's nice to meet you, Dr. Evans," Carly said. "I'm glad to put a face with the name, too. Your support means so much to Ray."

Dr. Evans's face had to hurt by now, she looked so thrilled. "The same goes for you. I'm so pleased for both of you. Congratulations on the big move."

Carly tightened her arm around Ray's shoulders. "Thanks. It's a big step, but honestly we took it months ago. Now we just need to stop making two mortgage payments for no reason."

Dr. Evans chuckled. "Sounds like a wise financial decision."

Ray kissed Carly on the chin. "And a wise emotional decision."

"Yes," Carly murmured, staring into Ray's eyes. "Very wise."

Dr. Evans cleared her throat. "You know, Ray, unless you've got more you want to talk about this week, we can cut this session short. I know you've got a lot to do before your sister gets there, so…"

Carly shifted slightly on her lap, igniting Ray's libido. Ray caught the flash of desire in her gaze. They wouldn't be playing Rock Band 2 anytime soon.

"Maybe that's a good idea," Ray said thickly, turning her attention to the webcam as calmly as she could manage. Which probably wasn't all that calm. "We've got plenty of boxes to unpack still."

Dr. Evans had an expression that told Ray she knew exactly where the mood in the office had shifted. "That's fine. I'll talk to you next week?"

"Yes." Ray hesitated, unsure whether to bring up something she had been thinking about. While she wasn't ready to stop therapy entirely, she wasn't sure they needed to meet weekly anymore. The panic attacks had subsided, nightmares were rare, and even when she fell apart, Carly was there to help her put back the pieces. Ray wasn't cured, and she still had challenges to overcome, but with Carly at her side, they didn't seem nearly as daunting. Maybe it was time to take another step toward independence. "I'd like to talk about our schedule."

"Oh?" Dr. Evans raised an eyebrow. "You know, I planned to bring up the same thing. Perhaps meeting biweekly would make more sense for a while. We can see how it goes. But you're a lot busier now, and I can't help but think that would be plenty."

Ray sat up straighter in her chair. "Great. We'll talk about it next time."

"Until then," Dr. Evans said. "It was nice meeting you, Carly."

"Nice meeting you, too." Carly waved at the webcam.

"Bye, you two. Have fun." Dr. Evans signed out and the video chat window disappeared.

"You realize she totally knows we're going to have sex now, right?" Carly murmured, tracing Ray's jaw line with her tongue. "You're so obvious."

Ray slipped her hand into Carly's shirt and caressed her breast. "Oh, really? I am?"

"Totally obvious." Carly giggled when Ray seized a nipple through her bra and squeezed firmly. "Or did you really want to keep unpacking?"

"No, not unpacking." Ray tucked her fingers under the top edge of Carly's bra cup and pulled the material down, exposing Carly's bare breast. "Undressing, maybe."

"See, I told you." Carly gasped when Ray pushed her shirt up and latched on to an erect nipple, sucking gently. "Obvious."

Ray drew away, releasing Carly's nipple with a soft *pop*. She fixed Carly's bra and pulled her shirt back over her chest, then gave Carly an innocent smile. "May I play the drums?"

"Excuse me?" Carly's face glowed pink and her words came out flustered.

"We were going to play Rock Band, right? I want to be the drummer."

Carly slipped off her lap and stood, taking Ray's hand. "You know we're not playing Rock Band."

"But I thought you wanted to school me?" Ray kept a straight face, even when all she wanted was to throw Carly against the wall and kiss the hell out of her.

"Oh, I'll school you." Carly led Ray out of the office by the hand and walked them to the bedroom. "Don't you worry about that."

"Worry?" Ray tugged on Carly's hand, pulling her back so Ray could push her up against the wall. She held Carly's wrists above her head and kissed her hard. Breaking away for air some time later, she whispered, "Right now I'm not worried about a thing."

About the Author

Born in a suburb of Detroit, Michigan, Meghan O'Brien relocated to Windsor, California, in October 2005. As a recent transplant, she's enjoying the moderate weather and gorgeous scenery of the Bay Area. Meghan lives with her partner Angie, their son, three cats, and three dogs. Yes, it can be just as chaotic as it sounds.

Meghan works as a Web developer, but her real passion is writing. From her humble beginnings creating numerous "books" out of construction paper and crayons as soon as she learned to write, to her two published novels and various anthology contributions in the past five years, writing is what makes her feel most complete.

Books Available From Bold Strokes Books

Battle Scars by Meghan O'Brien. Returning Iraq war veteran Ray McKenna struggles with the battle scars that can only be healed by love. (978-1-60282-129-3)

Chaps by Jove Belle. Eden Metcalf wants nothing more than to flee from her troubled past and travel the open road—until she runs into rancher Brandi Cornwell. (978-1-60282-127-9)

Lightbearer by John Caruso. Lucifer dares to question the premise of creation itself and reveals that sin may be all that stands between us and living hell. (978-1-60282-130-9)

The Seeker by Ronica Black. FBI profiler Kennedy Scott battles ghosts from her past, deadly obsession, and the evil that haunts her. (978-1-60282-128-6)

Power Play by Julie Cannon. Businesswomen Tate Monroe and Victoria Sosa are at odds in the boardroom, but not in the bedroom. (978-1-60282-125-5)

The Remarkable Journey of Miss Tranby Quirke by Elizabeth Ridley. When love enters Tranby's life in the form of a beautiful nineteen-year-old student, Lysette McDonald, she embarks on the most remarkable journey of all. (978-1-60282-126-2)

Returning Tides by Radclyffe. Insurance investigator Ashley Walker faces more than a dangerous opponent when she returns to the town, and the woman, she left behind. (978-1-60282-123-1)

Veritas by Anne Laughlin. When the hallowed halls of academia become the stage for murder, newly appointed Dean Beth Ellis's search for the truth leads her to unexpected discoveries about her own heart. (978-1-60282-124-8)

The Pleasure Planner by Larkin Rose. Pleasure purveyor Bree Hendricks treats love like a commodity until Logan Delaney makes Bree the client in her own game. (978-1-60282-121-7)

everafter by Nell Stark and Trinity Tam. Valentine Darrow is bitten by a vampire on her way to propose to her lover Alexa Newland, and their lives and love are placed in mortal jeopardy. (978-1-60282-119-4)

Summer Winds by Andrews & Austin. When Maggie Turner hires a ranch hand to help work her thousand acres, she never expects to be attracted to the very young, very female Cash Tate. (978-1-60282-120-0)

Beggar of Love by Lee Lynch. Jefferson is the lover every woman wants to be—or to have. A revealing saga of lesbian sexuality. (978-1-60282-122-4)

The Seduction of Moxie by Colette Moody. When 1930s Broadway actress Violet London meets speakeasy singer Moxie Valette, she is instantly attracted and her Hollywood trip takes an unexpected turn. (978-1-60282-114-9)

Goldenseal by Gill McKnight. When Amy Fortune returns to her childhood home, she discovers something sinister in the air—but is former lover Leone Garoul stalking her or protecting her? (978-1-60282-115-6)

Romantic Interludes 2: Secrets edited by Radclyffe and Stacia Seaman. An anthology of sensual lesbian love stories: passion, surprises, and secret desires. (978-1-60282-116-3)

Femme Noir by Clara Nipper. Nora Delaney meets her match in Max Abbott, a sex-crazed dame who may or may not have the information Nora needs to solve a murder—but can she contain her lust for Max long enough to find out? (978-1-60282-117-0)

The Reluctant Daughter by Lesléa Newman. Heartwarming, heartbreaking, and ultimately triumphant—the story every daughter recognizes of the lifelong struggle for our mothers to really see us. (978-1-60282-118-7)

Erosistible by Gill McKnight. When Win Martin arrives at a luxurious Greek hotel for a much-anticipated week of sun and sex with her new girlfriend, she is stunned to find her ex-girlfriend, Benny, is the proprietor. Aeros Ebook. (978-1-60282-134-7)

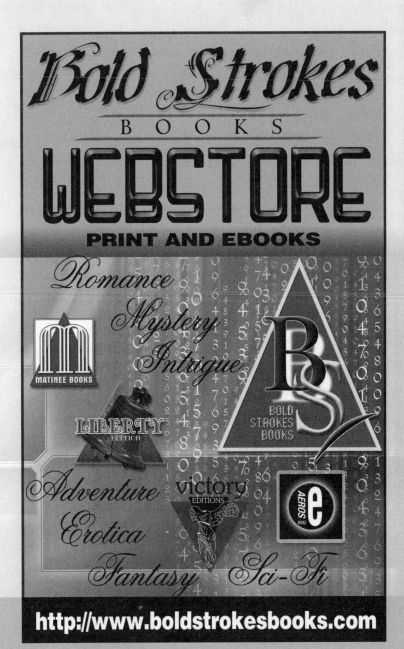